Wild Heart

Lacy Chantell

Copyright © 2024 by Lacy Chantell

All rights reserved.

No part of this publication may be reproduced, distributed, or transmitted in any form or by any means, including photocopying, recording, or other electronic or mechanical methods, without the prior written permission of the publisher, except as permitted by U.S. copyright law. For permission requests, contact Lacy Chantell at lacychantell.author@gmail.com.

The story, all names, characters, and incidents portrayed in this production are fictitious. No identification with actual persons (living or deceased), places, buildings, and products is intended or should be inferred.

Book Cover by Lacy Chantell

ISBN 9781088091494

Content Warnings

Stalking Behavior
Narcissistic Behaviors
Adult Language
Manipulative Parent
Sexual Content
Drinking
Sexual Abuse Trauma
Military PTSD

Dedication

I wanted to add a really powerful message about overcoming narcissistic and manipulative relationships, but then I realized I'm twenty-eight and still can't get over mine. Welcome to the start of my journey.

Chapter One

MARNI KICKS HER HEELS off and shoves them to the side of the open door. She slams it shut and hobbles on her sore, tender feet for the bottle of wine in the fridge. She starts for a glass to be more lady-like but changes her mind and pops the cork, taking the entire bottle to the couch where she lies back.

Ginger, her orange tabby, stretches her paws out on the back of the couch, interrupted from what Marni is certain is her tenth nap of the day. Marni presses the cold bottle to her forehead to ease the pulsing headache she received from her last meeting.

Budgeting, accounting, numbers—God so many numbers. Her eyes throb. She downs half the bottle until her headache eases, then stumbles through her apartment for a hot shower followed by comfortable clothes. She shimmies out of her pencil skirt and flowy button-down blouse. Panty hose should be outlawed, along with Spanx curvy women are expected to wear.

"They want us to all look like we know Victoria's secret. Well, let me tell ya, I enjoy a greasy burger as much as the drunk at the bar every evening and I don't see him squeezing his beer belly into Spanx." She huffs as she finally peels out of them and can inhale a deep breath.

"Much better."

The hot running water melts her tense muscles and her headache is completely gone by the time she emerges. Giving herself time for her personal life, she plops back down on the couch with her bottle and checks her messages that aren't work related. Those can wait until morning.

Her friend Tonya—well, once best friend until Marni moved away—texted her earlier that day. Just checking in like she does quite often. Marni sent back a quick, *I'm fine. Work is good, miss you too.* Then she scrolls through Facebook to see what other people are doing with their lives. There's nothing interesting, so with wine in hand, Marni heads to the kitchen.

Her apartment, while small, has a view that could take your breath away. She works for—actually co-manages—a reputable accounting firm in the city. She has the funds to get a bigger flat or an actual house, but she doesn't need extra space to keep clean.

She passes the wall of floor-length windows lining the balcony side. The remote curtains stay closed the majority of the time. At night, she opens them and stares at the lit-up city, pretending the illuminated windows dotting the landscape are stars like the ones that littered the sky back home.

In the kitchen, Marni prays she had been grocery shopping at some point and simply forgotten she had gone. Unfortunately, the fridge shelves sit empty minus a block of cheese, expired milk, and two lonely eggs.

"Looks like a cheesy omelet is what's for dinner." She puts a reminder in her phone to stop tomorrow for some essentials. The skillet sizzles when she adds a small amount of ghee so the eggs don't stick.

"Alexa, play Lana Del Rey." Her Amazon Dot turns blue and music flows at a low volume, filling the apartment with "Young and Beautiful".

While sitting at the island that doubles as a bar top, Marni continues her Facebook stalking.

"Looks like Parker's out having fun," she says and shows Ginger the picture of a male in a suit with clean cut hair and stubble with perfect lines, framing his chiseled jaw and piercing green eyes. A blinding white smile is spread on his face as a girl sits in his lap, leaning down, probably whispering something into his ear. Ginger lets out a meow.

"You're right, I am the one that keeps pushing him away. I have a successful career, my own place, you..." Her thoughts fade off as the wine quiets her mind.

She takes a peek at her schedule for work tomorrow. At eight sharp is her first meeting to discuss what was covered in today's meetings and then a follow-up at eleven to revisit what wasn't taken care of in the previous one. That leaves her an hour of desk work time to make heads or tails of it all. Then in big bold letters she has LUNCH written out, followed by a meeting with one of their pricier clients that she's sure will want to know every investment the firm has moved over the last year, down to the dime.

"My head hurts just looking at this." She holds up the empty bottle. "I know I shouldn't drink more. Water, I need water." Marni chugs a bottle of water and tosses it in the trash can. Ginger meows when she opens her next bottle of wine.

"Don't worry, I won't drink it all. Just a bit more. Besides, I've eaten and drank water." The feline gives her a disapproving look by licking its paws as if to say, *We'll see.*

Marni takes her wine back to the couch and gets nostalgic as she flips through pictures of her and Tonya on her phone. It seems like centuries ago. Their tanned skin covered by blue jeans, long hair, and cowboy hats.

They smile pridefully, sporting belt buckles they won at the local rodeo in team roping.

Dirt and sweat plaster their smiles. Marni's heart yearns for those days. Growing up has a way of sucking your soul and pissing on you in the process. From the outside looking in, people think she has everything she ever wanted; in truth, she has everything her mom wanted for her.

When Marni's mood shifts, Ginger pads her way onto her lap. Purrs vibrate through her as she rolls to her back, insisting on a belly rub. "There's my girl. What do you want to watch tonight?" Marni asks and tucks her brown hair behind her ear, clicking through Netflix. She picks an action movie—anything remotely romantic and this wine will have her in happy, sad, and angry tears. A stuffed-up head tomorrow won't do her any good.

***

ASLEEP, MARNI CRADLES THE emptied bottle of wine in her arms, with Ginger sleeping atop her abdomen. The light shines through the windows onto her closed eyelids. She jerks up, looking around wildly.

"What time is it?!" Her phone screen remains black when she frantically tries to check. "Shit!" Ginger goes toppling to the floor with the empty bottle when Marni jumps up and vaults over the back of the couch.

The clock on her night-stand reads six-thirty. She checks herself in the mirror. Her hair is a dumpster fire—curly in some places, straight in others. *This is the reason I never fell asleep with wet hair,* she scolds herself. She manages to tame it into a wrapped messy bun on top of her head and smears on some eyeliner, mascara, and primer to hide the dark circles under her eyes.

If looking like a truly sucked-dry, middle-aged adult is the goal, then I nailed it. It's a thirty-minute bus ride to the office. If she focuses, keeps her head down and walks with intent, she might just make it to the bus stop before seven. Marni glances at her watch; it's almost seven already.

"Damn it, I'll never make it." She tries to request an Uber but is met with the same black screen because she still hasn't plugged in the blasted thing. "Okay, what else can go wrong? C'mon, lay it on me! I'm right here!" She flails her arms around the room with her head thrown back. Ginger meows aggressively since her food bowl still sits empty. Marni carelessly tosses a handful of food into her bowl without measuring and grabs her dead phone and purse.

She shoves her heels into her purse and slides on comfortable flats since she will be walking—more like jogging—to get to work on time at this point. She bounces in place while the slow-as-Christmas elevator stops on every floor. *You have got to be kidding me!* Without minutes to spare, Marni rushes to the stairwell. Her quads burn after taking the twelve flights of stairs as quickly as possible. Outside, the cover of clouds hint at a chance of rain. *Oh, please no, just please,* Marni begs.

Walking anywhere in the city is faster than a car or bus by far. But by the way her legs burn and sweat pools on her back, she remembers why she never walks to work. Checking her watch, she has thirty minutes until her first meeting. She still needs to get to her desk, grab her laptop, make sure she has the correct files and presentation loaded, and find something to soak up the remaining wine in her stomach that is starting to churn.

With ten minutes to spare, she makes it to her office, and Parker leans against the door frame.

"I see you made it. Looking a little rough this morning, though. Bad night?" His confidence appears cocky and arrogant, which is one reason Marni finds herself drawn to him. While she second-guesses every decision and over-analyzes every task, Parker is so sure of everything.

"I may have drank one bottle too many last night," she admits. His eyebrows shoot up to meet his luscious dark brown hair that makes his sea-green eyes pop.

"Beer?"

"Unfortunately, not. Wine."

"Ouch, you have a wine hangover?" he asks. Marni nods and massages her temples, the headache growing stronger with each passing minute. "Say no more. Be right back."

She grabs her laptop and folder for the upcoming meeting.

Thank goodness I'm not leading this one. Stepping out of her office, she nearly misses Parker, and the thickly glazed donut he has outstretched in front of him.

"Easy, killer. Here, this will help."

"Thank you. I owe you." She says with her mouth full. The glaze of the donut sticks to the corners of her lips.

"Well, now you really owe me." After she devours the donut in three bites, he pulls a disposable coffee cup from behind his back. Just smelling the rich Columbian roast clears the fog in her head.

"I have to go before I'm late." She sidesteps him, not liking the feeling of owing him anything. The coffee coats her tongue as she sips the heavenly deliciousness. Parker shouts down the hall after her.

"I'll be calling to collect!"

Marni winces. She knows what he implies. He simply won't take no for an answer and will insist on taking her out *again*. She's tried letting him down easily. Tried flat out telling him she doesn't date, even tried avoiding him like the plague, but somehow he manages to keep coming back again and again.

The meeting drags on as they brainstorm ways to advertise and attract more clients, analyzing numbers for patterns in client fund withdrawals. They even discuss raising the threshold of the amount required before a potential client can schedule a consultation.

Money hungry bastards are all these people are, and I am one important cog on this well-oiled machine. I guess that makes me a bastard too.

Marni shifts her gaze down at her laptop when an email comes through from Tonya. She will not risk opening it here. Last time it sang *'Happy Birthday'* to her for the entire conference room to hear.

***

LUNCH ISN'T NEARLY LONG enough since Marni works during most of it. She gets caught up on voicemails and emails from clients. Apparently, one of the stocks dropped today, and it has everyone freaking out.

In her calmest, sweetest voice, she reassures the frantic clients that everything is under control and this is how stock markets work. They ebb and flow, rise and fall—all in a normal day's work. If it wasn't for the media, their clients wouldn't even know what was going on in the stock market.

They suddenly become professionals and think they know more than me with my two bachelor degrees and in-progress master's that will eventually turn into a doctorate. Just like Momma wanted for me.

She hit the nail on the head with the afternoon client meeting. He does, in fact, want every trade down to the penny to see if his money is being handled wisely. After questioning nearly every move the firm makes, he seems pleased with how it is done and leaves with friendly handshakes and gives Marni an even friendlier hug.

"He seems to like you," Boston, her boss, comments quietly. Boston comes from old family money and after it paid for him to get through college, he became a manager of this firm.

"Yeah, I caught that." Marni dismisses the thought with a wave of her hand. "He likes our numbers; that's all that matters."

"True, but it was your hard work. I am proud of what you did here today. Mr. Doyle is one of our first clients and now our wealthiest. That speaks volumes."

"Thank you, sir. I appreciate that." Boston gives Marni a rough pat on the back that sends her body forward with more force more than she anticipated. Her heels make her unbalanced and her laptop plus paperwork makes her top-heavy.

With one ungraceful loud stomp, she catches herself before she ends up splayed across the floor. The rest of the firm gives her looks of embarrassment and makes comments under their breaths. Marni, used to it by now, ignores them and holds her head high as she struts back to her office.

She shuts the door behind her and slides down into her office floor, trying to rub a migraine away. Another long day of talking about things she couldn't care less about. It is not a secret she has a gift with numbers. She can find patterns, algorithms, and equations in all the spreadsheets with a fleeting glance.

"Knock knock." Parker cracks the door open and peeks his head in. His eyes scan the room, then at her holding the door from opening further. "You look like you need a vacation," he muses.

"What's a vacation?"

"Yeah, I feel that. Want to go grab a bite to eat? You said you owe me." He gives her a soft smile, one he knows she can't refuse. She covers her face with her hands.

"I never said that. You said that." She stands and straightens her clothes. "Can I go home and get cleaned up first?" She feels gross from not showering this morning.

"I'll allow that. I'll pick you up in two hours. That'll give you time to get home."

"Sounds good." *I'll just have to go grocery shopping tomorrow. It's my day off, so I'll have more time, anyway.*

At least she can ride the bus back. Her quads are still sore from the walk this morning.

An elderly woman takes a seat next to her and makes idle chatter about the weather and whatever recent sports game they won or lost. Marni doesn't really listen. Her mind keeps drifting to Parker and the fact they are having another date tonight. He wants more than she can offer, more than she will ever be able to offer.

She knows he will try to make amends this evening, say all the right things, make her weak in the knees and prevent her tongue from forming any coherent thoughts. He'll walk her back home, slyly work his way inside, and then she will shut down again when he tries to kiss her.

Marni gives her cat several pets before taking a shower and giving herself a clean slate to work with for tonight's look. Her brown eyes stare back at her through the mirror while she places her earthy brown curly hair in all the right places.

Parker is promptly on time when a knock sounds on the door. Marni's phone chimes when she goes to answer it. Tonya texted asking if she had time to check the email she sent.

"Oops," Marni mumbles to herself. She'll have to look at it when she gets back.

Not yet. *S*he responds, then meets Parker's star-struck gaze.

"You look beautiful, Marni. I—like really..." He lets out a slow whistle. The compliment should make Marni blush or feel flutters and it probably would if she wasn't so damaged.

"That's sweet. You look very handsome tonight." He wears a dark gray tuxedo that accents his green eyes. His facial hair, as always, is short and tidy. Crisp lines angle from his ear, down his cheekbone, and to his lips. His hair is tousled in the way it makes men look wild and carefree.

"We could just order in?" Lust drips from his eyes, clearly ready to just skip the dinner and get to his real motive.

"And rob the public of us?" Marni brushes it off with a joke. "That would just be mean."

He gives her a forced smile and places a hand on the small of her back as they walk to the elevator. Marni grips her clutch and refrains from shying away from the touch.

"I got us reservations at Carmala's." He never asks Marni where she wants to go or what she likes, just decides for her.

"Sounds wonderful to me," she chimes. As if she had a choice.

The valet for her building pulls Parker's black BMW i to the front of the building. The car resembles the Batmobile. Parker has a taste for the finer things in life. He always strives to impress Marni at every chance he gets and while the car screams, *I have money*, sport cars just aren't what get her gears grinding.

It's a two door and so low-profile Marni falls into the passenger seat while Parker holds open the door for her. They zip through traffic as he accelerates. Marni can't deny it is exhilarating—the rush, the high speeds. Parker passes her a glance and notices the smile on her face. He hopes he can impress her enough tonight to stop the hot-and-cold thing they've had going on for the past year. She always pulls back just when he thinks they might finally be official.

Parker steps out of the car first and walks around to open the door for Marni. She loops her arm through his and the affirming touch sends hope pulsing through him. The inside of Carmala's screams expensive and fancy.

A pianist plays live music in the corner and the wait staff have perfectly folded white towels draped over their forearms. The women wear their best dresses and the men their full tuxedos, a requirement to even get in the door.

Parker and Marni are seated at a dimly lit booth in a back corner, like he requested when making the reservation. He needs tonight to go perfectly.

Marni takes in the romantic setting. She truly feels bad for not at least giving Parker a chance, a *real* chance. She hasn't been with a guy in two years and she honestly doesn't think she ever will be again. The pain is too raw and memories overwhelm her at the thought.

"You just...wow. You really are the most beautiful woman I've seen," Parker says.

"Parker...I—" Marni starts to put his expectations to rest, but the waitress comes over.

"Wine?"

"Yes please," Parker says.

It takes all of her willpower to not down the entire glass in one gulp. Instead, she sips and smiles at Parker before looking over the menu.

"What are you wanting to order?" he asks. Marni's anxiety gets the best of her when having to make any sort of decision. The menu seems to be in a foreign language as she tries to read over it, but she can't concentrate on making sense of it.

"I don't know. It all looks so good." She hides behind her menu.

"Would you like me to order for you?" Parker has observed the way her eyes shift, her hands fidget, and how she rereads the menu so many times she should have it memorized. The first time he offered, he was worried he would appear like a control freak, but she seemed so relieved. It is something he offers every time now.

"There's just too many things to choose from. That would be great. Thank you." She raises her wineglass to her lips. Parker orders a fancy steak for himself and a lobster for her.

"They have the most delicious lobster." He watches her as she places her now-empty wine glass back down. "I'll get us some more." He raises his arm slightly to signal the waitress over for more wine, then continues, "Listen, I wanted to talk to you about us." Marni freezes as Parker's words settle around her. The waitress fills her wineglass, and she gulps it down. Parker eyes her warily, her reaction from his statement not lost on him.

"Parker..."

He's heard that tone before. She uses it on clients when she has to turn them away. His heart hits his stomach. He proceeds to do what he always does: pacify her and rectify their hot-and-cold, back-and-forth relationship.

"It's fine if you don't want to. Forget I said anything." The waitress sets their food down. Parker pushes his steak and asparagus around his plate, then lifts his glass of wine to his lips. He ticks his tongue and purses his lips as he swallows the last bit.

It hurts Marni to keep pushing him away. She hates this is the person she has become. Hates that he fell for her.

"Do you like the lobster?" he asks.

Marni looks down at her fork. She was too caught up in her thoughts to even try it yet. She gets a forkful, and the flavor explodes in her mouth. The garlic butter coats her tongue and the tenderness of the meat practically falls apart as she chews.

"It's amazing," she gushes.

They silently continue to eat their dinner and empty two entire bottles of wine. The conversation died with Parker's question. Marni watches him with his shoulders slumped forward. His forced smile doesn't reach his eyes, and he plays with his food more than actually eating it.

He's attractive, sweet, caring—maybe if she forced herself to go through with it, she could get over her damage? But the thought of even going back to his place bubbles up a full-blown panic attack. Gulping more wine, she sits in silence.

Their waitress appears, reading the tension between them. "Can I interest you in any dessert?" Parker looks at Marni, who briefly meets his gaze.

The waitress notices the exchange. *How could she turn down a man like him? He is Ryan Gosling level hot. Maybe I can slip my number on his receipt.*

"The check is fine, thank you," Parker states. The waitress offers him a soft smile before leaving. Marni knows there is a chance that this is it. This is the last time he'll let her turn him down. The thought of him alienating her causes her chest to tighten. She doesn't want to lose him, but it isn't fair to keep stringing him along.

"Marni, I just...I wish you would talk to me, tell me why."

"I can't. I can't give you what you want. There are things about me...things you don't know." He opens his mouth, but she continues. "Things I won't discuss. I am sorry, Parker." She swallows down the lump in her throat. That was it—the final blow. The realization crosses Parker's face. No matter how many fancy dinners he plans, how many times he swoops in to save her, or compliments he gives her, it'll never be enough.

The waitress comes back and Parker's eyes shift from the numbers on the customer copy to meet the woman's gaze. She bats her lashes and turns so her ass is clearly in his view. Marni connects the dots easily enough. Maybe Parker will go back to her place tonight.

"I'll get a taxi home. Thank you for dinner." The tears burn, but she will hold them down, keeping the sobs at bay until safely in the cab. She sprints out of Carmala's, gripping her clutch with one hand and holding her dress up with the other. Her hair falls from the shocks of her heels hitting the ground. She holds her hand out and waves down a cab.

"Marni! Wait!" Parker breaks through the restaurant doors just as she closes the cab door behind her. Her hands shake and the wine-induced tears come out as choked sobs.

It shouldn't bother her that the waitress gave Parker her number; she had just turned him down again. A man that looks like him wouldn't be satisfied with her, not when she would have to say no every time he kissed a certain spot or touched her a certain way.

"Are you all right, miss?" the driver asks.

"I'll be fine, thank you."

He purses his lips but doesn't say anything more.

She closes her eyes and flashes of enraged brown, almost black eyes hover over her from where she cowers on the ground. Blood drips from the corner of her mouth. Pushing herself farther into a corner, she tries to find an escape. He pulls his hand back and swings it.

Marni jumps in the back seat of the cab as it takes a turn, her clutch chiming repeatedly.

Probably Parker trying to make amends again.

By the time she reaches her shower, her cheeks are smeared with makeup. A fresh bottle of wine finds its way into her hand to mask the pain she doesn't have the right to feel.

Chapter Two

MARNI TELLS HERSELF THIS was bound to happen. Parker tried to be more serious with her for a year. She knows she'd eventually have to squash that idea. She just doesn't expect it to hurt so much.

The hot water runs over her back as she sits on the tiled shower floor. She chugs the wine to keep the memories that are clawing to the surface locked inside her mind. There are rooms inside of her she refuses to ever open the doors to again. It is too painful—she wouldn't survive reliving it.

Ginger meows and swats at the shower door. Marni cracks it open and the defective cat climbs in with her.

"You really are the best cat."

The yellow tabby rubs up against her leg, totally ignoring the fact they're both wet. When the water turns cold, she shuts it off but continues to sit in the steamy bathroom. "Just you and me, Ginger."

She finally stands when the tile cools, wrapping a bathrobe around herself and putting her hair in a towel. She opens her laptop to the numerous emails, appointment reminders, and social media notifications pinging left and right. Her phone rings again from her clutch she discarded on the island. Not wanting to hear or see Parker's desperate pleas, she avoids all forms of contact and turns on a hopeless romantic movie since she's already heart broken.

***

HER HORSE SHUDDERS UNDER her as they stand in the box on the right side of the steer. Metal clashes against metal as the steer slams into the side of the chute. Brimstone's energy hums through the reins into Marni's hands. The smell of dirt, horse sweat, and livestock fill the air, mixing with the aroma of popcorn, burgers, and warm beer.

Tonya and Marni nod in unison at the man pulling the latch to let the steer run. It lunges forward as the gate slides open. Marni's heart thumps to the rhythm of her galloping horse as they run down the steer. She swings her lasso over her head and holds the reins with the other. Tonya snaps hers free and it catches the steer by the hind legs. A fraction of a second later, Marni releases hers and catches it perfectly around the animal's padded horns. Quickly, they wrap their ropes around their saddle horns and pull their horses back to stop, stretching the steer out to a halt.

The buzzer sounds and the girls both release their ropes as their time is called. They won, scoring the quickest time of 7.58 seconds. The crowd erupts to their feet and the roar of them puts Tonya and Marni on cloud nine. Their chests swell and smiles spread across their faces.

"YEAH!" they yell in unison as they pump their fists into the air. Tonya's parents drag them off their horses and swing them both around in celebration. Even Connor, Tonya's older brother, is there, smiling, with his hands in his pockets. His blue eyes track Marni while her parents sit in the bleachers. Her dad is smiling, but her mom rolls her eyes at the sight of them.

Marni rolls over in the king-size bed and rubs the dream out of her eyes. She always dreams of home in Wyoming when she is under stress. She covers her head with a pillow to hide from the sunbeams shining through the window. Her head pounds and her stomach swirls. Reaching out a hand, she pulls aspirin from the top drawer of her nightstand and dry swallows them before climbing out of bed. With each of Ginger's meows, a knife carves behind her eyes.

"I'll feed you, just give me a minute, okay?" she pleads, as if the cat knows what a hangover feels like. Marni shuffles to the bathroom sink. The cold water feels great against her face, and sharpens her mind. After taking care of Ginger, she opens her laptop to check her emails. Thankfully, Parker didn't resort to emailing her last night.

She scrolls through the spam and work emails, ignoring them until Sunday night when it's back to work time. Tonya's ranch name is bold in her inbox.

Shit, the email she sent. She clicks on Curston Ranch and pictures of a wild band of mustangs flood her screen.

This beautiful herd was rounded up two months ago, and I bought them from the kill pen. Some idiot rancher said they were a nuisance to his cattle and demanded they be "taken care of". The stallion—I've been calling him Commander—is a handful. I hope his offspring are easier to tame; they're built for the wilderness and survival. I think they'll make great working horses. I've attached pictures of all of them, even the adorable babies. Thought maybe you have forgotten what real beauty looks like being stuck in the city.

XOXO Tonya

Marni scrolls through each picture. She can practically smell and hear the horses on the ranch. Her heart aches for these majestic creatures, being tossed aside like garbage. A mixture of foals, three-year-olds with their lanky build, older mares, and their herd sire. He is a golden buckskin with two front socks and a white blaze down the center of his face. Marni ignores the ten missed calls and fifteen missed texts from Parker as she dials Tonya.

"Marni?!" her friend answers.

"Hey, T."

"Oh, my gosh! I haven't heard your voice in forever! How are you? Did you get my pictures?" Marni holds the phone a few inches from her ear as Tonya's pitch grows louder with each word.

"It has been a while. Sorry about that. You know, work. I actually was just looking at them, and that's why I called. They're beautiful, T, really. I'm glad you were able to save them."

"It's been an adjustment, that's for sure. Feed bills doubled and vet bills tripled, but it's rewarding. I've been able to re-home a few of the weanlings and yearlings. They aren't as wild. I have a few of the farm-hands working with the three-year-olds. They are quick to attach to one rider, though, which seems to be their flaw."

"Yeah, mustangs are known for trusting one person and being a one-person horse. That stallion is built like a tank. Has anyone been working with him?" Marni keeps his photo pulled up on her laptop screen. Something about his eyes draws her in, beckoning to her. Tonya snorts on the other end.

"Unfortunately, he's tried to kill basically everyone, even me. I worry he is too wild. I've not given up yet, but if he doesn't quit striking and charging us every time we open the gate, I don't know what else I can do. It's not right to keep him corralled all day. You know what I mean?"

"Yeah, I do," Marni mumbles as she inspects him further. He has scars on his chest and across his back, from protecting his herd, no doubt. Maybe even from another stallion. His muscles are sculpted and his veins are clearly visible in the photos. *Sheer power.*

"I wanted to ask you something, and before you say no, I want you to really think about it, okay?" Tonya asks. Marni eyes the phone skeptically and hesitates.

"Okay?"

"I would like to invite you to come to the farm. Just look at him, see if you can do anything. I miss you and I'd love to have you visit." Just like Tonya expected, Marni starts to say no before she even finishes her question. But her best friend has asked her to think about it, so she will.

"I have work, and meetings, and Ginger."

"Oh stop, when was the last time you took a vacation? I'm sure work can get on without you for a bit. You deserve a break, girl. I know you miss having your ass in a saddle. Bring your cat with you. I don't care."

"I'll think about it." She only says it to get Tonya to stop asking. It's almost a seven-hour drive between the city and the ranch. She also worries things will slip through the cracks at work if she leaves.

"Hey, I gotta run. Farrier just got here! Listen, really think about it. I'll call you back on Sunday night!"

After Tonya hangs up, Marni's stomach growls and the empty fridge reminds her of the grocery shopping she put off the night before. Since last night turned into the dumpster fire it did, she wishes she went instead of eating with Parker. "All right Ginger, I'll be back."

***

THE LITTLE CORNER MARKET is buzzing with bodies. Marni only needs to get the necessities, then she can hole up in her apartment for the rest of the weekend. She imagines she's back in Wyoming instead of here. On a clear, sunny day like today, she'd be trail riding, working cattle with Tonya's family, or fishing down at the river for trout. Instead, she inhales the scent of car fumes, and absorbs the sound of horns honking and people talking to themselves through ear pieces.

She grabs some bagels, eggs, frozen dinners, fruit, and a couple of bottles of wine. If she really is going to consider going to see Tonya for a bit, she'll need liquid courage. She looks for a female cashier and passes three empty lanes for the sweet elderly woman at the far side. "Good afternoon. Did you find everything you needed?" Her smile-lines wrinkle up to her eyes.

"I did, thank you." Her name tag reads Beth, and she is by far slower than the other male cashiers.

"Beautiful weather we are having today. Are you going to mosey down to the park? I sure would if I wasn't working." She scans the frozen dinners and bags them for Marni.

"I think I will just go home for lunch and have a lazy day today." Marni returns her smile and swipes her card.

"Well, I hope you have a great rest of your day, sweetie," Beth says to Marni as she grabs her bags. She keeps her head down as she heads back to her apartment. Several men stare as she passes, checking out her goods through her athletic shorts and tank top. A few try to say hey as she pushes by, but she doesn't respond or acknowledge any of them.

Ginger lounges on the back of the couch, and though she opens one eye when Marni walks in, she doesn't bother moving. Marni sits at the island and eats the pre-made cold cut she bought last minute.

Her phone chimes.

It's Parker, again.

She looks through the strings of *I'm sorry, please talk to me,* and *I'll do whatever I need,* but her reasons have nothing to do with him as a person. It's the things she has endured. She's watched a man change before her very eyes. *One minute he was loving, kind, a caretaker. The next...*She shudders at the thought and opens her laptop back up.

Tonya stands holding a foal while it's getting wormed. As cute as it is, Marni keeps finding herself sliding back to the picture of the stallion. His eyes are not trusting, but they are listening. His ears are perked toward the photographer and he's turned to face them with his head lowered a fraction, and nose pushed out slightly to show he is curious about what is going on. "You really are a beaut," she mutters to herself.

Ginger jumps up on the island and walks across the keyboard, begging for attention. "You are beautiful too, girl. What do you think about a little trip? Just you and me." She sits and cocks her head to the side, staring at Marni. "Yeah, I don't know about you traveling either." She closes the laptop and takes a couple of drinks of water. Migrating to the couch, she pulls up Netflix and starts her favorite series from the beginning again. It's like a favorite blanket or meal—it just washes all the stress away.

The intro to *Heartland* begins, and the song hits Marni's soul. It lulls her in and allows her to breathe. Even though it is scripted and there is no way that many unfortunate things can happen to one family, a lot of the horse knowledge is legitimate. The show only acts as background noise, though. In her mind, she is already in Wyoming meeting the stallion.

Could I really take a vacation? Would Boston give me a hard time? And would Ginger even be up for a trip? I mean, I just bought a loaf of bread and it'll go bad before I get back... Marni's mind races while Amy, the main character in the show, begins to *join up* with a black gelding her mom rescued from an abusive home.

She skims through her work calendar on her phone. There aren't any meetings that require her attention aside from Boston just wanting her to be there. Out of curiosity, she opens Google Maps.

A six-and-a-half-hour drive. She keeps her car parked in the garage attached to her apartment building. It is more of a hassle than it's worth to drive back and forth to work. She mainly uses it for out-of-town business.

"I could probably see if Mom and Dad would care to watch you. I'd just tell them it's a work trip. What they don't know won't hurt them." She chews on her lower lip, a habit formed from high anxiety and stress. *It's better than biting my fingernails. Less germs.* At least that's what she tells herself. "I'll call them, just to see if they have plans. What can it hurt?" After three rings, the call is answered.

"Hello?"

"Hey, Mom. It's Marni."

"I know, dear, your name popped up."

"Er, right. How are you?"

"We're fine. Your father is out fertilizing the yard." Marni's father, Gerald, is obsessed with his yard. Even when mowing, the stripes have to alternate every two weeks. "Did you need something?" her mom continues.

"No, just calling to check in."

"No need to fuss over us. We are capable people." Marni's mom, Gwen, seemed to have lost the maternal instinct.

"I wasn't fussing...I was just..." Gwen cuts Marni off.

"Well?" She remembers why she never calls her parents. They're the type that think once their child hits eighteen, they are done and the now-adult is completely on their own. Which is exactly what they did with Marni.

"Nothing, I'm glad you two are well. Love you both," she resigns.

"Yes, yes. Bye dear." Gwen disconnects the line. Marni stares at her phone and scoffs.

"Hey sweetie, how are you? How's Ginger? Oh, you want to go on a trip? We'd love to watch your cat, and you'll have to send pictures of those beautiful horses Tonya bought." She does her best impression of her mother's voice and says all the things she wishes her mom had. The only person to witness how cruel Marni's parents are was Tonya.

"Mom! Dad! I got in! I'm accepted into Southern Idaho for their pro rodeo team!" Tonya and Marni jump up and down through her house, waving the acceptance letter around like it's the Holy Grail. The two of them could finally chase their dreams in pro rodeo. Gwen pushes her brown bangs out of her eyes.

"You've already been accepted to the University of Wyoming, pursing your career in accounting. A real career," she sneers. Gerald stands behind Gwen and watches with hard eyes.

"Well, yeah. But Mom, this is a rodeo scholarship! I can get an education and continue roping with Tonya! She got in too!" Marni waits for the smiles to appear, for the 'congratulations', 'we are so proud of you' speeches. But she gets neither.

"That's very nice for her, but you are not going. I've already spoken with the dean at UW. Your room is spoken for and I pulled some strings, so you get one without a roommate. Easier for you to focus on your studies." Gwen glances at both girls with stone-cold eyes. Their smiles fade.

"But Mom, this is what I want. I want to team rope. I want to go pro." Marni knows her mom never approved of her lifestyle. She always hoped, if it paid for her education, she would let her go.

"It's time for your childish phase to be over and done. You're a grown woman, for God's sake. The rodeo is not a stable career choice. You are going to UW and that is the end of it."

In their stunned silence, Gwen steps forward and plucks the acceptance letter from Marni's hand. Before she can react, the letter falls to the floor, ripped into tiny pieces. Tears flow down Marni's cheeks as her mother crushes her dreams. The scholarship wasn't a full ride, and without her parents' support, she could never swing the rest. Tonya wraps her arms around Marni's shoulders; nothing she said would change Gwen Foster's mind. Gerald shows no signs of intervening or trying to help Marni, either. He just hides behind Gwen, not saying anything.

"Dad?" Marni pleads. Her voice cracks on the simple word.

"Go ahead, Gerald. Tell her I'm right and this is best for our little girl." He still says nothing. Marni looks at both of them with such hatred and resentment it would cut anyone down at the knees. Gwen, however, is unphased and, in fact, pleased that her daughter is cooperating so easily. Marni turns, and in that moment, she shoves down all her hopes and dreams. She becomes the version of herself her mom wants her to be.

Chapter Three

"WELL GINGER, IF I choose to go, it looks like you'll be going with me." Marni's mind wanders back to the ranch where she basically grew up. She spent every moment she could with the Curstons. They are the ones who gave her Brimstone for team roping, and the only condition was she had to take care of her and do some work on the ranch as needed. Which hardly felt like work to her.

She could use Zoom to attend her work meetings and take her laptop, of course, so she could work remotely. That would make her feel less like a deserter. "I'll sleep on it. T gave me 'til tomorrow evening to do just that—think on it." Ginger meows in response.

Across town, the city is already alive with people shopping, eating breakfast, and enjoying the cool air. Parker is rummaging through a flower shop to find the perfect mixture to say, *Please give me a chance*. He knows that Marni holds back. She has ever since he met her. When he feels like he is breaking through her hardened shell, she retreats again like he did something terrible.

Looks aside, she is a brilliant person, with a melt-worthy laugh, and the way she hides behind her hair to peek at him makes him catch his breath. Just the sight of her plasters a sappy, goofy grin on his face. He's never told her any of this, but he plans to today, and he will make her listen. He has to get this off his chest. She still hasn't returned his calls or texts.

"Can I help you?" The young girl wears a name tag that reads Molly, and below it, Florist.

"Good morning. I need something that pops, something that will take a woman's breath away."

"I'm glad you said so; those roses you're holding are so cliche and overdone. A woman won't show you, but she will internally roll her eyes at those. Follow me and I will show you the real jaw droppers."

Molly picks out dahlias in the softest of pinks, with hydrangeas that are the color of a purple sunset. Then filler flowers, Molly calls them, different greens and textures to fill the bouquet. At the counter she wraps it beautifully with white paper and white ribbons.

"Your total is one hundred thirty-five dollars; will that be a card or cash?" Without pausing at the amount, Parker swipes his visa, and walks a few blocks over to their local gourmet sweets store, Ocala Chocolates. Aromatic dark chocolate mixed with citrus and caramel hits Parker like a brick wall. *A menstruating woman's dream,* he thinks to himself.

He scours the multitude of options. *Does she prefer dark or white, or the kind with different flavors inside? What about nuts?* There are too many options for him to decide. His eyes hold a lost and helpless look as he reads and rereads the boxes.

"You look lost." The employee eyes the beautiful bouquet of flowers. *Whoever he is trying to impress will certainly swoon,* she thinks. Parker gives her a crooked smile and puffs out his cheeks as he exhales.

"I did not realize there were so many options for chocolate."

"Do you know what this special someone likes?" A nervous chuckle escapes him. To save him from his embarrassment, she goes with a safe choice. "Here, this is the best-seller, and it has a little bit of everything. Surely this will do the trick for you." And because he's ungodly attractive, she adds, "And if it doesn't work out, you know where to find me." She bats her lashes before sashaying away, ensuring she does it slow enough that he gets an eye-full of her backside.

Parker stares after her for a beat. Temptation burns in his stomach, but he shakes his head and leaves to walk toward Marni's apartment. He practices his give-me-a-chance speech. He isn't used to groveling or begging for a woman's attention. Maybe that is what makes Marni even more attractive—this playing hard-to-get game has him hook, line, and sinker.

His hands sweat, staring at her apartment door. *It is still early. Will she even be awake?* He debates waiting outside her door like a professional stalker, but takes a deep breath and lifts his hand. His knuckles barely brush the door when it swings open. Marni comes barreling out with a suitcase, laptop case, and her cat in some weird form of a space bubble on her back.

"Oh, gosh!" She stops and places a hand on her chest. "Parker, you scared me." Her eyes shift quickly from the gorgeous bouquet and elegantly wrapped chocolates under his arm. Her heart drops.

He's here to get me to give him a chance again.

"Um, I came to talk to you...I'm sorry. Is there a work trip I wasn't clued in on?"

"No...kinda. I'm taking a trip, but I'll still be working." She gives her suitcase another tug to get it sitting up and her hair falls in her face. He has the urge to reach out and tuck it behind her ear, but his hands are full still since she hasn't taken the flowers or chocolates.

"Where are you going?"

"Home. Well, to my friend's. She asked me for a favor so I'm driving down. I'll be back in a week. I already ran it by Boston. He said to not even worry about work but I still asked him to Zoom me in to meetings and I'll have my laptop ..." she rambles, as if trying to convince Parker it's okay if she goes.

"Oh, I see." He chews on the inside of his cheek.

"Yeah, so..." Awkward silence grows between them. Parker's nervous voice makes her jump.

"Marni, I wanted to tell you—I came here to ask you..." He sighs. "I want you to give us a chance. I bought these for you. The florist helped me pick them out, then the girl at Ocala picked these. Honestly, I didn't know what to look for. I hope you like them."

Marni stands with one foot in her apartment and one foot in the hallway. She woke in the middle of the night after a dream about the stallion being put down because he was too wild. She began packing right away and emailed Boston to let him know she was working remotely this week. She didn't even ask him, just informed him she needs some time away. It felt so invigorating to have the power to say what she wanted instead of hiding. Even if it was behind the safety of a computer screen. Have to start somewhere.

"Marni?" Parker still stands there, holding the flowers and chocolates.

"Oh, thank you. That's very sweet of you." She takes the box of chocolates and tucks it under her arm. "I'm not sure the flowers will make the trip, but I can put them in a vase inside. Here, let me take them." She grabs the flowers and jams the door with her luggage. She quickly fills the vase with water to place the flowers in.

"Marni, will you give us a chance?" He feels ridiculous having to repeat himself. Did she really not hear him the first time? She stops shuffling the flowers and places her hands on the counter-top. Marni stiffens as she holds the vase.

"I don't have time right now. I have to go." She avoids his eye contact as she picks her laptop case back up and grabs her suitcase. "I'm sorry. Thank you for the flowers and chocolates, really." She brushes past him on her way to the elevator. The last thing he sees is her cat lying happily inside its bubble on Marni's back.

The elevator door shuts and Marni's hands tremble on her luggage handle. She couldn't go back, and talk to Parker She'd end up in the never-ending loop of her letting him finish the conversation and somehow, she'd find herself going on another date and then retreating because Parker wants to go to the next step. She expects him to chase after her, try to convince her to stay or come with her. Either way, she won't tell him the truth. She made the mistake several times, and the pity eyes were almost too much to handle.

Her hand is steady on the steering wheel with Ginger's bubble carrier strapped in the passenger seat. She seems comfortable, stretched out in the sun. "All right girl, you ready?" Marni starts her tiny economy car and pulls out of the garage. For the first time in twelve years, she is leaving the city. Leaving the smog, leaving the rush of this life. She's finally going back home, and she couldn't be more excited and terrified.

She hopes to surprise Tonya. It is barely nine in the morning right now, so she should get there well before tonight when Tonya expects her call. She dreamed of the stallion all night, waking every hour to remind herself he isn't dead and she still has a chance to save him.

Her phone chimes and Parker's name flashes. Still asking if they could talk, wanting to know where she's going. Like all of his other messages this weekend, she leaves him on read and scrolls through her play list to find the perfect song for her mood.

'Long Live Cowgirls' by Ian Munsick and Cody Johnson vibrate out the speakers while she daydreams about the ranch. The pristine white two-story farmhouse with a wrap-around porch, framed with flourishing flowerbeds of the most vibrant colors. A pair of rocking chairs on each side of the red front door and a cattle dog lying in the shade at the foot of the steps. Off to the right is the red barn with silver metal roofing with two large rolling doors on the front. Hitching posts sit on each side of the entrance. Corrals, outdoor stalling pens, and dry lots scatter the back of the barn and melt into the lush green pastures of the valleys.

Tonya gathers her reins and leans forward in anticipation. "Wanna race to the river?"

"You'll lose." Marni gathers her own reins and tenses her legs around the bay mare Tonya's parents recently bought.

"Bet," Tonya snarks. In sync with each other, the girls squeeze their legs and click their tongues. Both horses launch from their rear legs, propelling themselves forward across the open field. At a gallop, only one of a horse's hooves touch the ground at a time, causing the four-beat galloping sound. They run to that same beat, matching each other step for step.

The river comes into view and Marni has the courage to do what Tonya never could. She lets the horse run with every ounce of its heart, releasing the reins, no holding back. Like flipping the turbo switch, the horse stretches her legs, reaching farther, pushing harder. Marni's heart pumps with each hoof beat. Tonya leans forward, urging her horse to go faster as Marni takes the lead, but she doesn't realize she still holds back; she still keeps the horse from running free.

Marni spreads her arms out to her sides and flies like any human being can. Her horse slows and splashes into the river and dips her nose to the water for a drink. Tonya, only four strides behind, pulls up beside her. Their laughs fill the open range with ecstasy.

"What more could you want when you have all of this?" Marni rubs down the bay's slick neck.

"I think she likes you." Tonya tilts her head toward the horse beneath Marni.

"She is pretty incredible."

"I bet my parents would keep her for you. Sweat equity. You are here enough anyway, and you need a good roping horse."

"We don't even know if she is a good header, and I couldn't ask that of your parents." They walk down the river bed, splashing water around them.

"Well, you won't have to, because I will. With a little practice, you can teach any horse to be a header. You have a gift." Marni rolls her eyes. Tonya likes to call her a horse whisperer often.

"Whatever you say, T."

Her mind comes back to the stretch of highway. That was the official day she got Brimstone, and she made one hell of a header for team roping. Her car dings, disrupting her daydream.

"Shit, don't crap out on me," she mumbles as she searches for the cause of the noise. Her low fuel light shines brightly.

"Right, gas." She exits the highway and by the way her stomach growls at her slowed speed, food isn't a bad idea either. She slips Ginger into her cat harness, not really knowing what to expect of this interaction.

Miraculously, she uses the bathroom with little convincing and doesn't fight the confinement. "You really are a defective cat." Marni smiles as she fills her collapsible water bowl.

After tucking Ginger safely back in her bubble, she enters the gas station. A man sits behind a glass barrier. Her palms sweat, but she has to get gas and some kind of substance for herself. She grabs cheese crackers, water, trail mix, and a couple of protein bars and places them on the counter. She opens her mouth to tell him she needs gas, but the words get lodged in her throat.

"Is that all?" He sounds annoyed, which makes her body stiffen. When she says nothing, he continues. "Okay, that'll be fifteen dollars and thirty-two cents." She clears her throat and tries again.

"I need gas." It comes out barely above a whisper.

"Okay, how much?" His fingers eagerly hover over the register. His phone vibrates on the counter; clearly, he is eager to read whatever texts are coming through.

"Um...thirty."

"Forty-five dollars and thirty-two cents, then. Unless there is something else you need?" She shakes her head and slides her card into the machine. A few beeps and she pulls her card out, then grabs her bag of snacks. She keeps her head down as she quickly shuffles to her car to start the pump. Her heart hammers in her chest. *He's not coming after you. You're fine, just breathe.*

Ginger meows like she was left for dead when Marni climbs back into the driver's seat. Her GPS has her four hours away. If Tonya's parents still run by their same routine, she will make it for dinner.

Marni's poor car groans in protest as she hits yet another pothole on the long gravel driveway. Ginger cries as it tosses her around her bubble pack. "I'm sorry," she says to both her car and her cat. Swerving to the right and left, she still hits one that makes a sound so harsh she cringes and rubs her poor dashboard in apology.

A large wooden arch towers over the last gate with a metal silhouette of a cutting horse working a steer. She takes a long, slow breath. This is her sanctuary. Bliss bubbles up her spine when she sees a field of horses grazing off to the right and a herd of cattle on her left.

Her car rolls to a stop when she pulls up to the front of the house. Time has not been kind to it or the barn as she takes them both in. Paint peels off the siding and a couple of aesthetic shutters hang crooked. The once silver-roofed barn is now more copper and orange from rust, the vibrant red of her memories dulled, like a faded t-shirt. No dog lies at the steps to greet her. In fact, she doesn't see a soul moving around.

The sun hangs low in the sky. Dinner-time will be when it's too dark to get any more work done outside. Which means people should start appearing soon. She steps out of the car and inhales two lung-fulls of the musty earth surrounding her. Horses, cattle, dirt, and fresh air make her moan in delight. "C'mon, Ginger. Let's see who we can find." She climbs the rickety stairs and listens to them creak under her weight. Pulling open the screen door, she knocks three times and the pitter-patter of feet shuffle to the door.

"I'm comin'!" a sweet, familiar voice sings. The door swings open and Stacy, Tonya's mother, looks at Marni in disbelief. Her gray hair is pulled back in a clip with wispy fly-aways landing on her cheeks. Tears prick at her gray eyes and she claps a hand over her open mouth. "Marni?" A smile spreads on Marni's face. "This is a wonderful surprise! Come here!" She pulls Marni into a hug that could warm the heart of Jack Frost himself. Stacy pulls herself back and eyes Marni up and down, noticing how skinny she has gotten, the muscles from her younger life long gone. She half expects her bones to rattle when she embraced her.

"It's good to see you, Mrs. Curston. I have missed you and this place." Marni looks around the interior of the house. Just like she remembered.

"Jack! Jack, come here! We have a visitor!" Stacy shouts. From the kitchen, Jack, Tonya's dad, ambles forward. His thick salt-and-pepper hair curls around his ears. A darker beard masks his face. The ranch life is hard on a person. He leans slightly forward and his knees don't bend like they used to. His blue eyes light up when he sees Marni in the doorway.

"Finally, our other daughter has come home for a visit. Took ya long enough." He grins and wraps Marni in a hug. His embrace melts away all her anxiety about showing up unannounced. He smells of tobacco, dirt, rain, and grass all mixed together.

"I'm sorry it took so long. Tonya called me and said she saved a band of horses. I wanted to come see them."

Jack releases her and steps back but keeps a hold of her hands. "I always knew it was horses that would bring you back. Tonya's still out tending to the back field of heifers this evening, tagging the new babies and vaccinatin'. They'll be along shortly. Would you like to join us for dinner?" The smell of a home-cooked meal has Marni's stomach fighting to go into the kitchen immediately.

"I'd love that. But can you show me where I'll be staying first? I have Ginger and although she traveled like a champ, she probably would appreciate more space to stretch." Marni turns to show them the bubble on her back.

"Well, isn't that a fancy travelin' case? Hello, Ginger, you are a pretty girl." Jack turns to mush over the fluffy feline. "The apartment in the barn is vacant if you would like to stay there, or we have a guest room upstairs. Although if I know you, you'll pick a stall if you could."

"The loft is perfect."

"We can help you with your things." Stacy starts toward the door, but Marni shakes her head.

"It's only my laptop bag and one suitcase. I can manage. I'll be back after I get settled."

Stacy and Jack watch as Marni takes her things to the barn, worried if they take their eyes off of her, they'll have imagined the whole thing.

"She's home." Stacy fights the tears that have burned her eyes since she opened the door. "She looks like she doesn't eat."

"Don't start your fussin'. She'll eat good tonight. Nobody can resist your cooking." Jack gives her a sweet kiss on the cheek and pulls her into a hug. The day Marni left was the day a part of both of them left as well. Marni will never understand how much of a daughter she is to the two of them. They love her just as they love their own flesh and blood.

Chapter Four

THE BARN APARTMENT ISN'T much, but it is all Marni needs. A soft, made-with-love quilt covers the bed. A nightstand table with a lamp, a vintage traveling wardrobe, and a chest at the foot of the bed are all that's in the room. There is a small bathroom with a standing shower in the corner. She opens Ginger's bubble, and she stretches with her butt high in the air. Marni fills her litter box in the corner before unpacking her clothes. She only owns one pair of jeans—she doesn't need them in the city—and doesn't have any boots. Tomorrow, she'll go into town and do a little shopping for this week.

She walks back down the stairs after getting everything settled. In the barn's alley, a horse squeals, followed by snorting and pawing at the ground. Out back through the double sliding doors is the buckskin stallion that haunts her dreams. Carefully, she approaches the panels, watching his movements. He has hay and water but is uninterested in both. He tracks her with wary eyes, putting on a show of power as he rears up on his hind legs and strikes out in her direction. Marni doesn't move from her spot, feet firmly planted. He stands at the far side of the corral and stares at her. His nostrils flare as he sniffs her out. Curious, he drops his head a fraction and pushes his nose out.

Marni slowly inches toward the gate while a man with a five o'clock shadow and a long duster landing at his mid-calves watches her have a staring contest with the malicious beast. His spurs chime on the heels of his boots as he approaches. He admires the woman from behind in her tight athletic shorts and tank top that show her bare shoulders.

Probably one of Tonya's tourists that wants the real cowboy experience. He leans against the barn doors, wondering if her face is as easy on the eyes as her ass.

The woman walks toward the gate and lifts her hand for the latch. He pushes off the door and with six running strides and slams it shut before she can slip in. The last thing this ranch needs are reports of a client getting trampled to death by a wild mustang stallion they had no business owning in the first place.

"Hey!" Marni whips around to face the person who sent the stallion into a frenzy. The mere size of the man causes her to lose the ability to speak and the anger in his eyes makes her cower and make herself invisible.

"You have no business being out here alone. That horse would kill you without a second thought." He spits his words like a viper spits venom. His Persian blue eyes slice clean through her and she pulls against his grip on her shoulders. Dirt is plastered to his face and a cowboy hat rests low on his forehead; little strands of hair poke out from under the rim.

Marni stumbles backward when he lets go. She wants to defend the stallion, but she can't, not with the anger being directed at her. Shutting down, she runs back to the house where Stacy and Jack are waiting for her to start dinner. In her panicked haze, she doesn't notice Brimstone tied in the aisle.

The man stares after her.

Better a crying client than a dead one, he tells himself.

Regardless, he knows Tonya will give him a verbal lashing for this when she finds out. If the client doesn't just disappear first. He pulls his saddle off Brimstone and hoses her down. Lucas, the farmhand, has already left for the day. He puts her in her stall and gives her feed and water when screams erupt from the house. He lunges for his rifle from his saddle sling and races to the house, heart drumming in his chest. Flashbacks of Afghanistan melt into the present with each stride. He squeezes his eyes shut to keep his focus.

Inside the farmhouse, Tonya embraces Marni and screams with delight that her best friend has, in fact, come to visit. And surprised her at that.

"You actually came! There is so much I want to show you! Oh, the stallion, he's out back! And then we have to go for a ride, of course. I just can't believe it!" She pulls her into another long hug that would be awkward if it was anyone else.

"I saw the stallion. He is even more beautiful in person," Marni states. Tonya pulls back just as the grizzly-sized man storms through the front door staring at her down the barrel of a rifle. On instinct, Marni tries to pull Tonya out of his line of sight, but she stands firm and squares her shoulders instead.

"Connor, you better get that out of my face before I shove it up your ass!" Tonya shouts. Stacy and Jack come from the kitchen to see what all the commotion is about and they pale when they see Connor, Tonya's older brother, looking as wild as the stallion with a gun in his hands.

"Jesus! Get that thing out of my house! For heaven's sake, you remember Marni, don't you? Jack!" Stacy pleads to her husband. He steps forward and pulls the gun from Connor's grip. It slips easily from his hands since he seems to be frozen in shock or embarrassment. His eyes land on Marni and her caramel brown eyes lock with his. He remembers her. She ripped his heart out when she left. He breaks their gaze and looks at his dad.

"I heard screaming. Thought something was wrong." His low sitting cowboy hat and stubble hide the heat that rushes to his cheeks.

"And your first instinct is to bring a gun? We're not at war here," Tonya snaps. She doesn't understand how deep the army planted its roots. His reactions are still hard-wired as if in the middle of war. Stacy intervenes before the siblings can start a blame game.

"Never mind that. Simple mistake. Come on, Connor, you're just in time for dinner. Tonya, set your brother a place. It's been a while since we've all eaten under one roof and it's complete with Marni here."

Marni's heart drums in her chest. She remembers Tonya's older brother, but she remembers a bean pole that couldn't be bothered with horses. Given his spurs, boots, and horsehair on his duster, that has obviously changed.

Marni watches Connor walk into the kitchen, not daring to have him at her back. His Wrangler jeans hug tightly to his muscled ass and thighs. A flutter forms in Marni's stomach. A feeling she hasn't had since...she shuts the door to that memory with an indignant head shake. They sit on opposite sides of the table from each other. The shock of the initial events has everyone silent as they pass the bowls around. Tonya breaks the tension with talk of the stallion.

"So, back to the wildie. What do you think? Did you get any kind of read on him?" Marni looks at the plate full of mashed potatoes from scratch, not boxed; canned green beans she knows Stacy spent hours on the porch breaking, then even longer canning, and a homemade bread slice with a perfect square of butter melting on top. She scoops a piece of meatloaf and lifts it to her mouth, then answers Tonya.

"I only saw him for a moment. He settled pretty quickly after I stood there for a few moments. I was, um, I got hungry and decided to save the next steps for tomorrow." She glances at Connor, who rolls some food around in his mouth and has a remorseful look in his eyes. Marni gives him a soft smile to tell him it's okay.

"Did you bring any riding clothes? I want to show you the herds we've built up and the other wildies that are in the back pasture."

"I actually don't have any. I was going to run to town and snag a few things. No need for boots and riding jeans in the city." She forces a small smile to brush off the sadness this admission causes. Connor notices her smile doesn't reach her eyes.

"I have plenty. I'm sure you'll fit in them. After dinner, I'll show you my cabin and let you try on a few things," Tonya says. Marni nods with a mouthful of the delicious buttery potatoes.

"How is life in the city treating you dear?" Stacy interjects.

"It's good. I have my own apartment with a window view and a good job. I actually have to work a bit while I'm here. Zoom meetings that I have to attend." She looks over at Tonya. "Other than that, I am all yours and the stallion's." She wears a genuine smile now. Excitement courses through her.

It's going to be very hard to sleep tonight and not work with the stallion after a catnap.

Connor decides now is not the time to start another argument about the useless wildies his sister insisted on saving. He has no intentions of letting Marni anywhere near that stallion, and Tonya is an idiot for thinking she could tame him enough for a home. The horse is far too wild; he'll be the one to do the breaking. Marni stands and helps Stacy with the dishes while Tonya and Connor step out to discuss ranch business.

"I'm sorry about Connor," Stacy starts. "The war did things to him. He hasn't been the same since he came back. He has a good heart still, and he is great with the ranch, but with people, not so much. You remember when he was younger, smiled all the time. He was such a happy kid. Now, he's hardened and has dreams where you need to stay far out of his way. He can be...well, what the army molded him to be."

Marni hadn't known Connor had joined the army or was even deployed. When she and Tonya did talk, it wasn't about him. Stacy gives her a soft smile when Tonya rejoins the room. Her face is red, like she just ran a marathon.

"Are you okay?" Marni asks.

"Oh, peachy." She waves a hand through the air. "You ready to go see my place?" Annoyance, laced with downright pissed-off, drips from her tone. The two of them walk outside to get in the old bench seat Ford and drive past her parents' house up a worn path.

"I just assumed you lived with your parents."

"Definitely not. I can't exactly bring guys to my parents' house at thirty years old." Tonya rolls her eyes and pulls up to a quaint little one-bedroom cabin with a full front porch.

"Hey, we aren't thirty yet! We still have a few years before we hit that life crisis." Marni laughs as she steps out of the truck.

"Welcome to my home."

Just the way Marni remembered Tonya's, organized clutter is scattered throughout the open floor plan in the kitchen and living area. Marni runs her hand along the wooden log walls. "It's gorgeous. It's about the size of my apartment back in the city. Is this real wood?"

"Yeah, all real. Sorry about the mess. I wasn't expecting company."

"Because that would have changed anything." Marni flashes her a sarcastic smile.

"Hey! I shove it all under the bed and in the closet when I have a man over. I could've done the same for you." Marni finds an empty spot on the couch and sits. The hours of travel and nearly dying from the panic attack Connor induced earlier are catching up to her.

"Wine?" Tonya opens her dorm sized fridge and holds out two wineglasses.

"Yes, please. So, your brother...?" Marni raises her eyebrows toward Tonya.

"Oh, my brother," she sighs. "He's a mess. Has been since he's been home and decided he was going to run the ranch. He's older, so he has dibs. I don't mind as long as he keeps his hands away from the wildies."

"He doesn't want them here?" Marni's mind focuses on the way his Persian blue eyes heated a fire inside of her. They were fierce when he slammed the gate shut and full-blown feral in the house with a gun.

"He's a cattle rancher. He sees a waste of hay and space." Marni lets that simmer for a moment. A trigger-happy individual around horses he doesn't care about puts her on edge. Apparently, Tonya can read the worried look on her face. "He won't kill them or harm them. Just bust my chops about them until he's blue in the face." That makes some of her uneasiness subside, but the ferocious man she met at the corral panel and then in the house with a gun scares her, nonetheless. "Anyway, enough about my broody brother. Any guys in your life back in the city?"

"Not really. There is Parker, a work friend. He actually showed up at my apartment as I was leaving this morning with flowers and chocolates."

"That's so sweet! Is he sexy? Good in bed?"

Marni cringes at that mental image. "No—I mean, yes, he is attractive, but we've never done anything more than go out to eat. He repeatedly states it known he wants to be more. I just can't do it. Not after..." Marni lets her thought trail off. Tonya knows where her mind is going and she scrambles to pull her attention elsewhere.

"Well, I refuse to settle for any of the men around here that can't do much with what God gave them."

Marni snorts out a chuckle.

"Besides, I don't need anyone trying to tell me what to do," Tonya adds.

"Cheers to that!" They clink their glasses together before gulping down their wine.

"How have you been, really?" Tonya is the only person who knows about what happened to her. She came to the hospital to be with her and the days that followed she helped her get settled in back at home.

"I'm okay. Still have my moments, but I'm excelling at work and Parker has helped with getting me out of my apartment. Maybe that is why I keep stringing him along." Marni lays her head back and looks at the ceiling. "Ugh, I hate that I do it, but I enjoy his company and the restaurants he takes me out to are divine. Like full-blown ball-gown and tuxedo level."

"So why not give you two a chance?"

"He wants to take the next step. I don't know if I'm ready."

Tonya mulls this over like the wine she sips.

"How about this? We go to Turnpike tomorrow night, get you loosened up, find your confidence, flirt a little, and then...I don't know what else."

Marni can practically see the gears turning in Tonya's mind on how to *fix* her friend.

"I don't know, T. I can't talk to guys...Parker doesn't count."

Tonya jumps off the couch and disappears to her room.

"But I have the perfect dress for you! Look!" She comes out holding a sparkling sapphire cocktail dress. "Try it on!" Obliging her fantasy, Marni strips down and slips into the cocktail dress. It hugs all the right curves and falls right at mid-thigh, accenting her long legs.

"T, it's beautiful." Marni poses in the floor-length mirror, twirling with her hands out like a child playing dress-up.

"I have the perfect heels to go with it!" She disappears again and comes back with a pair of black heels that certainly don't belong in this part of Wyoming.

"Is Turnpike a fancy bar or are you shooting over the top here?"

"Maybe we should stick to boots and jeans. I can find somewhere this weekend for you to wear that and I'll wear this." Tonya holds up an emerald green dress that swoops to the small of her back.

"Why do you have these?"

"The local prom dress store went out of business and had a closing sale. I figured why not? But here are these for tomorrow." Tonya stacks jeans and shirts on top of a pair of worn, brown cowboy boots. "I need you to prove Connor wrong. Commander isn't a lost cause. He keeps saying I'm the reason we are in a financial bind and not the market."

"Give me 'til the end of the week and I'll have him singing a different tune," Marni states, holding her head high and a smile forming at the corner of her lips.

"Is that how long you're staying? I was hoping for more. If I'm honest, I was hoping you had the wild hair to quit your job and stay." Marni's heart sinks. No amount of time with Tonya is long enough, but dwelling on the fact she'll be leaving in seven days is not how she wants to spend it.

"T, I—"

"Don't worry, it's the wine talking," Tonya cuts her off. "You're here and that's what counts. I'll drive you back to the loft. Breakfast is at sunrise, just like always." On the drive back, Marni sees the silhouette of a man in a rocking chair on the back porch. "Looks like Connor hasn't gone home. Probably waiting to pounce me to finish the conversation I cut short earlier."

The brim of his hat shifts as he looks up when they get out of the truck. His rifle leans on the table beside him.

"Hey." Tonya snaps Marni's attention back to her. "The farm-hands will be here early, so don't freak out if you hear people."

Marni wraps her arms around Tonya's neck and holds her tightly. "I've missed you, T."

"I've missed you too, Mar."

Connor watches as the two women laugh and hug. Marni enters the barn and the loft light flicks on, her shadow moving across the window. He told Tonya what he thought about the stallion and that only led to her becoming red-faced and unreasonable. She's hellbent on saving every single one of those horses, but the hoof-shaped bruise on his back from the stallion just solidifies his point.

Tonya drives off and gives him a captain's salute. Clearly, she isn't in the mood to come to an understanding between them.

"Sweetie, are you going to bed?" Stacy peeks her head out of the screen door.

"I'll be heading home soon. Good night." She gives him a knowing smile. She saw the way he stared at Marni when they were younger, and knows how much it hurt him when she left. Now she is back, and her first impression of him is treating her like an infidel and waving a gun in her face.

Chapter Five

Connor rubs his calloused hands across his face. He won't be able to sleep tonight, not after his manic episode. He sits at his regular spot at Turnpike, orders his usual, starting with whiskey, then switching to Michelob.

"Needed a release again, Stout?" The bartender saunters over and leans forward as she stares into Connor's eyes. The top button of her blouse busted open, barely covering her nipples. Her blonde hair falls forward and skims the bar top.

"Another, Christy," Connor requests and she slides a glass down the bar to him. He tosses it back and lets the burn spread through his limbs. His running mind settles and he switches to beer. He can't get trashed tonight. He has to go home so he can babysit Marni with the stallion tomorrow. Since Tonya won't listen to reason, he has no intention of letting Marni anywhere near him alone.

He scans the crowd from his perch as people flood in and out. Some disgustingly trashed, others dancing on the floor having the time of their life. This isn't a high-end bar, that's for sure. The low-lifes have a way of creeping in here when it is late like this, looking for scores or a way to make a quick buck.

"Your place or mine tonight?" Christy bats her lashes as she wipes down the bar in front of him. Her Daisy Dukes and tied button down, topped with cowboy boots scream slutty cowgirl wanna-be. He never takes her to his place, but that never stops her from asking.

"I can't tonight. Just needed to take the edge off." He tips his beer towards her, then chugs before pulling out cash to pay his tab. She comes out from behind the bar and pushes his leg between her thighs. From the height of the bar stool, his jeans rub against her lips and it's obvious when she rocks her hips slowly while talking to him.

"C'mon, I get off in thirty minutes. Stay, drink, then we can have some fun." She runs a hand down his chest and licks her lips. Against his better judgment, he hardens at her warmness inching closer to his lap.

"Back room," he resigns, and she happily sashays her way to open him another beer. Maybe he can use Christy to get the captivating brown eyes out of his head.

Last call comes and goes. Then she's leading him behind the bar to the stock room downstairs. Eagerly, her clothes hit the floor before he has a chance to even work her up.

He pushes her against the wall and hikes up her right leg by the back of her knee. With a couple of tugs, she has his belt undone and grips his length, rubbing her hand up and down. She opens a condom with her teeth and slides it on like it's as easy as undoing her bra. Maybe it is for her. He holds back the moan that wants to escape him. This is just a quick fuck, nothing more.

He thrusts deep inside of her, digging the brick wall into her bare back. She moans like he's the best lay she's ever had, but he only focuses on the warm, wet desire that caresses his cock.

"Yes!" Her scream bounces off the walls. Connor buries his head in her shoulder, his eyes shut, keeping himself from seeing the woman he's inside of. She scratches her nails down his back and he shoves the full weight of himself into her. With each rock of his hips, he pours out his flashbacks from the war, the fear that swelled up when he saw Marni about to challenge the stallion and the way her eyes froze with panic when he stared her down the barrel aimed right at her.

Christy wraps both legs around Connor's waist, giving him the leverage to go even deeper. She peaks on a half-scream, half-moan, and Connor holds the full weight of her up while he follows suit. He grits his teeth and holds his breath, refusing to give her the satisfaction of making him come. He slides out of her and she has to lean against the wall to hold herself up. Quickly, he buckles his pants and adjusts himself.

"You're just gonna leave a girl wanting more like that?" Christy purrs as she saunters her naked body over to him.

"I have an early morning. Get home safe."

"I'll remember this next time you come to me for a pity party. I'm just an easy fuck to you, aren't I?"

Connor winces at her revelation. "I told you from the beginning, no emotions, just sex," he states coldly.

"You can't just fuck someone like that over and over and not give a fuck about them." With tears in her eyes, Christy hastily pulls her clothes back on.

"Christy, I..." Guilt sits heavily on Connor's chest. In the back of his mind, he knows she is developing feelings. She watches him constantly at the bar and doesn't flirt with the other patrons like she used to.

"Save it, Curston. I don't need your pity. You and your baggage can stay the hell away from me." She shoves past Connor and stomps back up the stairs. "Get out so I can lock up!" she shouts behind her. Connor rakes his fingers through his hair and slides the cowboy hat back low over his eyes.

He pauses as she stands with her hip cocked out, holding the door open. "I wish you the best, Christy." She scoffs and slams the door closed behind him.

***

MARNI WAKES AT FIVE thirty on the dot. She checks her emails and her first meeting is at eight. She could go work with the stallion now and get a couple of hours in before showering to look presentable on the Zoom call. Bounding down the stairs two at a time, the smell of leather and horses filling her nostrils.

Heaven. This has to be what heaven smells like.

At the sound of her footsteps, horses stick their heads over their stall gates and nicker, requesting food immediately. Marni smiles at them and tosses flakes of hay over each gate with a pitchfork. Tonya will have to show her the feeding schedule; since she is already here in the mornings, it's the least she can do.

She grabs the lasso from the hook and walks toward the corral where the buckskin beauty displays aggravated snorts and pawing.

"Hey boy, remember me?" She leans against the panels while he runs around stomping, rearing, pinning his ears back, and showing every ounce of his raw power to scare her off like the predator he thinks she is.

"Easy boy, I'm not going to hurt you. I'm here to help, even though you don't know it yet." He settles down but watches her from the far side of the corral. His ears flick from side to side, scanning his surroundings for an ambush. He has even more scars than the pictures showed. He must be a real slugger to have this much damage and still have his band of mares. Marni observes him from the gate, checking for any signs that he's going to attack.

He swings his hindquarters so he stands facing her. She pulls the lever of the gate and it creaks as she steps inside. He lets out a warning snort and strikes the ground, but doesn't advance.

Letting her body language do the talking—she keeps her shoulders relaxed, arms down, and gives him plenty of space. She slides the lasso down her arm into her hand. "We're just going to run a little. You like to run, right?"

His ears perk at the sound of her voice and her movement. He holds his head high as Marni slaps the lasso against her leg and barely clucks for him to move. When he bolts and nearly runs into the panels with his full chest, she heads to the center of the pen to keep him running around her.

They dance in tandem with each other. When he slows or tries to stop, she clucks and gives the lasso another slap to keep him moving. His eyes and ears constantly look for an escape, not giving Marni any part of his mind.

After several laps, he turns one ear toward her, watching with one white-rimmed eye of distrust. She backs up to cut him off and sends him across the corral to run counter clockwise now, but the stallion has a different plan.

He never cuts away from her; instead, he barrels straight at her and she has to scramble up and over the panels before he makes contact.

"Touché," she lets out breathlessly, and shakes the adrenaline out of her hands.

Back inside the corral, she picks him up at a run and let him slow to a trot. After several laps, she backs up again to cut him off. When he rounds the circle, he lowers his head, preparing to charge. Marni throws her hands up and waves the lasso.

"Hah!"

The stallion backs down and turns to the other side of the panel with a sidekick in Marni's direction for good measure. Getting a second wind, he madly dashes around the corral, bucking and kicking in annoyance that he just lost the game of chicken.

"Settle, easy. There you go," she coos to the stallion as he slows to a controlled trot.

Marni drops her arms and backs up from the horse's space. He stops and looks at her, his ears twitching and nostrils flared. When he drops his head and takes a deep breath, she knows she has him. Not today, certainly not tomorrow, but by the end of the week, she will be on his back.

Once she closes the gate, she hangs the lasso back up. Sweat trickles down her back. Her arms and legs burn with the intense form of groundwork. She tosses fresh hay into the corral and fills his water bucket. Stiffly, she walks back for a shower, but spots Tonya and Connor leaning against the barn doors. Heat rushes to her cheeks, realizing she was being watched.

"That was incredible! I knew you could do it!" Tonya beams.

"I haven't done anything yet."

"You got in there and out in one piece. That's more than anyone else has done," Connor retorts, his voice gruff and deep.

"You missed breakfast, but I put a doggie bag upstairs for you," Tonya says. "Your cat hissed at me when I came in. I tried to pet her, but she wasn't having it."

"She isn't used to anyone besides me. I'm sorry I missed breakfast. I'll have to apologize to your parents." Tonya waves her hand in a dismissive gesture.

"We all knew where you were. Connor missed breakfast, too, but he drank too much last night." Tonya jabs at his ribs.

"Don't you have new calves to tag and record?" He stalks off toward his bay mount, and the star on its forehead sparks a memory in Marni's mind.

"Brimstone?!" Connor pauses before swinging his leg over. "Is that really you?" Marni rushes to rub her hands across her star and down her neck.

"You know my horse?" Connor asks, perplexed. The word *my* throws Marni back. Of course, when she left, someone else would have taken over her ownership.

"She was Marni's header when we competed," Tonya interjects. Connor notices the water pooling around Marni's eyes, but she blinks them away before they fall. How had he forgotten this was her horse before she left?

"Oh, well, I can get another one. Leave her for you?" Connor peers back at the barn and runs through the available working horses to choose from. Marni shakes her head when he reaches to unbuckle the saddle.

"No, it's fine. She looks good and likes you. I have to work anyway. It was just a shock to see her."

"I'll have Lucas pull Turbo out for you and when you finish your meeting. You can meet me in the back pasture. Do you remember how to get there?" Tonya smiles and Marni's lips turn at the thought of riding a horse, not to mention getting to work cattle.

"I'm sure I can manage." They both giggle, knowing Marni has no sense of direction and is notorious for getting lost. "Fine. If I get lost, I'll call."

"Deal."

Connor mounts Brimstone while Marni walks back inside. She gives one fleeting look over her shoulder at the cowboy who now has the claim of her horse.

***

JUST AS MARNI PREDICTED, she wasn't needed in the meeting. She kept herself muted the entire time and listened as they discussed growth and different rises and drops of current stocks. When she comes back downstairs and enters the barn, a saddle with a note on top of it in the middle of the aisle.

Thought you might need this.
Welcome home
Stacy & Jack

Tears well in her eyes as she runs her hand over the handcrafted leather saddle. It's hers from before. They kept it all of these years and it's in great condition. It looks brand new, like years haven't passed.

"Marni?" A man's voice startles her, and she squeals, nearly knocking the stand over. A boy about eighteen or twenty with tan skin and blond hair poking from under his cowboy hat reaches out to steady her. "Sorry, I didn't mean to scare you. I'm Lucas, one of the ranch hands. Tonya asked me to help with getting Turbo saddled for you."

"You're fine. I'm fine. It's fine," she blubbers out. She takes a deep breath and tries again. "Tonya told me you would be here. She said I would ride Turbo today, but I don't know which one that is."

The barn of twelve stalls is nearly full, after all. Lucas gives her an amused smile and leads her over to a stall with a stocky chestnut gelding catching a nap.

"I already brushed him off for you. I'll go grab his bridle."

Marni isn't used to having someone do these tasks for her. She rubs Turbo down, getting a feel for him. He has a quiet mind, humble eyes, and a good disposition. Once Lucas has him saddled, he goes into the tack room and comes out with a box.

"This has your name on it. I'm not sure what it is."

She opens the box and pulls out a new cowboy hat with a leather braid around the hatband. She slides it on her head—a perfect fit. There's no note or anything to say who it is from.

"Thanks. How does it look?" she asks Lucas, tipping it down like the cowboys in movies when they say howdy.

"You look like the real deal," he says with a genuine smile. She smiles in return and swings her leg over Turbo, her glutes hugging her saddle like an old friend. The clip-clop of horseshoes echoes as she walks Turbo across the rocky pavement. Her body vibrates with anticipation of running, to feel the wind blow through her hair and help her soul soar. The wild stallion squeals as she rides by him.

"Fix your attitude and this could be us!" she hollers back at him. He snorts, as if understanding her meaning. Once they reach the grassy field, she picks Turbo up to a canter toward the back pasture.

Connor's eyes follow Marni as she gallops from the ridge. One hand on the reins, the other on her new hat. He watched her from the shadows this morning. Tonya caught him red-handed, but was nice enough to not say anything. His mom gave him the hat box when he grabbed leftovers, since he missed breakfast. He bought her the hat as a *congratulations* for going pro rodeo, but fate screwed him and he never had a chance to give it to her.

"This is a new look for you, Curston. That filly has you all sorts of scrambled." Hocks rides up next to him, eyeing Marni as she streaks across the open field.

"Let's get to work." Connor grumbles. Hocks turns to head toward the herd, but Connor gives her one last glimpse as she disappears into the woods.

Marni slows to a walk as the smell of pine trees and fresh running water fills the air. The river runs alongside her and she will have to cross it to make her way to the back pasture. The sound of birds singing and Turbo's deep breaths is music to her ears. No traffic horns, no people chattering, just peace.

Wildflowers bloom in yellows, purples, and reds while rabbits dart across the trail, scurrying to their hidden burrows. She ducks under a low-hanging branch and finds the path to cross the river.

Marni stands atop of a slope and sees Tonya and five others below. Two are holding a calf down as it screams for its mother, while the other three people remain on horseback to protect the two on the ground from the wrath of the protective cow. Smoke rises from the small fire for the branding iron and Marni canters down to get in on part of the action.

"Finally, someone who can rope worth a damn!" Tonya shouts out. The ranch hands chuckle at her declaration.

"I wouldn't get excited. I haven't done it in years," Marni states and gets a feel for the lasso in her hand.

Tonya gestures toward a scrawny, red-haired boy on horseback. "Anything is better than Wes."

"You wound me, T." He holds his hand over his heart like he's been shot. He turns his gaze to Marni. "I get the job done, but it's not pretty." He flashes her a smile, which highlights his freckles.

"Okay, what do you need?" Marni pulls her hat lower and sits up in the saddle.

"Turbo is a decent cutting horse. I need you to rope the babes without tags first. There's a couple of five-month-olds that continually give Wes the slip if you could help with that." Marni nods and pushes Turbo toward the herd. She spots a baby without a tag. Wes and the other two hands focus on keeping the herd rounded up while Marni cuts out the one she needs.

Testing the stiffness of the lasso. She loops it around her head a few times; the weight sliding through her hand. On her fifth swing, she releases the rope, and it hits the ground next to the calf, causing it to spook and run to its mom in the herd.

Tonya watches in anticipation. Her best friend's confidence has been doused since she left the ranch. This week is just as vital for her as it is for the stallion. Tonya intends to get her friend's fiery spirit back.

"Try again!" she calls. Marni lets out a huff and pushes through the herd for another calf. She spots one of the older ones that gave Wes the slip and points Turbo on it. He cuts him away from the herd, then the chase is on. Unlike the steers they chased in team roping, this calf is young and not nearly as strong. Marni swings her lasso above her head as Turbo canters to keep up. She releases the rope; the calf cuts a hard right but Marni's loop is wide enough. It slides right over its nose and tightens as she wraps it around the horn of her saddle.

The boys let out a chorus of *whoops* as they circle the calf from the herd. Once its hide is singed with the Curston Ranch brand and its ear pierced with an identification number, Tonya releases Marni's lasso and she rolls up the slack.

"Now go get 'em." Tonya smiles at Marni. Her eyes sparkle with adrenaline as she and Turbo work as a team. After several hours of cutting, roping, and releasing, the group loads up their gear and heads back to the house for lunch.

"Wes, she made you look terrible!" A boy wearing a black cowboy hat with light brown hair rides up next to Marni. "It's like you speak to cows and know what they are going to do!" A huge smile adorns his face.

"I don't talk to cows. You can read their body language. Your horse can too, if you work enough."

"No, *you* can read their body language," Tonya chimes in. "It's your gift, just like with horses. I like your hat, by the way." Marni reaches up to touch her hat as she dismounts from Turbo.

"It was in a box with my name on it in the tack room. Your parents set out my saddle, so I assume the hat came from them, too."

"Well, it fits like it was *made* for you."

Lucas and the other hands take the horses to untack and hose off. Marni just stares after them. "I feel weird, like I'm not finishing the job."

"They're cheap labor, chasing the pro rodeo life. Bull riders mostly, although Wes wants to do team roping with Lucas. They need a lot of work. I guess I kind of made you a legacy with them. Meeting you today put them on cloud nine. They've gawked at our trophies and ribbons hanging in the tack room."

"I'm nothing special. I didn't even go pro." Marni's voice drops. Reminded of the dream, she never got to chase.

"You are special, regardless of any of that. And you made those boys' day," Tonya says. Marni smiles as she catches the guys watching the two of them walking away.

She snickers. "I think they think we're hot." Tonya turns and the boys fall over themselves, trying to look busy. She gives her hair a flip before walking to the house.

Chapter Six

MARNI SLIDES HER BOOTS over her socked feet to do night checks on the barn and stallion before going to bed herself. She tops off the water buckets hanging in the stalls and gives the hardworking horses another flake of hay. The stallion paces his corral and whinnies for his herd on the other side of the ranch. Tonya said during dinner she wants to take Marni out there tomorrow to see them.

"Hey pretty boy, you're all right." Marni leans her arms against the panel and the stallion stops pacing to watch her. "There you go. You just don't like being alone, do you?" She drags a square bale over to sit beside the panels. The air has a chill to it since the sun went down.

Connor stops as he enters the barn to check the horses when he sees Marni with her long hair blowing in the gentle breeze, talking to the stallion. He didn't believe Tonya when she told him about Marni's gift, but watching the stallion now with his head low and ears forward, Connor knows she will form a bond with him. But what happens to him when she leaves? It'll take the next owner just as much work, if not more, to form this kind of understanding.

The chances of this stallion finding a new home are slim to none, and that's exactly why he pressured Tonya into letting the whole lot be someone else's problem. The ones they can't re-home will be right out there in the back pasture, eating the grass meant for cattle and costing the ranch money.

Once he is sure Marni has no intentions of getting in the pen with the stallion tonight, he retreats to his truck. His headlights spook the stallion as they swing around, flashing his eyes. "Easy boy." Marni calms him again before turning her head to see who else is out so late. She recognizes the faded blue pickup as Connor's and lays her head back to look at the stars that litter the sky.

She names the few constellations she can; Big Dipper and Little Dipper, some man's belt, and the North Star. A shooting star darts across the sky and Marni closes her eyes to whisper a wish. The sound of hooves stepping closer alerts her, but she doesn't jump. In her peripheral vision, the stallion has taken a couple of steps closer, sniffing in her direction.

"I see you," she whispers, and his head jerks up at the sound of her voice. She giggles and closes her eyes as a barn owl hoots in the distance.

***

MARNI STANDS FACING THE stallion with the lasso hanging down by her leg. Both of them glisten, wet with sweat. Marni shrugs out of the pullover she thought she'd need when they started early this morning.

Unfortunately, horses have no sense of time, and when working with one, you need an I-have-all-the-time-in-the-world mindset. Which is exactly what she told the stallion when he struck out at her an hour ago.

"You are making this so much harder than it has to be!" She struggles to keep the irritation from turning into full-blown pissed at this point. "I am hungry, thirsty, and hot," she whines, but clicks her tongue to pick him up at a trot again. One ear remains turned on her while he watches her with his inside eye. After a couple of passes, she backs up for him to turn across the corral. Like he has done every time today, he kicks out at her and pins his ears back in an attempt to scare her.

"Get your ass over there!" she shouts, throwing her arms up at him. The stallion mimics her rage by snorting and raising his tail high in the air as he bucks around the panels. She pushes him to run harder around her, demanding the same respect she *was* showing him. Lucas stands in the barn aisle in awe of the ball of fury Marni has become. She seemed so quiet and couldn't even make eye contact with him before, but she is not backing down now.

"Don't you have stalls to clean?" Connor pops up behind him, his tone even.

"Um, yes sir, sorry." Lucas tries to recover as he creates space between him and the intimidating older brother. There are stories about him. Like he killed a man with his bare hands. Nobody dares ask him about it, though.

Connor walks over to Marni with a peace offering of a cold bottle of water and a granola bar. His mom insisted he bring it out to her and wouldn't take no for an answer. When Marni spots him, her blazing eyes fall to the ground and her shoulders lower. As if trying to turn into herself and become invisible. Not the actions he'd expect from the spitfire he just saw.

"Mom said you missed breakfast again and might need this." He hands her the bottle and bar through the panels. She chugs three quarters of the water before stopping, then wipes the excess and sweat with the back of her hand.

"Thanks," she says breathlessly. She takes a bite of the granola bar and sags against the panel, her head resting on the rail. Connor shifts uneasily, trying to find the courage to say what he needs to get off his chest. He hates that she seems so scared of him.

"Marni, I'm sorry about Sunday. I didn't know it was you. All I saw was a girl about to get herself killed. I shouldn't have grabbed and scared you like that." He waits for her to meet his gaze, but she doesn't.

"It's okay. It was an accident." She fidgets with the wrapper.

Connor attempts to change the subject. "Having a harder time today?" He turns his attention to the stallion, not completely trusting it won't try to take advantage of Marni's weakened state and attack.

"He's just stubborn and doesn't want to trust me. I think he's acting out because he knows he can trust me, but it pisses him off."

Connor snorts. "He told you all of that?"

"Not exactly. I can just...tell." She stuffs the wrapper in her front pocket and downs the rest of the water.

"Well, I'll let you get back to it. Don't want to interrupt. If you plan on missing lunch, let someone know so we can bring you something." His voice is less rough than the first time she saw him. There is a tenderness to it.

"I don't think he has another two hours in him. At least that's what I keep telling my sore muscles." Her brown eyes trace the lines of his face. It is easier to talk to Connor when the conversation revolves around horses. His blue eyes lock with hers. A second passes before Marni breaks their connection and walks back to the middle of the corral.

Progress, Connor thinks to himself.

Chill bumps scurry up her arms even in ninety-degree heat. She risks a glance behind her as Connor walks to the barn, his hands stuffed in his pockets. Her own curiosity piques as she takes in his tight-fitted Wranglers and broad shoulders stretching his button-down tightly across his back. She turns to the stallion. He pins his ears back and paws at her. Pushing all thoughts of Connor aside, she slaps the lasso. "All right, let's keep going."

***

EVEN THOUGH THE STALLION submitted before lunch, the hot shower Marni required to soothe her sore muscles, plus her comfortable bed, lulled her to a deep sleep that even Armageddon couldn't wake her from. To prove that point, Tonya snuck in to bring her lunch, but quickly retreated when she saw her sleeping with Ginger curled up next to her.

Her phone rings later that afternoon and wakes her. She rolls over to see Parker's name and in her sleepy state; she forgot she was screening his calls and hits accept.

"Marni? Where are you? You haven't answered any of my texts or calls."

Crap, Marni whines to herself as she sits up in bed, pushing her wild hair out of her face.

"Hey, I'm fine. Visiting...family. What time is it?" She licks at the disgusting film covering her teeth. Her body feels heavy, like she's been asleep for days.

"You missed the two o'clock meeting. I was worried. Are you drunk?" He seems more annoyed than worried to Marni. She pulls open her laptop to see an email from Boston who sent her the minutes, so she is up to speed on the meeting.

"Hello? Marni?!"

She rubs her eyes and readjusts the phone.

"Yeah, I'm still here. I just fell asleep. Boston said the deal was done with Robotics Developing. That's great." Marni skims to make sure there isn't anything vital she needs to know.

"Yeah, they did," he says curtly. "When are you coming back?"

"This weekend, why?"

"I think we need to talk about what you expect from us. It's not fair to keep stringing me along and then you disappear for weeks at a time with no communication," Parker snaps. Instantly, Marni feels guilty about the whole situation.

"Parker, I can't give you what you want. I'm—"

"Damaged. I know. You say it every time. Just give me a chance to show you I'm different." Marni cringes at his tone. Last week she would have groveled, apologized for hurting *his* feelings, but now a rage burns at the way he dismisses *her* feelings. Parker continues.

"Just tell me when you will be back and I'll come over to talk." Impatience drips from his words.

A spark ignites within Marni's chest. Maybe it's from the fact that she just got a twelve-hundred-pound horse to listen, so dammit, she can make him listen too. "No. I don't think you should come over and we don't need to talk. I'm sorry, Parker, truly, but I don't think we should speak outside of work." She figuratively high-fives herself and forces a deep breath into her lungs.

"Wait, Marni. I'm sorry, I shouldn't have been so cross. I just want to talk. Just let me know when you'll be back and I can take you out to eat. Maybe that place that's your favorite?" His voice is sweet as honey, drawing her in like a moth to a flame. She says whatever she has to just to get him off the phone.

"I'll call you when I get back. Talk to you then." She hangs up the phone and tosses it across her bed. Ginger meows at her distress.

Why won't he just take no for an answer?

She wants to tell him to go to hell and to stop manipulating her. She thought he was her friend. Now she sees he's never been a friend—it's all a game to get more. She jumps at a knock on the door. Before she can say anything, Tonya peeks her head through the crack.

"Hey, you're up. Are you still wanting to go to Turnpike tonight?" Tonya eyes the untouched food and the heat in Marni's cheeks. "What happened?" Marni lets out a sigh.

"Parker called. He demanded I tell him when I'll be back so we can talk about us, but only after he shamed me for missing my afternoon meeting that my boss didn't give a rat's ass about. Being here, feeling like me again, I see it for what it really is."

Tonya makes a serious face, like she is thinking hard about something. "Is that a yes to Turnpike or...?" Marni launches a pillow at her and laughs. "Okay, well, let's go to my place to get ready." Marni purposefully leaves her phone so Parker can't spoil her fun.

Connor watches the two of them giggle like teenagers from the barn aisle.

He came to check on the horses when he heard her on the phone upstairs. He tried not to eavesdrop, but as her voice raised at *Parker*, it was hard not to listen in on the anger in her voice. After hearing her talk to Tonya about him, he has to remind himself her personal affairs are none of his business. He fills the water buckets and gives hay to the stalled horses. The stallion rears at his approach.

"Easy, bud. I'm just here to give you water and hay. Marni is in charge of your ass kicking." The stallion eyes him cautiously, but he bends down and takes a bite of fresh hay. "Well, look at you, eating your hay. It's a damn miracle." Connor chuckles and the stallion snorts and bends to take a fresh drink of water to prove his point.

Feeling restless, Connor picks out the stalls, starting at one end and making his way to the other. He's working on the last stall when Tonya's truck pulls out of the driveway and takes a right down the highway. "Wonder where they're going?" he asks Brimstone as he rubs down her neck. He finishes up, then heads to his cabin for a much-needed shower.

***

TONYA AND MARNI SING *'Don't Stop Believin'"* by Journey at the top of their lungs. Dragging out *people* like they can actually hit the high notes. Marni's hair is in a half up-do and curled while Tonya let her long, naturally curly locks hang free. Tonya did their makeup, accenting her green eyes and Marni's brown. Even though they love the dresses, they chose Kimes Ranch blue jeans paired with cowboy boots. Marni topped her outfit with a burgundy lace blouse and Tonya picked a deep red fitted button-down that accents her God-given chest.

The bar smells of burned cigarettes and watered-down beer mixed with sweat. A long-haired blonde behind the counter pours shots and pints for the drooling men.

"How about a drink?" Tonya grabs Marni's hand and drags her over to the bar. She looks at her options; she hasn't touched anything harder than wine since she and Tonya got drunk in the loft the night her mom ripped up her acceptance letter.

"Well, if it isn't baby Tonya." The bartender wipes down the bar top and gives Marni a once-over.

"Marni, this is Christy," Tonya introduces. "My brother's frequent booty call and nothing more." Heat flushes to Marni's cheeks. Christy could be a beautiful woman with her big doe eyes and hourglass curves, but the way her body language screams *desperate* makes her disgusting.

"I actually ended things with him. He wasn't good enough for me, and him constantly begging for me was exhausting." Christy says.

Tonya snorts a chuckle and tries to cover it with a cough. Christy seems unphased, and a smile creeps across her face.

"We'll have two shots of tequila," Tonya states after clears her throat. Christy sets the glasses down too hard and the liquid sloshes over the sides. Tonya hands one to Marni with a grin.

"Even she can't ruin my mood tonight. Bottoms up!" Tonya taps her glass to Marni's and they throw their heads back and let out a hiss as the liquor burns down their throats.

Marni coughs. "That was a lot smoother when I was younger."

Tonya lifts her hand and shouts down to Christy. "Two tequila sunrises!" She rolls her eyes as she mixes the drinks. Tonya grabs Marni's hand and leads the way to the dance floor. Luke Bryan sings *'Country Girl'* and Marni shakes her ass with her hands raised over her head. The alcohol is doing its job as her limbs loosen and all her tension melts.

The floor gyrates with bodies, moving in masses around one another. A hand finds her and she looks up to see hazel eyes set into a chiseled face with a five o'clock shadow. Like all the other men in here, he wears a cowboy hat and a button-down. "Well, look who made their way back to town! Marni?" He flashes her a dimpled grin that even on this man she could never forget.

"Dillon?! Look at you!" He takes a step back and spins slowly with his palms held out to allow her to eye all of him. She seemed to miss how the Wranglers fit the men out here perfectly.

"Look at you! Radiant, gorgeous. Are you still breaking hearts?"

"I just added one to the list this morning, actually," she teases. In elementary school, the two of them got married on the playground and promised themselves to be best friends forever. Obviously, that didn't happen.

"I think you owe me a dance." He holds his hand out and Marni slides hers into his grasp. Morgan Wallen belts the beginning of *'Whiskey Glasses'*, and Marni downs her drink to go dance. Dillon spins her around the dance floor with finesse and grace she didn't know was possible in square-toe cowboy boots. She finds herself getting lost in his eyes, and a genuine smile works onto her face as they sway together.

Dillon doesn't miss a beat singing the chorus, Marni throws her head back with laughter then picks up the chorus with him. She feels a tap on her shoulder; Tonya is standing there with her bottom lip stuck out.

"I'm empty!" she shouts. "Let's do another shot." Marni nods and Dillon keeps a hold of her hand as they weave back to the bar. "Christy! Two more!" Tonya side-eyes Dillon, who just shrugs. "Make that three!" Christy sets out three glasses and pours silver tequila to the rim.

"Ready?" Marni asks as she raises her glass and tosses her head back. "Oh man, that is good!" Dillon smiles down at her, his eyes lingering on her lips a second too long. The anxiety takes hold, and Marni backs away from his brick wall of a body.

"Hey, don't go." He grabs her hand and pulls her close again. Marni's breath quickens and Chinese war drums beat in her chest. She jerks her hand away again, and an arm drapes across her shoulders.

"Hey girl. Breathe. Need some fresh air?" Tonya whispers in her ear. Her nerves settle some. Tonya won't let anything happen to her.

"I'm fine. Sorry." She gives Dillon a sheepish smile; in return, she gets more dimples.

"How about a beer?" he offers. Marni nods and he hands her a long neck Michelob. She takes a few gulps and looks up at his hazel eyes. Tonya escapes to the dance floor with her own version of a hot cowboy. "Do you want to dance?" Dillon asks her. Marni's smile is the only confirmation he needs as he takes her back to the dance floor.

The side entrance of the bar opens as Connor walks in. Christy's eyes find him instantly, like she's been staring at that door, just waiting for him all night.

"I thought I told you to stay the fuck away from me," she snarls with her arms crossed. Connor just gives her a soft smile.

He knows what game she is playing, and she won't get the reaction she hopes for. He sits at the bar and waits for her to acknowledge him.

"Will this be on your tab or adding it to baby sister's?" she finally asks. Connor's blue eyes widen. "Tonya?"

"Well, yeah, unless that Marcie girl is your sister, too." Connor immediately scans the crowd. It doesn't take long to spot Marni holding a beer in one hand and dancing with Dillon, of all people. The same guy, Marni, cried over in Tonya's room because he asked another girl to prom.

"How much have they had?" he asks, not hearing whatever Christy said.

"Oh, they won't be driving," she chastises as she hands him a beer. He lets out a sigh. Christy leans forward, giving Connor a clear view down her blouse. Jealousy courses through her when he doesn't take his eyes off of Marni on the dance floor. "So, is she your sister too, then?"

"No."

Marni's hips ebb and flow with the rhythm of the music perfectly. His blood runs hot as Dillon's hands slide down her hips, then back up her abdomen under her blouse. He takes a long drink of his beer, once again reminding himself her personal affairs are not his business. Marni's eyes remain closed, completely free of the self-doubt he's seen her wear since she's arrived. The song fades into a slower beat. Dillon turns Marni to face him and he cups her cheek.

Marni's body language changes instantly, her fluidity turning to stone. She puts her hand against his chest and pushes with no force in her drunken state. Connor is already weaving through the crowd when Marni's eyes grow wide with fear and Dillon swallows her scream.

Without thinking, Connor grabs the collar of Dillon's shirt and whips him around.

Marni's scream unleashes when he pulls Dillon off of her. Confusion crosses Dillon's face right before Connor's fist cracks across his jawbone, causing him to stagger backward. Blood drips from the corner of his mouth. Tonya looks for the source of everyone's panic and sees Marni frozen in fear as her brother grips Dillon.

Chapter Seven

"CONNOR!" TONYA YELLS. HIS feral eyes shoot to Marni's first. Her hands tremble across her lips.

Dillon recovers and stands tall to square up to his attacker. Hesitation shoots through him when he sees it's Curston that landed the ear-ringing blow. "What the hell, man?!" he yells. Connor keeps his back to him, focusing on breathing and unreeling his clenched fists. His eyes stay on Marni's. Her vocal cords are knotted from having Dillon's lips on hers. She feels the involuntary movement coming as saliva pools into her mouth and her stomach clenches. She throws a hand over her mouth and sloppily runs out the side door Connor came through.

Tonya chases after her, leaving everyone staring at Connor to see how he will react to the onslaught of insults hitting his back. He tips his hat at everyone in one motion as if to bid them a good night, then grabs his half-empty beer. He leaves cash on the bar that'll cover more than their drinks and follows his sister.

"You're really going to put on that kind of show. Get me all hot and bothered, then just leave?" Christy calls out like a siren to a sailor. Connor opens the door as if he didn't hear her at all. He finds Tonya holding Marni's hair with one hand and rubbing her back with the other as she uses the wall of the bar to hold herself up.

Marni vividly remembers now why she doesn't drink anything besides wine. Footsteps approach and she freezes, trying to decide if she should run from the unknown advancement or put her head in the sand like an ostrich.

"What the hell was that, Connor?" Tonya pulls Marni's hair slightly as she half turns to face her brother.

He looks past his annoyed sister. "Marni, are you okay?" His tone is coated with worry.

"Wait, what did I miss? Did he do something to you? Do I need to chop his dick off? Better yet, I have our bander in the truck." An image of a rubber band being tightly wrapped around anyone's balls makes Connor cringe.

"I'm fine. I'm fine," she repeats. "Don't band anyone or chop anyone's dick off. I drank too much...it's fine." Marni squeezes her eyes shut, and the world tilts and spins as it rushes to meet her face.

"Easy there." Connor grabs her forearm to steady her before she falls forward. She pushes at the foreign male grip and makes a whimpering puppy sound.

"Mar, it's okay. It's just Connor. He's going to get you in the truck. I'm right here." Connor passes his sister a sideways glance and raises his eyebrows. She shakes her head, dismissing his silent question, and opens the door for her to get in.

"Are you okay to drive?" Connor uses one knuckle to raise Tonya's chin and tries the follow-my-finger act, but she swats it away like an annoying fly.

"I'm fine. I've drunk more than this on a Tuesday." He chuckles at the fact it is Tuesday. She spins on her heel, proving she has her balance, and stomps to the truck like a toddler.

Marni dry heaves and Connor rushes in to toss her an empty feed sack from the back seat before he has a sour smelling tequila-soaked truck. Her head throbs with each breath she takes. "I'm sorry."

"Why are you apologizing?" He fires up the truck and checks that her door is latched.

"For ruining everyone's night."

"Are you seriously apologizing for Dillon forcing *himself* on you?" He grips the steering wheel. That image will be burned into his mind forever.

"I drank too much. I knew better."

"None of this is your fault. How can you think that?" She lays her head against the window and lets out a sigh that fogs up the glass. She smirks and draws a smiley face.

"I'm damaged. Broken. My brain is in fragmented pieces. I overreact."

She doesn't make any sense to him. He didn't see a woman who overreacted—he saw a woman who didn't want to be kissed and made that fact known.

"I don't follow. He kissed you and you didn't want him to. That's not broken..."

"I see him, every time. It replays in my head. His eyes, cold as steel, hard as stone...the pain..." Her voice breaks off and her eyes go wide as she comes into focus with Connor in the driver's seat. "Oh god, I'm sorry. I didn't mean...forget I said anything." She tries to recover. The shadows hide his clenched jaw.

Had Dillon done more before he got there? Was it more than a kiss?

"He won't touch you again," Connor seethes. He slams the truck into park and opens the passenger door to help Marni upstairs. Tonya pulls in behind him and leads the way to her apartment. He takes each step with grace, Marni cradled to his chest. She's on the verge of passing out now as he settles her softly on her bed.

Tonya places a trash can, aspirin, and a glass of water on her nightstand in case she wakes up in the middle of the night. Her brother quickly retreats downstairs like he can't get out of there fast enough.

"Hey! I think you need to tell me what happened back there. You look like you're ready to kill someone." Tonya steps between Connor and his truck door.

"Move." His eyes dare her to stop him. Unlike the rest of the town, his sister doesn't back down from his icy stare.

"Not until you tell me why you went all Rocky Balboa on Dillon." He takes his hat off and rakes his fingers through his hair.

"He kissed her." Tonya raises her eyebrows. Connor continues, "It was obvious she didn't want him to, but he was too drunk to notice. Then on the way here she said..." He lets out a rage-filled growl and slams his fist down on the bed rail of his truck. "She said she kept seeing him every time she closed her eyes and blamed herself. Said she was damaged and continued to apologize." The pieces click for Tonya and she relaxes her stance.

"It's not Dillon. Let's go to your place and I'll tell you what I know." Connor studies his sister, all the fire wanting to castrate someone at the bar gone. If it's not about Dillon, then who? A million questions fill his head, but he nods and follows his sister to his cabin.

Inside, she makes herself a cup of coffee and places a cup in front of Connor. "T, what the hell is going on?" She chews her lip, her telltale that she is conflicted.

"It's a lot. And I need you to listen until I'm finished. I won't go into details because it's not my story to tell. The only reason I'm telling you anything is to save poor Dillon's face." She pauses, studying his reaction, making sure he will listen. It's no secret Connor pined over Marni when they were teenagers, and how he watches her now, it's obvious he still does.

"When Marni went to UW, she met a senior. They clicked; he was perfect to her. After they moved in together, something changed in him. I should've seen the signs. She had an excuse for everything—why I couldn't come visit, why she couldn't, where her bruises came from when we video chatted. She'd wear long sleeves and sunglasses, even inside. Claimed she had a migraine coming on." Tonya's hands shake around her coffee cup, and Connor swallows the lump forming in his throat.

"It wasn't until I got a call from the hospital that I learned how bad it was. I was her emergency contact. They said I needed to come right away." Tears spill over her cheeks now. She gives a loud sniff and wipes them away before straightening her posture. "She was so small...barely recognizable from the bruises and swelling. She cowered at any touch, like a beaten dog. I stayed with her afterward until she could take care of herself. She hasn't been right since. I see flashes of her here—with the horses and the stallion."

Connor stares a hole into his coffee he hasn't touched. Distantly, Tonya asks something, but he only sees Marni lying limp on a hospital bed—defenseless, beaten and battered. His heart shatters in ways he didn't know was possible.

He pushes to his feet so quickly the chair clamors to the wooden floor, causing Tonya to jump. He steps out to the porch and places both hands on the railing as he rocks on his feet. Tonya silently stands in the doorway to give him his space.

"Why didn't anyone say anything?" His voice is full of pain as it squeaks out.

Tonya wraps her arms around herself, not daring to hug her brother, who will either shove her off or break from the embrace. She couldn't handle either. "You were in Afghanistan. Telling you wasn't important at the time."

"Where is the guy now?" He stands tall and clears his throat.

"Why, so you can kill him? Hah, get in line. She won't tell me. Just says he's gone. Are you going to tell her?"

"Tell her what?"

Tonya gives him a you-can't-be-serious look. "That you're in love with her and have been since high school?"

"Now is hardly the time to discuss that," he says sternly to end the conversation, but in classic Tonya fashion, she doesn't back down.

"If you keep waiting for the right time, you're both going to be in the ground. If you had told her then, maybe we wouldn't be having this talk." Her words slap him, but she meant them. "Time to buck up."

She walks to her truck and gives him an encouraging smile before heading back to the loft. He knows she will sleep there tonight to make sure Marni is all right.

His body hums with rage, and he has no healthy ways to get it out of his system. He can't run to Christy and take it out on her. Not with Marni on the ranch. His sister saw right through his facade and called him out on what he knew all along. He loves her, and he hates himself for it. She'll go back to the city and he'll go through hell all over again.

***

STACY BEATS A DOZEN eggs in a bowl vigorously. The clanking of metal against the glass bowl chimes throughout the quiet house.

"What did those eggs do to you?" Jack asks and pours himself a cup of fresh coffee.

"Something happened last night. Marni isn't up yet, and I saw headlights flash through late."

Jack's chair groans under his weight as he pulls out his newspaper. "The girls went to Turnpike. We knew that."

"There were two sets of headlights and I might have peeked to see Connor packing Marni upstairs." Jack's attention snaps to Stacy over the top of his paper. Stacy continues, "Then I saw Tonya make a beeline in front of them leading the way. Poor girl probably couldn't hold her liquor."

"Hmph." Jack grunts in disappointment.

"Then Tonya and Connor went to his place, and a while later, Tonya came back to the loft."

"Jesus, woman, did you sleep last night?" Jack lays his paper down now.

"A little." She pours the scrambled eggs into a skillet and they sizzle from the heat.

***

MARNI ROLLS OVER AND sees Tonya sprawled out on the floor, still in the same clothes as last night. She rubs her head like that is the magic cure for the crippling hangover she has. She spots aspirin and water and swallows them both. Careful to not wake Tonya, she tip-toes to the bathroom and digs out her toiletries. Finally, finding the mouthwash and toothpaste, she rinses her mouth out twice.

Unfortunately, she wasn't drunk enough to forget everything that happened last night, and she sits on the cold tile floor with her head between her legs in embarrassment. She also needs to wait and see if vomiting is in her future or not. When she seems in the clear, she turns the shower on.

A replay of Connor punching Dillon plays in her mind. Then she cringes when she remembers she had already puked everything up last night.

She can still feel Dillon's lips on hers, pushing extremely too hard. Some bruising and swelling remains. Next thing she remembers is Connor driving her home in his truck.

Oh god! I said stuff. I talked about Vance. Marni groans as she lets the water run over her face. *Maybe I will hide out or just go back home.*

A horse squeals loud enough she can hear it over the water.

No, she has a job to do. She'll finish it, then go back to the city. After packing two bottles of water down the stairs, she realizes the sun is pretty high for her early morning routine. She checks the tack room clock.

"Holy shit!" It's after one—this is the longest she has slept in years. Her stomach growls, but she prefers to avoid the walk of shame into Stacy and Jack's at this hour. Brimstone's stall is empty, so at least she can check running into Connor off her list.

She reaches for the lasso, but the bag with her name under it catches her attention. Inside are two carefully wrapped sausage biscuits and a bottle of orange juice. "Thank you, Jesus." She sighs as she unwraps the first one.

"Just me." Connor leans against the door frame and gives her a sideways smirk.

With her mouthful she mumbles. "You did this?" A few biscuit crumbs fall out of her mouth as she asks.

"I thought you would need something when you woke up." He shrugs like it's no big deal.

"Thank you, that was sweet. I was debating on the walk of shame into our parents and decided that was a hard no." He chuckles at her. "About last night..." Connor abruptly stands and takes a step back, adding more space between them.

"We don't have to talk about it," he insists. Marni presses her lips together. She knows why he was there. Tonya told her about Christy and, by the way she acted about Connor, he was probably there to make up with her and who knows what else.

"I didn't mean to pull you away from your evening plans."

Connor looks confused, but her squealing, impatient stallion cuts him off from asking what she meant by that.

"I think he misses you," he states instead.

"He thinks that until we get to work," Marni snarks. She grabs the lasso and her other wrapped sandwich. Her name on the bag flips a switch in her head. The same swoop at the beginning of her M, followed by lazy letters. "Hey, did you...?" When she looks up, Connor has already walked away.

He gave her the hat, not Tonya's parents. She rushes to the barn aisle. Her head swivels back and forth, looking for him. She jogs to the back of the barn in time to see him disappear on Brimstone over the ridge top. She'll just have to thank him later and talk to Tonya about how she feels about it.

"Hey boy, are you ready to play?" The stallion paws the ground and snorts as she opens the gate. She knows him better now, and he knows her. He won't try to trample her, but he still doesn't want to give or fully commit to this relationship.

Today, it takes less time for him to settle into a controlled trot around the pen. His veins protrude from the exertion of the exercise. He tosses his head a few times to express his annoyance.

She backs up for him to switch directions, and he only kicks out once—so, progress. They continue this dance for nearly an hour and Marni smiles in satisfaction. She stops and turns to face the opposite direction of the corral, allowing him to make the first move. The stallion breathes heavily while he stands, waiting for Marni's instruction. She takes a step backward, toward the stallion, shortening the distance between them.

"Shit!" Tonya exclaims from inside the barn. The stallion loses his focus and rears at the intrusive sound. Marni lets out an aggravated sigh and exits the corral to see what has Tonya all out of sorts.

"Good morning sunshine." Marni greets. Her friend's makeup is smudged under her eyes and she squints like she's never seen the sun in her life.

"What time is it?" Tonya slurs.

"Way past lunch. Here, I didn't eat this one. Looks like you need it more than me." Marni tosses her the extra biscuit.

"You're a lifesaver." She moans and her eyes roll in the back of her head as she takes a bite.

"Don't thank me, thank Connor. He had them waiting for me in the tack room." Unexpected heat rushes to her cheeks when she says this out loud.

"Did he now?" She bats her lashes at Marni in mockery.

"His handwriting matches the writing on the hatbox. I tried to thank him, but he was literally riding away when I went to find him." Tonya tilts her head and lifts both eyebrows, and Marni feels like she just silently called her dumb. "You knew?"

"I promised I wouldn't meddle. Dad made me and Mom swear to it when you arrived."

Marni pretends to be offended. "Best friend code!" she shouts. They've been using this since elementary school. They never kept any secrets between the two of them.

Tonya only rolls her eyes. "How about I go shower, you saddle up, and we will talk about this on a trail ride?"

Marni looks at the stalls. Horses of all colors crane their heads over, begging for attention. "Deal."

Chapter Eight

Marni legs up on a dappled gray mare while Tonya rides a bay that reminds her a lot of Brimstone. Thank goodness her best friend's cluttered way of life doesn't spill over into the barn. The tack is labeled with the horse's name, so finding the right bridle was easy enough. "So, where are we headed?" Marni asks as she gathers her reins.

"You want to go see the rest of the wildies?" The pictures Tonya sent flash through her mind.

"Absolutely."

She kicks the gray mare up to a canter as they ride toward the far side of the ranch. Tonya looks sideways at Marni and gives her a daring smile, one Marni has seen a lot over their lifetime. Both women squeeze their legs and push their horses to a full-speed gallop. Their bottoms barely kissing the saddle as they run.

Like muscle memory, Marni moves as one with the horse, leaning her body forward to flatten against the saddle. She lets go of the reins and her horse pushes harder, taking the lead and only slowing to a stop once they reach the gate.

"How?! Like what the actual hell? You literally picked the slowest horse in the barn! How can you still beat me?" Tonya half jokes as she waves her arms around. Marni wraps one hand around her abdomen and laughs hysterically at Tonya's show. Her friend's annoyed frown lines only exacerbate her laughter more. Tears leak down her reddened face, and she uses both hands to wipe them away.

"You let me take the slowest horse?" Marni pants out between laughter.

"Well, yeah. I thought I'd have a chance," Tonya grumbles.

"You still hold back, T."

Tonya swings the gate open and they both ride through. "I thought, just maybe since it's been like years, literally years, I would have a chance."

Marni gives her an apologetic smile. "So, to continue our conversation earlier. What is going on with Connor? And don't give me that look again."

"What look?" Tonya raises her eyebrows and shakes her head slightly.

"That's the one."

"If I tell you, pinky swear you won't tell him you know." Marni refrains from batting away the childish gesture and wraps her pinky around Tonya's. "He bought you the hat before you left. It was meant as a congratulations for Idaho, but then your mom happened, you left, and he went to war. Poof, here we are."

"But why did he get it in the first place? He never talked to me and he hated horses back then."

"Do you really not see it? The way he looks at you. The sideways glances he gives you. The reason he clocked Dillon for kissing you?"

Marni's face is blank. She thought he was just being nice, acting like a protective big brother to his little sister's friend. Tonya can't contain herself anymore.

"Listen closely. My brother, dear Lord help me,"—she pauses—, "has been in love with you for years and never told you." Marni's mouth falls open as she processes the declaration.

"No, he isn't, he can't...I would've noticed."

"Well, you haven't, so, I guess not. How do you feel about it?"

Marni ponders her question.

What does this mean to her? She felt the flutters in her stomach when he stared at her, noticed the way he fills out his Wranglers, and how he makes a duster seem irresistible. His crooked smile makes her breath catch and the way he seemed vulnerable earlier turned her to mush.

"What about Christy? Isn't that why he was at Turnpike last night?"

Tonya's face scrunches up in disgust. "There is nothing there. She likes to act like there is. Yes, my brother has slept with her," she gags as she says those words. "But she is nothing."

Marni lets her mind wander again. She imagines Connor's rough hands caressing her face. Maybe it's because she grew up with him, but the fear she normally feels with men isn't there. Could she actually be falling for her best friend's older brother?

"Earth to Marni!" Tonya cups her hands around her mouth.

"What?" she asks innocently.

"Oh, you definitely feel things," Tonya jokes. "I have to tell you one more thing. Last night, I had to tell him about Vance. Not everything, just enough to keep him from killing poor Dillon. Apparently, you said something in the truck and made Connor want to drive back to Turnpike and do God knows what."

"T! Oh my god." She places her face in her palms. "That is why he was being so nice to me this morning and brought me breakfast. It was a pity fest."

"Stop right there. It was definitely not a pity party."

"But he'll think I'm damaged goods and want nothing to do with me," Marni resigns.

"Do you want him to have something to do with you?" Tonya cocks her eyebrow at Marni in curiosity.

"T!" Marni swats at her and laughs. "Okay, serious for a minute. How did he take the information and how much did you tell him?"

"I told him about the hospital. I didn't go into how extensive detail or what all had happened. Figured you'll tell him if you want him to know."

"What do I do now?"

Tonya laughs and shakes her head. "Now, we go look at the adorable babies. You can process your emotions, and if you want nothing to change, it won't. Connor won't make a move...well, ever. It's been driving my parents crazy for years."

"Your parents?!" Her cheeks are full crimson now.

"Oh yeah, they've always been team Marni."

How does everyone know but her? She doesn't stop asking herself that and looking for the signs in her memories until they reach the herd of wild horses.

Foals with the zoomies top the cuteness overload radar for Marni. Their tiny bucks and rearing on their hind legs just scream adorable. There are five current ones still nursing, and the rest are weanlings. One particular palomino paint foal catches Marni's eye as it stops running to watch the two women on horseback.

"They're beautiful." Marni gasps. The palomino paint whinnies and rears, putting on a show.

"I think that one likes you," Tonya says.

"She's a real prize. I can't believe someone would just discard them like trash. What if you kept the mares and trained the babies to be working horses? They'd bring income and serve a purpose. The foals look really nice."

"I've thought about it. It's just too much to take on."

Too bad, Marni thinks to herself. Marni's gears turn as she tries to find a way for the farm to prosper from these amazing horses. After they watch the herd and pretend to name the babies, they head back to the barn.

Lucas magically appears to untack their horses and hose them off while Marni goes to the loft to check on some things for work before dinner. Her phone shows a missed call, and for once, it isn't Parker.

"Marni! Good to hear from you! I thought you might've gotten lost out there in the country." Boston's voice sings from the other end.

"It's good to hear your voice, too. Not lost at all. I needed this. Thank you for being understanding."

"You sound good, lighter. I may need to get me a dose of country air, too." His laughter bellows.

"Come on out, I'll stick you on a horse and show you the real beauty of Wyoming." Marni giggles at the picture in her head: Boston in his tailored suit and dress shoes awkwardly scrunched around the horses terrified of the four-foot fall.

"I wouldn't get on a horse if my life depended on it, sweetie. I wanted to call and check in on you. Looking at next week's schedule, we're pretty dead. Nothing Parker can't handle. If you want to extend your trip another week, you can." Her heart rises, and she silently pumps her fist into the air.

She controls her tone as she double-checks, that he is sure. "Are you serious? You don't need me?"

"Don't go that far. I'll always need you, just not next week. You've earned it."

"Thank you! Are there any meetings I need to attend via Zoom?"

"No, no. We have it all handled. Unplug, recharge, then I'll see you soon." She stares at her blank phone screen.

An extended stay! She gets another week with her best friend, the ranch, and the stallion.

"Woo-hoo!" she shouts in delight as she collapses back on her bed. Ginger jumps at the pitched tone and gives Marni a death stare from the chair in the corner.

An old-fashioned dinner bell rings from the farmhouse's front porch. Marni pulls back the curtain to see Stacy smiling when she spots her. Marni lands at the bottom of the stairs and slams into a brick wall, bouncing off it like a pinball. Rough hands grab her arm to keep her from tripping over the feed bucket behind her feet. Once steady, her eyes travel from the hand, up the flexed forearm, and meet the Persian blue gaze hidden under his cowboy hat. Her mouth goes dry. Everything Tonya said earlier floats to the front of her mind.

"The hat," she blurts. He eyes her, confused. *Crap, that isn't right.* "Thank you for the hat. I know it was you. The handwriting this morning matched the box."

"It was no big deal. Couldn't have the sun blinding you while you were out trail riding. You might fall off a cliff." Connor winces. Why couldn't he just say you're welcome and admit he gave it to her because he likes her?

"Right." She stares at him and he at her. A throat clears, and he abruptly releases her arm, causing her to lose her balance again. Only this time, in her daze, she falls flat on her ass.

Lucas looks mortified on her behalf. Connor whips his head back around when he hears the thud, followed by a yelp from Marni. Her face reddens as she sits on the floor.

"Sorry," Connor mutters as he holds his hand out to help her up. She ignores it and pushes herself up.

"I'm fine." Marni waltzes past Lucas to the house. She refuses to rub her bruised cheeks until she is out of their sight. His eyes are so captivating. How has she never noticed before?

Tonya studies her when she enters the farmhouse. "Red cheeks, dazed eyes, inability to walk. Were you and Connor...?"

"Would you please stop looking at me like it's your lifelong dream for me and him to roll in the hay?"

"Would that be so bad? We could be sisters, legally!"

"You are skipping so many steps there, T. Besides, what happens when I go back to the city?" Tonya's elated smile fades. In the back of her mind, she knows her time with Marni is not forever. "I don't want to hurt him."

"He's a big boy who can make his own decisions, so if you want to give it a chance, let him decide for himself."

Marni opens her mouth to argue, but Stacy shouts from the kitchen, "Dinner's ready!"

One thing is for sure, I'm going to miss these home-cooked meals, Marni thinks to herself.

In the middle of the table, a roast rest on a bed of carrots, potatoes, and yellow onions cooked to perfection. Cornbread, from scratch, sits in a cast-iron skillet on a hot plate.

After they're seated, the screen door bangs shut and Connor steps in, removing his hat, before sitting at the end of the table. His and Marni's eyes lock for a brief second before Jack steers his attention to the cattle sale they're going to this weekend. While the men talk business, Stacy strikes up a conversation with Marni.

"So, dear, I've been avoiding this question. I won't lie, but how long do we have your company for?" Tonya stares at her lap and Connor is no longer listening to his dad as he waits for Marni's answer.

"Actually, my boss called this afternoon during our trail ride," she says, looking at Tonya. "He insisted I take another week off before returning to work. So, if it's all right with you, I'd like to stay longer?"

Tonya's face lights up like a Christmas tree, and Stacy clasps her soft hands in delight. "Of course you're welcome to stay! Oh, this is wonderful!" Marni risks a glance at Connor to see his reaction to the news. Relief softens the hard lines around his eyes as he fights the smile that wants to form on his face.

"Thank you, I appreciate it. Being here has been wonderful. I wish I could stay permanently."

"Why can't you?" Tonya objects.

"My job, for one. My apartment. My life is in the city," Marni says robotically.

"You mean your mom's life?"

Marni flinches at her aggressive tone.

"Tonya, that's enough," Stacy hisses, and places a hand on Tonya's arm to silence her. Her daughter flings it off and continues.

"From what I've seen, this is the life you are meant to live; this is where you belong."

Marni looks at her best friend, at a loss for words. It just isn't that simple to uproot her life. "I'm sorry, dinner was delicious. I'm going to head back for the night." Marni leaves before anyone can say anything more. Her heart yearns to be here, to live here. But her mother would never allow it and would never let her live it down.

Throwing your career away to chase ponies? Preposterous! She could hear her mother now.

Marni is financially stable, independent, has a good job with a good boss and good pay. She'd be dumb to throw all of that away. She slumps down on the hay bale by the stallion's pen.

"Why does adulting have to suck so much? All our lives, we rush to get older, to have a say over what we do, but it never happens. As long as we have parents, their input, manipulation, their feelings are always taken into account." She lays to look at the purple-blue sky. Stars are barely visible as they peek through.

The stallion walks over and sniffs under the panels where Marni lays. She holds a hand out, and he backs away at the gesture. "I don't think Commander fits you. You just don't look like a Commander." She turns her head to the side. "I'll think about it. How does that sound?"

Night falls and the barn owl's hoots stir up the night. Something skims across her arms, and she jumps when a shadow looms over her. She throws her arms out, ready to run.

"It's just me." Marni's eyes focus on Connor, holding his hands up while backing away to give her some space.

"Sorry, you scared me." She picks up the blanket he placed over her and wraps it around her arms. A cedar smell flows from the fabric. "What time is it?"

"After midnight. I just got back from...town."

"You mean the bar? I'm not a little kid anymore that believes your omissions." Marni snarks. Her chest tightens at the thought of him with Christy. "Well, thank you for the blanket. I should probably go sleep in my bed." She looks up at the stars. There are so many of them. How could she choose to leave all of this for the city?

"Orion's Belt is bright tonight," Connor mumbles.

"Orion. That's the name I couldn't remember," Marni whispers to herself. She looks over at the stallion, who watches Connor with wary eyes. "Orion," she says more firmly. The stallion perks his ears and snorts at her.

"Orion?" Connor asks, puzzled.

"That's his name now. He looks like an Orion, don't you think?" Connor studies the feral creature with untrusting eyes and a mean temper. Does she even see the same horse when she looks at him?

"Sure, I guess. It's a good thing you're staying another week." Marni's heart flutters. Is he finally going to tell her what she already knows? Does she really want him to? Connor sees the internal debate flash across Marni's face. "You'll need another week to tame this one." He jerks his thumb toward Orion. The butterflies sink to the pit of her stomach.

"Right," she recovers. *Get a grip, Marni. He has Christy to scratch his itch. He doesn't need someone who is leaving in less than two weeks.* "Still don't think I can do it?"

"I think you are capable of so much more than you give yourself credit for." He shoves his hands in his pockets to keep from reaching for her. The blanket wraps around her like a present with a bow and he wants to unwrap it, slowly, to see what is under all of those layers. Instead, he takes another step back to lessen the feeling growing inside of him.

Taken aback by his compliment, she faces him. "Really?"

"I've witnessed what you did with Brimstone. She wasn't wild, but she was feral as they come. Now, she's the best working horse on the ranch." The damn butterflies are back in her stomach doing intense acrobats. He appreciated her horse and cared for her when Marni left.

"Thank you. That's...that means a lot."

The blanket slides off her shoulders as she takes a step forward. Confidence blossoms inside of her. She feels safe with him. She trusts him.

Connor stiffens at her advance. He saw how she reacted to Dillon and doesn't want to cause her that pain. He lets her make the move, even though his body screams to embrace her and kiss her immediately. She stops with only inches separating them. He slides his hands out of his pockets and brushes her cheek with his thumb. How could someone blemish her porcelain skin?

Marni's breath catches at his touch. His rough, calloused hands have a softness about them as he is ever so gentle with her. She gets lost in his eyes, drowning in want for him. She's never felt this, not even with Vance. These emotions are like the moon pulling the tide—they can't fight them. The blanket falls as she places her hand over his and flicks her gaze from his eyes to his lips. She lifts herself up to her toes and leans in, pressing her lips to his.

He's careful not to go too far. Waits for her to change her mind and push him away. When she laces her fingers through his hair, pulling him to her, he closes the distance and tastes her. Marni's world spins and fades away. She can't hear anything but the drumming of her heart mixed with labored breaths.

Connor holds one hand at the small of her back; the other tangles into her mahogany hair. A growl vibrates from his throat and his grip tightens. Just when she thinks he is going to whisk her off her feet, he pulls back. The cold night air replaces his warmth. She wraps her arms around herself. Chill bumps race up her arms and tingle her spine.

Connor lifts the blanket from the ground and shakes it out before handing it to Marni. He doesn't meet her gaze. She doesn't try to grab it. The pained look on his face makes her run back to her apartment and lock the door.

Ginger meows at her abrupt entrance, and Marni slides to the floor, replaying the feeling of him. The touch of his hands on her body. Her cheeks are raw from this scruff, and her lips burn for more.

Hell, her entire body burns for more.

She wishes he would knock at any second, but headlights shine past her window and Connor's truck drives off. She refrains from seeing where he goes. If he heads toward the highway, he'll be going to meet Christy, and she can't handle that.

The way his eyes fell to the ground when he pushed her away... Was it not what he expected? Does he not feel the same burn inside like she does?

Chapter Nine

"Hey, hey!" Marni uses her gruff tone to push back against the stallion's advance. For the most part, he keeps enough distance between them but occasionally he gets a wild hair—one of his many—and tries to see how far he can push her. After thirty minutes of complete spaz attacks, he settles and acts like he has a brain.

He finds his rhythm in a slow trot and turns on cue, only pinning his ears to show his annoyance with the repetition. Marni drops the lasso in her arms and turns to face the opposite side of the corral, giving him her back.

"Whoa," she drags out in a soft, low tone. Now she waits. She waits to see if today he gives in to his curiosity and takes one step forward, one small step that will change everything. She lets out a long breath and hears him mimic her from behind. The sun beats down on both of them. Sweat runs down the middle of her back and across the band of her hat.

She turns her head slightly to see him in her peripheral vision. His ears are perked forward, head lowered, nose pushed out toward her, and his body faces hers. All good signs.

C'mon, you can do it. I'm trusting you. Now trust me, she urges in her head. Minutes pass during the battle of wills. Hesitantly, he steps one foot forward and, to Marni's surprise, a second. His breath blows out on her back. Jubilation fills her chest, and it takes all of her willpower to not throw a fist in the air and cheer.

"Hey, pretty boy," she whispers. He doesn't move as she slowly turns to face him.

Marni doesn't hear the black sports car kicking up dust and rocks along the driveway. She holds her hand out to Orion for him to smell.

Connor watches the two of them from the ridge. He finished working the registered herd of heifers earlier than he thought he would. His eyes catch the swift movement of the car, driving incredibly too fast for any locals. Picking Brimstone up to a trot, he grabs his gun—more for show than actually to use. A plume of dust covers the car as it skids to a halt.

A clean cut, suit wearing, pampered monkey of a man that reeks of the city steps out. Probably a developer, someone coming to convince his parents to sell the family ranch. Connor glances at Marni, who is completely oblivious to the stranger as Orion smells her hand. The man leans back down in his car and three sharp honks echo through the valley.

In a split-second Marni turns to see what the noise came from and Orion rears, his front hooves level with her head.

"Marni!" Connor shouts from the hillside. He kicks Brimstone into a run.

The air whooshes by her head and she ducks to shimmy under the corral panels just as Orion stomps on the ground. She stands and tries to calm him down as Connor and Brimstone slide to a halt next to them.

"Hey, easy, you're okay. Settle, settle." Marni's voice is velvety soft toward the stallion.

"Are you hurt?" Connor instinctively grabs her hand, but just as quickly drops it when her eyes meet his. Dust and dirt cover the front of her body.

"I'm fine. He didn't try to hurt me. He just got startled."

"Yeah, I saw that. Stay here while I go see who this is." He packs his rifle in his right hand and Marni falls into step next to him. "Still don't listen, do you?"

A smug smile twitches at the corners of her mouth. When the well-dressed man removes his sunglasses, her jaw drops and annoyance makes her blood boil. He wears a Cheshire cat smile and winks at Marni.

"What the hell?! You almost got my head bashed in laying on your horn like that! This isn't the city. We don't use those things unless it's an emergency!"

Connor's taken aback by the furiousness in Marni's tone, and by the man's wide eyes and open mouth, he didn't expect it either.

"I didn't know." Then his eyes change from shock to anger. "Why are you in there with that wild beast that could kill you, anyway? That's not smart, Marni. What happens if you get hurt? Who takes care of you?" Marni takes a step forward with a clenched fist, but Connor's voice interrupts her thoughts.

"Who are you?" Connor asks the monkey.

Marni answers for him. "Connor, Parker. My co-worker." This is the guy she and Tonya were discussing in the loft.

"Co-worker? You know there's more to it than that, Mar." He holds his hand out to Connor for a shake, ignoring the elephant-sized killer piece of steel weighing him down. "I'm more than a co-worker. We haven't exactly labeled it yet, but we're working on it." He flashes a smile at Marni. How did she miss he was so arrogant in the city?

"No, we're not. I told you that. Before I left." Ignoring Marni has even said anything, his eyes stay on Connor.

"You know women. They don't know what they want."

With one motion, Connor swings the lever of his rifle and the *cha-ching* breaks the tension. Parker drops his hand and stands up straight.

"Marni, let's go talk. I drove all the way here to see you."

"I'm working right now. I have to go fix the trust you just broke between me and that stallion."

Parker scoffs, and Connor steps forward to square up with him. Parker's eyes shift from Connor to Marni. Connor is just itching for a reason to deck this cocky bastard.

"Marni, honey, can you come here for a moment?" Stacy shouts from the porch steps. She sees the tension brewing like a flash flood thunderstorm. Marni places a hand on Connor's forearm and he relaxes a fraction.

"This is how it is? You leave the city to come out here and hook up with a smelly cowboy? Couldn't give us a chance, but you jump at the first sign of interest from him?" Connor takes another step forward and Parker flinches back. Before he can power up his punch, Marni steps between them, her voice low and dangerous, knocking Parker off his high horse.

"Get in your car and leave. When I get back, we are co-workers and that's it. We won't *talk* outside of work; you won't *see* me outside of work. Clear?" Connor stands behind her, rifle in his left hand and his right on her shoulder. Parker seethes and straightens his suit jacket before sliding his sunglasses back on.

"Fine. Like you said, you're damaged anyway." He slides back into his car and Connor and Marni shield their eyes from the dust cloud as he leaves.

Marni's body shakes.

Stacy, now satisfied that Connor doesn't have anyone to kill, goes back inside to give them some privacy.

Connor's hand grasps hers; her charged nerves vibrate through him.

"I've been trying to say that for a year and he wouldn't listen. This is exhilarating." She looks up at Connor, then at the cocked rifle. "Were you going to shoot him?!" Her mouth drops open.

Connor Shrugs. "Only if he put his hands on you." Marni's cheeks flush and last night replays in her head. The ball is in his court. She made the first move, so now it's his turn.

Stacy's heart warms at the sight of their smiling faces through the kitchen window.

"You're spying, Stace." Jack wraps his arms around her waist and rests his chin on her shoulder, also watching the two twitterpated kids outside.

"I can't help it. They give me the warm and fuzzies. Look at him! And who I presume was Marni's fling from the city was just here. He left in a heated puff of smoke." Stacy can't hide the smile that reaches her eyes.

"Don't go getting your hopes up. She still has plans to return to the city, remember?" She swats him away with her dish towel and stares at Marni and Connor as if she can will fate itself.

***

CONNOR FINDS THE REBEL Brimstone grazing ten feet from where he left her. Orion settles back to watching Marni's every move. She enters the pen, and the stallion lowers his head and lets out a nicker as if to ask, *Are you okay?*

"I never thought I'd see him like this, with anyone."

Marni hears the compliment, but she stays focused on Orion. She was so close to touching him before Parker arrived.

"Hey, boy. I'm okay, you're okay. It was just a dumb man." She keeps her voice low, soft, like talking to a slumbering baby. She holds her hand out and pauses, watching for any signs that Orion is going to spook.

He sniffs the air around her hand and lets out a squeal. Connor tenses his hand around the gate latch, ready to leap for Marni if he has to. Orion lowers his head again, and the whiskers around his muzzle tickle Marni's hand. Her heart leaps from her chest at the trust he is showing. She forgot how it felt to have a horse give you their trust—to bond with you and be willing to work with you.

Brimstone blows out her nostrils and shakes her head from behind Connor.

Marni giggles at the display. *Big deal,* she seems to say. Marni slowly lifts her other hand and gently places it in the center of Orion's blaze. His skin twitches under her palm. Scared to breathe, she stands frozen as he smells her. Reluctantly, she backs away, not wanting to push him and have him freak out again. Connor opens the gate for her and when he closes it, she wears a goofy grin like a girl who got a pony for her seventh birthday party.

"You're happy," he comments. Everything about her demeanor has completely changed from what he just witnessed with Parker.

"I'm...just...gosh. Being here. I feel like I'm finding myself. He's helped me do that." She gives the stallion another glance. "Thank you." He nickers before trotting over to eat hay.

"Marni..."

"No, wait. I need to say this before I fall off this high I'm riding." She pauses and takes a deep breath. Connor holds his own, waiting for her to tell him that what happened last night was a mistake. "I don't want to hurt you. I will go back to the city. Back to my job. What happens if we catch real feelings and then I have to leave? I was reminded you are an adult and I need to let you make your own decisions, but I'm scared. Scared of hurting you, but also scared of falling for you."

Connor keeps a blank expression while inside. His heart feels like it is going to explode from his chest. He doesn't care if she goes back to the city. He'll worry about that when, or if, it happens. He wants to feel her, taste her, have her all to himself. Is that selfish? After everything she's been through, what does that say about him? Before he can say anything, she continues.

"T told me you know about my...past. If you don't want me after that, I understand. It's pretty fucked up. I think I've come to terms with it. Living in the past will make you insane. I need to look forward and not be hindered by things out of my control."

Connor was never good with words. Instead, he tilts her chin up to see her rich brown eyes. His gaze flicks to her lips and she parts them slightly, inviting him in. He leans down and gently brushes his lips across hers. Gripping his biceps for balance, she steadies herself on her toes and reaches for more. She wants so much more, a feeling she has never experienced before, the need to have him cover every inch of her.

"Connor..." she whispers out a moan as he ravages her mouth. His facial hair rubs against her skin while his rough hands hold her gently, being careful not to blemish her ivory skin. "We have to stop," she says breathlessly.

He quickly pulls back. He drops his gaze and his hands. Defeat hits him like a wave—she changed her mind. Just like that, he isn't what she thought she wanted, and he blew his chance.

"No, not like that." Marni quickly tries to salvage the hurt she sees in his eyes. "Brimstone needs to be put up before she wanders away completely." Connor turns to see she's meandered a way, eating as much grass as she can. He smirks and his shoulders rise as he stands straight again.

"Tonight, will you come to my place?"

Her stomach doesn't just flutter, a category five hurricane rages in the anticipation.

Connor reaches out to hold her hand, terrified this is all a dream and he'll wake up in his cabin. He pulls her close and presses his lips to hers, for good measure. "Had to make sure this was real." His left dimple appears and Marni giggles as she places her feet back on level ground.

She leans against Orion's pen as Connor saunters to where Brimstone happily grazes. She lets out a sigh and heads to her room to get cleaned up before dinner.

Staring at herself in the mirror, she runs a hand over her features. Her lips are red and swollen, and her eyes look wild, desire dancing around them. Maybe they could just skip dinner and go to his cabin now? She lets out a love-struck sigh as she turns on the scalding shower. Her hair sits high on her head in a bun to keep it from getting wet. She shaves her legs twice, just to make sure she doesn't miss any spots Connor might find later.

After brushing out her wavy hair, she quickly runs a straightener through it to hide any frizz. She side-eyes her makeup bag.

"You are eating at his parents' for dinner like you have every night. No need to go overboard." Ginger meows as if to agree and she settles with just a hint of color on her eyes and mascara. She double checks herself in the mirror, and once satisfied, she slides her boots on over her socks.

***

MARNI PUSHES THE COLESLAW and green beans around her plate. She keeps peeking up at Connor, who is doing the same to her. Stacy eyes the two of them and hides a smile behind her napkin as she wipes her mouth before she breaks the silence. "So, was that a friend of yours earlier?"

Connor shifts uneasily in his chair.

"He's a co-worker. He thought we were more than that or hoped, I'm not sure. I think I made it clear now, though."

"I see. How did he know where you were?" Stacy presses.

"I ran into him when I was leaving to come here. I've talked to him about Tonya and the ranch—I guess he looked it up."

Tonya snorts. "If, *ran into,* means he brought you chocolates and flowers to win your approval, then yeah, you ran into him." Marni's cheeks flush at her too-much-information spill.

"Really?" Stacy coos, but looks at Connor to see how he reacts to this information. He seems unphased, which is odd, considering the pissing match she witnessed earlier between the two of them. Marni's voice reels her attention back to her.

"I told him then that I didn't want to be more than friends. I don't know how much clearer I can make it."

Now Connor smirks, but he still doesn't add any commentary on the subject. Stacy notices the way his eyes continually flit to Marni's and the secret exchanges the two keep having.

"Well, I think he knows now." Stacy smiles as Marni pulls apart her fried chicken. "How is it going with the stallion?"

Marni's smile lights up the room. "I actually gave him a name. Commander didn't suit him." She shrugs at Tonya. "Sorry." Tonya waves her hand, eager to hear about their progress. "Connor actually helped. I was looking at the constellations and he mentioned Orion's Belt. When I said Orion towards the stallion, he nickered and seemed to like it." Tonya looks to her mother with a knowing smile and Stacy returns one of her own before Marni can catch sight of it.

"I love it. It definitely suits him better, I think." Tonya agrees.

"As far as progress, I was able to pet him today. He walked up to me and sniffed my hand. I had to keep from jumping up and down. I was so happy." Her cheeks blush as she remembers the moments that followed that exchange.

"That's awesome! I can't wait for you to ride him! Do you have any idea when that will be?" Tonya asks, and she and Marni dive into her training schedule and what her plans are. Connor dismisses himself from the table. His mother enters the kitchen behind him while he scrapes the leftovers into the trash can.

"Things seem to be good between the two of you," Stacy begins.

"I don't know what you mean." He tries to play dumb at his mom's game of match-maker, but the smile he can't contain tells her everything she needs to know.

"She seems happy here. Her eyes shine again." She pauses for a moment before continuing. "Don't break her heart, son."

"Ma, I don't think she'll be the one with a broken heart." There is a sadness to his tone she didn't expect. She gently places her hand on his shoulder. Since he came back, he isn't the same huggable son she once knew. He always tenses up or shies away when someone tries to offer a comforting touch.

"She will go back," Stacy says evenly. He nods as he looks out the kitchen window.

"I know." He turns and gives her a soft smile before going outside on the porch. Stacy sighs and places her hand over her heart. Tonya comes in from cleaning up the remains of dinner.

"What's wrong?" She notices the sad look in her mother's eyes.

"They're gonna break." Stacy looks out the kitchen window as Marni slides into Connor's passenger seat. He keeps his headlights off to try and remain incognito in their little adventure, but it doesn't work.

"They're both adults." Tonya washes the dishes that have piled in the sink.

"Yes, one is my son, and the other is practically my daughter. And one or both of them will be left broken when she goes back to the city."

"She could stay, if she would pull her head out of her ass and realize it."

"Tonya Faeye, your tongue."

"Sorry," Tonya grumbles, not at all sincere.

"I hope she will stay too, but her mother is ingrained in her so deep. I just don't know how far she will take this newfound backbone of hers."

Chapter Ten

CONNOR WALKS AROUND AND opens the door for her when they reach his cabin. It's the same layout at Tonya's, just with less clutter. A wood stove sits in the corner of the living room with a couch that looks like it's never been sat on. If she stumbled upon this place herself, the dirty coffee cup in the farmhouse sink would be her only sign anyone actually lives here. She freezes on the welcome mat, afraid to move, afraid to mess up the order of things.

"Are you going to come in?" He stands off to the side, giving her plenty of room.

"Are you going to act like I'm breakable all night?" Marni tilts her head at him. He slowly approaches her, making her squirm under his intense gaze. Her palms sweat and her stomach flops at the way he undresses her with his eyes. He pulls his cowboy hat off and hangs it on the rack.

"I don't think you're breakable," he whispers as their bodies push up against one another. "But if you need me to stop, tell me." Her mouth goes dry and she can only nod. He smirks and grips both hips with his large hands. He tosses her over his shoulder, and she lets out a string of giggles.

Connor shoves the door shut with his boot and packs Marni to his bedroom.

"Connor, I can walk!" she laughs. He smacks her ass, and electricity shoots through her body. Her stomach tightens at the desire coursing through her. "Oh," she whispers as her giggling fit ceases.

He gently lays her back on his king-size poster bed. He slides up between her legs and stares at her with both hands pressing into the comforter on either side of her head. She notes the size of his arms as he braces himself over her, careful to not touch her—yet.

She fingers the hem of his shirt and slides it up his muscular back. Connor rises to balance himself on his knees and finishes pulling his shirt over his head. A gasp escapes Marni before she can stop it.

Scars litter his chest and right shoulder, raised with uneven jagged lines. Connor sets his jaw and avoids Marni's gaze. She lifts a finger and traces each one. A shiver runs down Connor's spine and Marni drops that finger to skim across his waist. He sucks in a quick breath and her wanting eyes meet his.

Connor—painfully, slowly—unbuttons her blouse and slides it off her shoulders. He left the bedroom light on, and she shies away from him, drinking her in. She wraps her arms around her midsection.

"You don't have to hide with me. You're beautiful and should never feel otherwise," he whispers. Connor weaves his fingers through hers and slowly lifts them over her head. He lowers himself until their lips are inches apart.

Marni closes the distance. Connor brushes his lips across hers before moving to her neck. Bursts of pleasure radiate between her thighs. Her toes curl at the way he takes his time. She isn't used to this—Vance was always violent, like he was trying to take all of this anger, stress, any problems in general, out on her.

"Connor..." she moans, not really sure what she means by it. Her mind is reeling.

"Tell me what you want. Tell me what you like."

"I don't know." She gasps as he unclasps her bra and sucks her nipple into his mouth. He leans back and looks down at her, confused.

"You've never...?"

She tilts her head. "Never...?" she repeats in the same questioning tone.

"You've never had an orgasm, like during sex?"

Heat rushes to Marni's cheeks and the instinct to cover herself again rushes forward. She shakes her head, avoiding his eye contact.

"Well then, it's my job to change that." His dimples pop as he smiles, so sure of himself, so excited. Connor stands from the bed, and then her boots thud to the floor. He slides her pants down her legs and she applauds herself at how smooth her legs are as she rubs them together.

Connor gives her a mischievous smile, grabs the edge of her panties and rips them down the sides.

"Hey! I need those. I didn't pack extras," she playfully scolds him. He only smiles wider and hangs them on his bed post as his trophy. He lifts her foot to his mouth and kisses the inside of her ankle. "Oh, my," Marni lets out a moan. Who knew that a place so random would be attached to her oh-god-fuck-me button?

Connor trails up the inside of her leg, sucking and nipping as he goes. His mouth crests her inner thigh, and she squeezes her knees together.

"What's wrong?" Connor watches her carefully.

"Sorry, it's just...intense," she says breathlessly. Connor throws Marni's legs over his shoulders, and she knots the comforter in her hands when his tongue rolls over her clit. "Fuck!" she squeals, and Connor only rolls faster.

She bites down on her bottom lip to contain the moan that writhes inside of her.

She has had an orgasm before, but it was always with a vibrator or in a dream. Being the one not in control, like this—it's a whole new level of pleasure. The desire builds inside of her, and just when she thinks she can't take anymore, Connor amps it up and begins sucking and biting. She arches her back and her abdomen clenches. His fingers slip inside of her and she looks down to see the fire burning under his eyelashes.

"Connor...I can't..." She looks around the room as if to find a way to escape this storm inside of her.

"Just let go, Mar. Come to the sound of my name." The crest comes and when she tips over the edge, she throbs around his fingers inside of her and moans. Her legs shake as he keeps twirling his tongue around her clit to ride the wave all the way to the end.

She lies on her back breathless, her mind reeling at what just happened. Connor kisses her inner thigh and stands to remove his own jeans and boots. Marni watches, gravity keeping her weighed down to her spot.

Her eyes go wide when he slides off his boxers. She licks her lips, buzzing with a new feeling of wanting to taste every part of him, especially his hard cock.

"Come here," Connor purrs and holds his hand out to pull her up from the bed. Her legs hang off the edge and he steps to her. "Only if you want to." He runs his fingers through her hair. He did it for her and it felt so damn good—she wants to do the same for him.

"I've never done it," she admits shyly. Connor leans his head down and presses his lips to hers. He smells and tastes like her.

"Just no teeth." He smirks, and she grabs his thick cock, testing the waters by only taking part of him in. His precum coats her mouth, and he instantly gets harder as she slides her mouth down. A gasp escapes Connor as he wraps his fingers in her hair and she can't help but smile because she fucking did that; she is the reason he is moaning right now. She finds her groove and takes him all the way to the back of her throat, fighting the urge to gag but enjoying the way his body is responding too much to stop.

"Marni..." The way he purrs her name sends chills over her skin. She looks up through her lashes and slides his cock out. She stands to meet his gaze, and her hardened nipples brush against his chiseled chest. "I have to have you now. I want all of you." His Persian blue eyes swirl with desire. He grabs her hips and places her back on the bed, pushing himself up between her legs.

The time for taking it slow is over. He needs to feel her all around him, to drown inside of her and not come up for air. Her back arches to meet him as he thrusts inside of her. She gasps, and Connor bites her shoulder as he pumps harder and faster. She is so tight around his cock and her mouth already had him so close.

"I'm going to come. Are you on birth control?"

"What? No!" Marni moans as she rocks her hips in time with his. When his release comes, he slips out and explodes up her abdomen. He comes so hard it lands between her supple breasts. They lay together, lost in an ecstasy high.

Connor lifts himself from the bed and leads Marni to the shower. Steam quickly fills the cool bathroom, and he shuts the door to keep the heat in. He turns Marni's back to him and runs a soapy washcloth over her chest, palming each breast.

“Is it possible to want more?” she asks over her shoulder. A chuckle sounds from behind her, and she pushes her back into him and looks up at his euphoric smile.

“Only when it’s that good.” He kisses the top of her head and continues to wash down her body. She squirms when he reaches between her thighs. He steps around her and bends down as he washes each of her legs. Her head falls back at his gentle touch. When he stands, he wears a satisfied smile and lifts his knuckle to tilt her chin back. Water filters its way through her tangled hair.

“Was it that good for you?” She didn’t want to ask, but what else is she supposed to talk about when she is still riding the high of ecstasy? He combs his fingers through her hair and it takes her a fraction of a second to realize he is actually washing her hair. All of this is so different from what she has ever experienced.

“I don’t know how it gets much better,” he murmurs while he gently untangles the strands that fall down her back.

“Better than Christy?” Marni regrets the question the moment it leaves her lips. She hadn’t intended to ask, but it had been racing in the back of her mind.

He pauses from massaging her scalp. “The day my sister stays out of my business, hell will freeze over. I didn’t realize you knew about that.” He tilts her head back again and rinses out the shampoo.

“You didn’t answer my question,” Marni presses. She can’t backtrack now—might as well get the truth out of the way. With her hair suds free, he cups her cheek.

“She has never been here, to the ranch. She has never stepped one foot into my house, or my truck, for that matter. I don’t have any feelings beyond that of a quick fuck." Marni winces at the harshness of his tone. He tries again, gentler this time. "I'm sorry, I just...I need you to believe me when I say there is no comparison to you. You are beyond incredible."

Marni grabs the wash cloth from where he laid it and maneuvers him to stand under the falling water. She only smiles as she adds soap to the cloth and begins doing the same to him as he did to her.

"That's a fine answer. Can I ask another question?" The suds slide past the scars on his chest.

"Anything," he responds confidently.

"What are these from?" She brushes her thumb across one of the larger scars. His muscles tense. She has the urge to kiss them, but by the way he is responding to her touch, she waits.

"Afghanistan. My team and I walked into an ambush. The building was rigged with explosives. These are minor compared to what others endured." Pain flashes across his eyes, but not the physical kind. The kind that takes you to a dark place where you want to curl inside of yourself and beg death to take you. Seeing his pain, she leans forward and trails kisses over the scars. With each press of her lips, a shudder goes through him.

"Is that why you drink?" she asks. He lets out a rough sigh. "I'm sorry. If that's too personal."

"No, you're fine. Just haven't talked about it before." He clears his throat as Marni reaches down to wash between his thighs. "Yeah, I drink to forget, to sleep, to not see the horrors I've witnessed. I wish it was different, that I wasn't like this. But we won, and I came home." There is a far off look in his eyes and Marni wraps her arms around his waist. She looks up at him, smiling.

"What's so funny?" he asks, perplexed.

"You're too tall for me to wash your hair as elegantly as you did mine." He lets out a chuckle.

"I can handle that." He rakes the lather through his wavy toffee brown hair. It's lighter than his facial hair; and he wears his hat so low she hadn't noticed before.

Her eyes scan down the lines of his muscles, the way his hips dip into a V leading to his front. Her eyes linger on his cock—not completely soft yet. Connor's head is tilted back as he rinses his hair. She kneels down and takes his cock in her mouth. A surprised moan escapes Connor and, like before, a smug smirk of appears on her face. He steadies himself with one hand on the shower wall and buries his fingers in the very hair he just untangled.

He doesn't pull her away this time, and she is glad he doesn't. She wants to do this for him. Take away his pain, make him moan in pleasure and delight. Taste him as he gives in to the sensation of it completely. She peeks up at him through her eyelashes. He's biting his bottom lip and arching his own back at her touch, her caress. She is surprised at the power she has over him when like this. It makes her feel sexy as hell to have him weak in the knees and needing to support himself. She doesn't stop until he comes inside of her and she drinks him down.

***

GINGER MEOWS IN ANNOYANCE when Marni creeps into the loft so early in the morning. She and Connor want to be as discrete as possible on the ranch and just enjoy whatever is going on between the two of them. Her hips ache from the numerous orgasms and new-to-her positions Connor had her in.

She lays back on the bed in total bliss. The kind that has her mind full of air and a wide goofy grin on her face. She sighs in full contentment and giggling randomly as she replays each moment of mind-warping sex she experienced.

Her phone chimes, and she snatches it from the nightstand. Six missed calls dances across her screen, all from Boston. Her stomach drops. What did Parker tell him after yesterday? Would he go so far as to ruin her career with some smooth-talking lie, or worse, spin it so she is the obsessed narcissist?

She redials and waits, her palms slick with sweat while the phone rings.

"Marni! Thank God! Parker was in an accident and was rushed to the hospital last night. I need you to come back for a meeting with Highbridge first thing in the morning." His words echo through her head on a loop.

"What?" Her mind is racing. She eyes the trash can as her stomach churns and wants to expel all of its contents. Parker wrecked after he left—after she turned him down.

"Highbridge will be here at eight tomorrow. They are a huge potential client. This is our only chance. Parker was going to do the pitch. I can get you a flight if that's easier for you."

"No, no, I'll drive." Her voice is hollow as she says it. She was leaving...already? She doesn't want to leave, especially after last night. But this is reality—her job, her career. Connor is a fantasy that would not last. She was going back to the city eventually, right? Just happens to be sooner than she expected.

"Great. I will see you at seven tomorrow to prep for the pitch." Boston hangs up without so much as a thank-you for her cutting her trip short. Marni looks out her window as Connor walks to his parents' house for breakfast. Her heart aches. She didn't expect to feel this deeply for him this fast. She kept telling herself it was a fling and nothing more, but now that she's leaving, she wants more. So much more.

***

MARNI LOADS HER SUITCASE into the car and leaves her hat on the pillow along with Tonya's jeans and her boots. Ginger slightly protests at being put in the bubble. She wipes her sweaty palms on her jeans as she reaches for the farmhouse door.

This is going to suck.

The family chatters around the table, making plans for the day to come. Silence falls when Marni steps in. All eyes land on her and she wants to break down right there, but she forces herself to get through this and make it as painless as possible. She promises herself she will come back to visit, but will she go back to being the same meek person once she inserts herself into the city life?

"I have to leave...work needs me. My co-worker that was here..." Tears spring to her eyes and a lump in her throat cuts her off. Tonya stands and walks over to take Marni's hands in hers.

"What's going on?" Her voice is thick with concern.

"He was in an accident. My boss called and needs me to come for a meeting in the morning. I'm sorry, I have to leave. Now."

Connor's chair scrapes the floor as he pushes away from the table. He grabs his hat and walks out the back door without so much as a word or look in Marni's direction.

"Will you be back? After the meeting?" Tonya grips Marni's hands while tears form in Stacy's eyes.

"I don't know. I don't know when Parker will be back at work. I made him so angry. When he left here, he wrecked and I..."

"No, don't you dare," Tonya interjects. "You have come too far this week to blame his shortcomings on you. Connor told me about the altercation and he doesn't sound any better than the last guy." Marni's eyes trail out the back door where Connor disappeared. "Go talk to him." Tonya steps aside and Marni takes the painful steps toward the only guy she truly cares for.

He is leaning against the porch column, his hat pulled down over his features, staring out over the fields of the ranch. "Connor, I'm sorry. If I could stay I..."

"You can." He faces her now. "You can choose to stay."

"My job, and my boss, need me. I don't have a choice." He steps towards her and cups her soft cheek in his rough hand.

"You can choose." Her heart lurches. If she could separate her heart from her body and leave it here, she would. Her eyes beg for him to tell her to stay, to not leave the choice up to her. Put down his iron fist and refuse to let her leave. Tears blur her vision and Connor leans down, pressing his lips to hers. The fire that burned between them last night reignites with vengeance. He throws careful out the window and pulls her hard against him.

The pain of losing her drives his passion. She can't leave. Not after the flood gates she opened within him. He won't let her slip through his fingers again; he won't let her just walk away. Her tears wet his own cheeks, and he pulls back to see the war raging inside of her. She won't stay. He can see it.

Maybe she'll be back, but at least he doesn't let her leave without knowing how he really feels this time.

Marni backs away and races through the house she loves and locks the door of her car, as if that can cage her heart and keep it from shattering. Ginger is sleeping peacefully in the passenger seat and Orion lets out a shrill, high-pitched squeal from his corral. Through her tears, Marni sees Stacy and Jack embracing one another for comfort on the porch. Tonya holds up a hand, not committing to a wave goodbye.

She puts her car in drive and watches as they grow smaller in her rearview mirror. A gaping hole of pain explodes in her chest and she grabs it with one hand to try and hold herself together. Connor's blue eyes, the star-filled sky, the horses, her best friend, her family—everything she could've had if she had never listened to her mother.

She stops at the highway and rests her head on the steering wheel. A blood-curdling scream expels from her body, unleashing on the universe. On her mom, Parker, her ex. Anger swells alongside the heartbreak, warping into something so ugly and unrecognizable.

Brimstone breathes heavily on top of the ridge. Looking down at the entrance of the ranch, Connor spots the brake lights shine. A beacon of hope. "Just turn around. Come back, please," he whispers to the wind, willing it to carry his pleas to her. He finally knows what it feels like to kiss her, touch her, to have her and be hers. He won't survive without her. He needs her like a drought needs rain. "Come back." Brimstone whinnies a plea of her own.

Marni lifts her head. The sobs have quieted, but the anger still rings. She checks her rearview mirror. If he chases her, she'll go back. If he asks her to stay, she will. She stares, willing headlights to appear. Several minutes pass.

She lifts her foot off the brake and pulls onto the pavement. Silent tears continue down her face until the ranch fades into the distance.

Chapter Eleven

"It's been wonderful doing business with you, Marni. We greatly appreciate your help and feel confident our investments are in capable hands." Mr. Wong bows and Marni returns the gesture. Her professional, but fake, smile is plastered on her face. She's been wearing it since she got back. A mask to hide her anguish.

"It's been a pleasure. I'll be in touch." She closes the door to her office and clicks the lock into place. This was her second meeting with Highbridge. This time, the actual owner, Mr. Wong, graced them with his presence.

Dragging her laptop with her, she collapses on the floor and scrolls through the pictures of the wildies. She stares at Orion, the ache in her chest still just as raw and open as the day she left two weeks ago.

Tonya has called a couple of times, asking for advice with Orion since she took over his training. She never mentions Connor and Marni doesn't ask. She slams her laptop shut and shoves it into the carrying case. Changing her heels for flats, she steps out of her office and locks the door behind her.

"Marni?" The male voice stops her dead in her tracks. She thought she was prepared for this, but hearing his voice, her defenses shatter. Parker stands in the middle of the hall, one arm in a sling and a bandage above his brow. He isn't even supposed to be back at work yet. He saunters toward her and she shrinks back. His eyes seem just as shocked to see her as she is to see him. "I just want to talk to you, please."

Marni scans the office; they seem to be the only two left. "What do you want?" she snaps, and he stands taller, reflecting more of a predator now than an injured man.

"I want to apologize for my behavior. Seeing you with the cowboy, the way he sized me up, it messed with my head and I'm sorry." Marni just eyes him warily. "I mean, you're back, so obviously I have nothing to worry about. You chose. We can put all of this behind us and go out to eat like we always do. I have a rental—it's a newer BMW than the one I had. Very nice. Leather heated seats. They even *vibrate*."

"How hard did you hit your head when you wrecked?" Marni's voice cracks and he takes a step toward her. He reaches out for her hand, but she jerks back. "No, I told you back at the ranch. We are co-workers, only to see each other at work and talk about work. That didn't change because I came back." Something flashes in his eyes that he's never shown her before. They look...just like Vance's

"We can discuss work over dinner. It'll be completely professional. Come on, Mar. I just want to have a night spent with a friend. Entertain me. It's not like you have anything else to do." His words drip with arrogance. Fear shudders through her. She looks behind her and sees the exit is still a good distance away.

"No." Marni grits her teeth. A snarl replaces his cocky smirk, and her body goes cold with terror. She backs away from Parker's towering body. As much as she wants to stand up for herself, years of being broken down makes it impossible.

"Marni?" Boston pokes his head out of his office, and like a switch, Parker goes from lethal to his charming self. Even his stance changes. *A telltale sign of a psychopath*, Marni thinks to herself. How was she ever so dumb to fall for his tricks? She sidesteps Parker, hearing him huff as a smirk appears on his face.

When she enters his office, Boston sits at his desk, shuffling through papers and massaging his left temple. He lets out a low whistle and leans back in his leather office chair. "I've arranged for you to get on a plane tonight. The New York firm wants to meet in person and they got me by the balls about coming here. Here are your plane tickets. I'll email you their files." Marni can't keep her jaw from falling open as Boston holds out a hand with two airline tickets.

"What?" she blurts out. Do all the men here just think they can tell her what to do? Is this how it always was and she just didn't realize it?

"These are your tickets. Your plane departs at eight-twenty. You'll meet with the firm at ten a.m. Eastern time tomorrow. Is something wrong?" he asks, but his eyes don't meet hers as she places the tickets on the desk in front of her. He begins typing away on his laptop. Marni scoffs and slides her fingers over the two tickets.

"No." It comes out as a whisper, but the keys stop clacking and he looks up at her.

"Pardon?" he says sweetly, but his eyes harden.

"I mean, I can't. I have plans this weekend. I am going back to the ranch." A lie, but it isn't a totally absurd idea now. Boston smiles and types again.

"I need you on this. You're the best there is." He uses the same manipulative tone Parker does. She's had enough.

"No, send someone else." She stands to leave the office, but Boston cuts her short.

"All right then. This is no longer a request. You are going to New York or don't show up on Monday." She spins on her heel at his ultimatum. Like rapid fire, her response triggers before she can think it through.

"Are you fucking serious? You don't know your head from your ass when it comes to finances. I balance your books! I do everything around here! All of those clients are because of me and my reputation, and you're going to try and pull this shit?!" His blank expression revs her temper even higher. "Fine, fire me. We will see what Jennifer has to say when she finds out. We both know where you'll end up then."

Marni slams the door behind her and Parker looks at her with disgust, actual disgust, as if she is lower than the crud on the bottom of his shoe. For good measure, she flips him her middle finger and walks past, leaving the shit-hole of a job she hated, anyway.

***

Her apartment door slams, rattling the frames on her wall. Ginger jumps off from the couch, losing one of her nine lives to a heart attack. Marni slings her clothes in the suitcase she just finished unpacking the night before. Her phone rings, breaking through her blinding rage.

She doesn't even take time to see who is calling before answering. "Hello?"

"This is what a jobless, middle-aged woman sounds like." Her mom's cynical tone stops Marni short as she stomps to the bathroom.

"How the hell do you—Boston called you?" It isn't a secret to Marni that Gwen's connections got her into the big-city investment firm in the first place.

"Watch your tone, young lady. Yes, he did, and thank God he did, so I can stop you from trying to ruin your life again."

"Ruin my life?! You'd rather I let a man push me around and make decisions for me?"

"Well, clearly you can't make sound decisions for yourself. Call Boston, tell him you will go to New York. I'll send a driver for you now to take you to the airport."

Marni grips her phone and chucks it across her apartment, smiling in delight as it shatters to pieces on the floor. With the invigorating rebellion coursing through her, she reaches for Parker's dead flowers and launches the vase in the same fashion.

A war cry fills the empty space of her apartment as she slams her suitcase shut. Most would call her unhinged, having a mental breakdown, midlife crisis, or simply gone crazy. Quite the contrary, she feels enlightened. Never surer of herself. She slides her suitcase and Ginger into her car and squeals her tires from the parking garage to the highway.

'Mama's Broken Heart' by Miranda Lambert plays from her radio and she cranks it so high her speakers crackle along with her voice as she sings—well, more like screams—at the top of her lungs. She pushes the limit as she makes her way back to where her heart belongs. Only stopping to fill up on gas. Caffeine isn't necessary. The venom that spreads through Spiderman's veins has nothing on her adrenaline high.

"I just quit my job! Holy shit, Ginger! I quit my fucking job!" Her cheeks hurt from smiling as the mile marker signs rush by. Adele's *'Hello'* comes on the radio and almost makes her lose it completely. She feels like a wild animal being released from years of restraints. No longer fitting in the perfect square box her mother built for her, she's a fucking Valkyrie. Ready to take to the skies, kicking ass and taking names.

"I want to fight something! Like you see on TV. Or break something." Bubbles of hysteria work their way up her abdomen and a witch-like cackle erupts from her mouth. Maybe she really has gone crazy. She pushes the pedal to the floorboard. Excitement courses through her as she gets closer.

Her eyelids grow heavy when she finally makes it to the ranch. Through her exhaustion, she doesn't notice Connor's truck parked at the house. She picks Ginger up from her seat and makes her way to the barn. The loft stairs creak under her weight, her bed calling to her with its embrace. The knob sticks and she jerks it open.

She sets Ginger down, letting her out to stretch. Marni reaches for the light switch, but the sound of a rifle being cocked makes her freeze. Her eyes widen and her heart drums in her chest.

"You best make your way back down those stairs and off this farm. There isn't anything here worth your life." His voice sends shivers down her spine. Flashes of his body pulsing against hers. She turns with her hands in the air. The moonlight casts shadows on his chiseled jaw. His eyes widen when they land on hers. "Marni?" He lowers his gun, and she wants to jump into his arms, snuggle in close to him, relive all the amazing things between the two of them.

"Who the fuck is Marni?" A nasally voice comes from under the covers. Marni sees her blonde hair first, then she turns her head. Christy stares at her through slits for eyes. Marni whips her head between the two. Connor is quick to grab the sheet to wrap around his waist, but Marni is quicker to get Ginger and escape the room. Her rage was spent on three other people. She doesn't have any left.

"Marni! Wait!" Rushed footsteps chase after her as she races to her car. She grips Ginger tightly to keep herself held together. "Marni, please, just wait!" The part of her heart she left here at the ranch is dust on the wind. She pants as she tries to catch her breath, not from the running but from the colossal ache attacking her entire body.

She sits Ginger down in the passenger seat and turns when Connor comes out of the barn in nothing but his boxers. Her eyes act as traitors when they catch the outline of him and how his toned hips dip down. She gets wet at the sight of the moon dancing through the clouds on his body. Her fingers twitch to trace the lines of his hardened muscles. His eyes shine with the same shock he wore upstairs, but now there is sorrow, pain...regret.

"I'll just go stay with Tonya. Sorry to bother you." She hates the way her voice wavers.

"I didn't know you'd ever be back," he whispers, his hands held out, palms up, like Marni does when approaching a cautious horse.

"I would have called, but I broke my phone...quit my job...pretty sure my mom will never talk to me again...Oh God. I need to stop talking now." Word vomit explodes from her, along with the tears she tries to hold back. Connor takes a step closer, but she wraps her arm around herself. Her knees shake and her car is the only thing holding her up.

"It isn't what you think. We aren't...we didn't..." Marni holds her hand up at the same moment Christy comes out of the barn, the comforter the only thing covering her body.

"Connor, come back to bed," she coos with a shit-eating grin on her face. Marni wipes her tears away and slides into the driver's seat.

***

TONYA'S DOOR CRACKS OPEN and the barrel of a pistol pokes out first. "Does everyone have a gun out here?" At Marni's voice, Tonya jerks the door open and stares in disbelief.

"What the hell are you doing? Get in here!" She wraps Marni in a hug and the two of them sit on the couch. Like the great cat she is, Ginger doesn't leave Marni's lap while she tells Tonya everything, including Christy. As Marni dumps all of it on her best friend, the load lightens off her shoulders.

"Whoa, that's a lot to process. Are you okay? Obviously not, you showed up here with red puffy eyes." She paces the floor while Marni tracks her with her eyes. Exhaustion from the drive, the events, and the pain of it all hits her like a ton of bricks. "And your mom. I never liked that woman and Parker...well, he deserves the injuries from the car crash. Don't worry, we'll find you a new job. We'll figure it all out. You can stay here as long as you need, of course."

"Thanks, T. Do you have any wine?" Tonya nods and pulls one bottle for each of them out of the fridge. Marni definitely deserves one of her own. She relives the details of standing up to Boston.

She clings to the high she felt to push away the betrayal of finding the skank in *her* bed. Connor told her she meant nothing, that she had never been to the ranch. Clearly, something changed in the past two weeks.

Marni finishes her bottle of wine and lays her head on the arm of the couch. Ginger curls up beside her.

Tonya stops and turns to see Marni, her worry lines gone as she is cuddles with her fluff ball of a cat. Her heart breaks for her best friend, but this is all years in the making. Connor—on the other hand—that she could do something about. Right on cue, headlights shine through her windows and she slinks out the door before his knocks can wake her.

"What the hell were you thinking? Bringing Christy here? And to the fucking loft? Are you completely all out of functioning brain cells?!" She keeps her voice low, but he still winces as if she is screaming.

"It wasn't like that. I got in a bad place. It's been two weeks since I've seen her or talked to her..."

"And whose fault is that? Did you try calling her? Telling her how you feel?" She pauses, but he doesn't answer. "No, you didn't."

"Please, I need to talk to her, to explain."

"She's asleep, and she's had the shittiest day of her life. Your skank was the cherry on top." He slides both hands into his pockets. He wants so badly to cradle her in his arms and protect her from ever being hurt again.

"What happened? Is she all right? What made her come back?"

"It started with Parker, then her boss, then ended with Gwen telling her she was ruining her life. Marni threw her phone into a wall at that point and drove straight here." His fists clench at the mention of Parker.

"What did he do?" he asks through a tight jaw.

"Oh, chill. Marni handled it. It seems the stallion taught her as much as she taught him. She quit her job when her boss told her she had to fly to New York. Then her boss called Gwen, and we all know how that went."

"How do I fix this?" His tone sounds like that of a worried child.

"She is pretty forgiving. Just be honest with her. We all know Christy means nothing. Hell, even Christy knows, and she still sleeps with you. Talk to her tomorrow." He nods.

"I think I love her," he says, his voice barely above a whisper.

"We all know that too, dumb-dumb. About time you catch up." He kicks a rock with the toe of his boot. He has to fix this. Connor leaves his sister to go to sleep and keeps his headlights off as he makes his way back to the loft, hoping to not wake his parents if he hasn't already.

He strips her bed and piles the quilt and sheets in the corner. Fixing the bed with clean ones, he lays her hat, jeans, and boots back how he found them.

A couple of days after she left, he came up here and saw her clothes. The air smelled like her. That's when he started to sleep here. Then tonight at Turnpike, Dillon came in and tried to pick a fight. Connor drank more and more, trying to drown out her memory, the way her brown eyes captivate him. Before he knew it, he could barely walk to the bathroom to piss.

Christy offered to drive him home when he was too drunk to even open his truck door. He doesn't remember much else after that.

Not able to fall asleep after his royal fuck-up, he watches the sun peek over the mountain tops and listens to the stir of horses as they wake. Car tires crunching on gravel grab his attention and he hurries to the barn door to see Marni's car passing the house toward the driveway. Refusing to let her slip through his fingers again, he hops in his truck. Acting on pure impulse, stuffing down any doubts he has about how she will react or even if she still wants him, he floors it and races after her.

She is almost to the highway when he slams on his horn. Her brake lights shine brightly before her parking lights flash. The driver door opens, and she steps out wearing a thin tank top and those delicious athletic shorts. For a moment he just stares, not sure what to say or do now that she stares back at him.

"What are you doing?" She furrows her brow and bites her lip. She wants to run into his arms, to feel his lips on hers again, but then she also wants to slap him at the same time. What happened with Christy? Does he no longer want her? Was she just a conquest to be conquered and now her allure is gone? Silence fills the gap between them.

Connor suddenly takes three long strides and plucks his cowboy hat off with one hand, wrapping it around her waist, and tugs her against his body. With his free hand, he grabs her hair and tilts her head back, then crushes his lips to hers.

His urgency presses into her, heat spreading from her abdomen through her limbs. The initial shock of his touch wears off, and she grabs the waist of his jeans and pulls him between her legs, pinning her against the side of her car. His mouth leaves hers and trails down her neck, across her collarbone. He nips and sucks her exposed skin, causing the want between her legs to drip. A moan escapes deep in his throat and she thinks he is going to take her right there. Instead, he pulls back. Lust fills both their eyes.

"Don't leave. Stay. Come back with me, please." Marni is taken aback by his plea. She wants to slap the puppy-dog look off his face for finding him with Christy this morning. Instead, a giggle escapes her before she can stop it. Hurt settles as his shoulders slump forward.

"No...I'm not laughing at you, although you might deserve that or a slap across the face for this morning," she gasps out. Trying to regain control, she forces a quick deep breath. "I was just going to get a new phone." A smile cracks the serious worry lines on Connor's face and he pulls her to his chest, inhaling the scent of cinnamon and citrus from her hair.

"A slap?" A chuckle rumbles through his chest. "I thought you were leaving."

"I debated it. Then I saw the sunrise over the ranch and I just couldn't." She looks past his truck as the sun clears the mountains now. "This is heaven on earth. Nobody can change that for me."

"Would you like to grab breakfast in town? I can take you, or if you don't want to, that's fine, too." Marni looks into his eyes for a moment. How could she hold last night against him? She showed no signs of coming back and didn't give anyone a heads-up.

"I'd like that."

Chapter Twelve

Stacy is working on mending a hole in a pair of Connor's jeans when Jack comes in from working on the ATV that has a miss. He notices Stacy's humming and a blushing smile on her face that seems stuck there for good. She even lets out a satisfied sigh to boot, like the jeans she is mending are her greatest pleasure.

"Stace, you hate sewing. What's into you?" She sets down the needle and pants and looks up at him with a beaming smile. He flashes to when they were younger and she came out of the bathroom wearing that same smile, holding a positive pregnancy test. "Okay, you're starting to freak me out."

"Susan called. You know, my friend at the Malt and Toffee?" She refers to the local breakfast and coffee restaurant in their little town.

"And they have your favorite dish as a special and I should take you?" He grasps at straws to find the hint he is obviously missing.

"Oh, stop." She leaps from her seat and clasps her hands over her chest. "Connor was there this morning...with Marni." She raises her eyebrows as if there is a hidden message somewhere within her eyes.

"Just spit it out, woman." She lets out an aggravated huff and places her hands on Jack's shoulders.

"He was with Marni and they couldn't keep their hands off each other. Holding hands, stealing kisses, sitting on the same side of the booth. I think this is it, Jack!"

"Now just slow down and don't be starting any wedding bells. Marni wasn't even here. How is she in town with Connor?"

"Exactly what I thought. So I called T, who informed me she quit her job yesterday and arrived early this morning while we were all asleep."

"You should have your own private eye TV show, Stacy. You can find anything with a dial of that phone." He tries to hide his joy by picking at his wife.

"Oh, I can barely contain myself! I should plan a huge dinner. What were her favorites? Do you remember? Oh, never mind, she loves all of my food." Stacy dances through the kitchen and pulls pots and pans from various cabinets. Jack stands on the front porch looking down the driveway, admiring the view and thanking God for everything He has provided.

***

"So, CAN I ASK one thing?" Marni asks as they walk down the street, a new phone bag swinging in her left hand.

"Shoot."

"Why the loft? Why didn't you take her back to your place?" Connor gives Marni a sideways glance. He lets outs a breath and chooses his words carefully.

"She's never been to the ranch. I didn't lie about that before. I honestly don't remember anything after leaving the bar last night. She drove me home, and I woke up to you coming in the door."

"You two didn't...?" His cheeks turn red and he clears his throat. Marni backpedals. "You don't have to answer that. It's not my business."

"We didn't. I'm sure she tried, but I was too far gone to do anything...performance-wise."

That makes her feel better. At least she just has to burn the linens and not the whole bed. They make their way back to the truck, and Connor opens the door for her. Before she steps in, a voice catcalls from across the street.

"Connor! There you are!" Christy bounds toward them, looking right past Marni like she doesn't exist. Marni's lips twist into a smirk and she rubs her hands together.

"Do you need something?" Connor asks, not taking his hand off the passenger door. Marni stands between the two of them, and Connor shows no sign of stepping forward.

"I think I left my bracelet at your place this morning. I thought maybe I could come later and look for it?" She lowers her head, bats her eyelashes, and bites her lip in one flawless motion. Marni turns toward Connor and mouths *your place,* with raised eyebrows. She waits for Connor's answer. Is he going to fall for her ruse to get back in the loft?

"I've already torn that room apart and washed the linens. There wasn't a bracelet. You must have lost it somewhere else." Well, sounds like she won't have a victorious bonfire after all. Christy finally acknowledges Marni's appearance.

"So that's it? She's back and you're going to toss me aside until you need something?" Christy crosses her arms and Connor stutters to find the right words. Marni decides that's enough from her cunning mouth.

"He won't be needing your help with anything anymore. I've got it taken care of from here. Thank you for getting him home safely last night. That will be the last time you ever set foot on our ranch." Marni gives her a venomous smile and slides her hand into Connor's back pocket for good measure. Christy's gears lock in place and she lets out a stream of unintelligible sounds before stomping off like a two-year-old who just got told no.

Marni removes her hand to step in the truck, but Connor grabs her wrist before she can. She turns to see if she had taken the *our ranch* comment too far. Feverish lips crush into hers and his arms wrap around her waist. He slides his hands down her back and firmly cups her ass cheeks, lifting her into the truck seat where he sports the biggest smile that shows his dimples.

A truck horn blows as it drives by. "Go, Curston!" Hocks shouts and Marni giggles at the spectacle.

"Friend of yours?" she asks.

"Worse. He's an employee." Marni's mouth falls open.

"Your mom!" Connor laughs at her revelation.

"Oh, I'm sure the gossip tree already rang when we went to the coffee shop. Odds are Christy was the last to know." He climbs into the driver's seat and fires up the engine. "Just to clarify, you aren't planning on leaving anytime soon, right? No matter what comes through that phone when you activate it?" Marni stares down at the bag. No telling what slander her mother has left on her voicemail and Jennifer...has Boston told her she quit yet? Connor grows worried with her delayed response. He places his hand on her thigh and snaps Marni back to reality.

"It's okay. I know what I'm signing up for." He gives her a confident smile.

Great, she thought, *because I have no clue what I'm doing with my life at the moment.*

Marni drives her car back to the farmhouse and Tonya's parents rush out the door to embrace her.

"Oh sweetie! You're back! I'm so happy to see you! What happened? Are you okay?" Stacy fuses over every inch of Marni.

"Mom, you can cut the act. We know Susan called you and that you've talked to Tonya."

She gives her son a knowing smile. "I don't know what you mean." She hustles back to her busy kitchen. Jack wraps his arm around Marni and kisses her head.

"It's good to see you back. You can stay as long as you want. The loft is yours unless you need to stay somewhere else...?" He looks at Connor as he says the last part. Apparently, they know more than just about her being back.

Marni smirks as Connor lets out a huff and rolls his eyes. "The loft is fine. Thank you, though."

"Well, if you change your mind, we have the whole upstairs inside the house. Connor, can you make time in your busy schedule to come help me with the ATV? I can't figure the engine out."

"Yeah, I'll be right there."

Marni lifts her suitcase from the car and carries it toward the loft stairs.

"I'll get it." Connor plucks it from her hand before she can object and walks behind her to the landing of the loft. He takes a step inside and sets the luggage on the floor. He watches Marni with curiosity. Her long hair flows down her back, rich brown waves that he wants curtained around him.

"Things look different since I was here last," she jokes. She picks up her hat up from the pillow and slides her hand around the brim. She sets it down on the bedside table and moves the jeans to the drawer of the wardrobe. Connor's eyes track her across the room. Stealing kisses in public is easy. Here—completely secluded, with a bed—she wants to pounce him and make him forget the blonde.

"So, about earlier. You have me taken care of?" Connor asks. Heat builds in her stomach. She bites her lower lip as heat rushes to her cheeks.

"I didn't...I just wanted to get under her skin and shut her up."

Connor closes the door and hangs his hat on the doorknob. Marni's breath quickens. The loft suddenly feels so much smaller with his eyes stalking her.

"So you don't want me then?" His voice is low, almost a growl. A smile creeps up to his eyes and his fingers brush her bare skin below her tank top. "Say it," he whispers in her ear.

A shudder runs through her, desire begging him to take her now. To not play around with the fire, he is slowly kindling inside of her.

"You have to say it, Mar. How will I know otherwise?" He kisses her cheek and places a knuckle under her chin to bring her eyes to his.

His eyes are wild, laced with want for her. A want she hasn't seen a man have for her before. Not possessive—he wants her as his equal. He wants to hear that she wants him just as much.

She swallows loudly, her mouth and throat both dry. Her lips part, wanting to taste his. She reaches up on her tiptoes, but he pulls back just out of reach.

"Say it," he repeats, definitely a growl now. His own restraint faltering.

"I want you," she whispers, his eyes not leaving hers.

"Where do you want me?" Her breath hitches as he slides his fingers below the waist of her shorts. She is already dripping wet from the stare-down between the two of them. "Tell me," he almost begs. Like he needs her permission to do all of the things she is imagining.

"I want you inside of me. I want all of you." Connor slides two fingers between her thighs and holds his lips inches from hers.

"You're already so wet for me. Do you want it?" He slips his fingers inside of her and pulls her hair. She moans and Connor presses his lips to hers, dancing his tongue across the inside of her mouth. "Tell me," he says against her lips. Her eyes roll back when his fingers find her clit. He pinches and circles quickly around it.

"I want your cock inside of me. Please. Please."

He jerks her shorts down her long silky-smooth legs. He tosses her back on the bed and she squeals in delight. Connor chuckles as she rips her tank top and bra off in the same motion. He leans down and kisses her abdomen, teasing her while he unbuttons his shirt and pants.

"You'll be the death of me," Connor murmurs as he slides his body up against her. He guides himself in, and with each thrust, Marni moans out and her back arches, allowing him to get deeper, to be completely and totally devoured by him. She tangles her fingers through his hair and wraps her legs around his waist, rocking her hips in rhythm with his.

She lets him push all her worries out of her. Each time he presses his body into hers, she feels lighter. She takes a page from his book and moves one hand down her abdomen and rapidly trails her fingers around her clit. A whole new wave of ecstasy crashes around her as she quickly climaxes and her body spasms under Connor's weight.

He pounds into her hard, riding out the wave of her orgasm while she throbs around his cock. Seconds later, he feels his own climax and pulls out to stake his claim on her body before rolling over onto his back.

The room smells of sex and heat. Marni lays with her eyes closed and a smile spread across her face. He leans up on one elbow and runs his thumb across her lips. Her chocolate eyes find his and his heart bursts with how happy she looks in this moment.

"Shower?" He nips at her bare shoulder and she giggles.

"I don't know if I can move. I feel like one giant noodle." Connor leans over and kisses her swollen lips. He notices the redness of her skin around her breasts and neck. His beard is the culprit, but damn, he loves leaving his mark on her.

"I'll carry you." Before she can object, he whisks her up in his arms. He catches their image in the mirror and notices the small bruises forming on his collarbone and shoulder. Her bites left her mark on him too, and he fucking revels in it.

***

MARNI PLACES HER HAND on Orion's blaze. His eyes watch her for any sudden movement. His breaths are rapid and he's nervous about the touch. She has a halter over her right shoulder and a lead line slung around her arm. She really doesn't want to use the lasso to make him to submit to the pressure before being able to halter him.

While staying at his head, she brushes one hand down his neck. His body twitches, but he doesn't move. She grips the lead and rubs it over his neck and shoulder, giving him time to get used to the feel. Marni slides the halter down her shoulder and Orion jerks his head up at the clank of the metal buckles.

"You're okay, boy. It's just me," she purrs to the stallion. She holds the halter out for him to smell and slides it over his nose and ears. He snorts at the restraint but doesn't pull away. Once it's latched, she backs up a few paces to wait for his blow-up at the new pressure around his head. Orion follows her instead. One step at a time.

"Okay?" She looks at him with distrust for the first time. Never has a wild horse who has just been haltered willingly followed the person. At least not in her experience. But Orion does. Marni stops and he stops in front of her. She rubs his head at first, then continues down his neck and to his back. She drapes her arm over his back, and though he gives her a side-eye, he doesn't run.

"You're tempting me." Her tone is wary, but full of excitement. She drapes her other arm over his back and rubs his flank on his off side, trying to push his limits. She bears her weight down across his back. He wiggles from the discomfort, but as soon as he settles, she removes her pressure. After a couple more times, he doesn't move at all.

"This is incredibly stupid of me." She jumps around his side and in his space, but not touching him. Just flailing her arms around trying to get him to spook, to test if he really is this calm. He looks at her as if she's crazy. Marni lets out a huff and wiggles her jeans up.

"Well, here goes stupid." She brings the mounting block over from the gate. She hadn't planned on riding him today, but she can't let this moment pass her by. Marni stands on the top step and rubs him down until she's satisfied.

Seconds pass after she drapes her midsection over his back. Holding her breath, she waits for him to bolt, or try to kill her.

"Good boy." Her voice comes out shaky, her adrenaline getting the best of her. She pushes her body upright, feeling his spine and withers between her legs. "Easy, good boy."

Once she clicks her tongue to move him forward, Orion leaps from a standstill. Marni squeezes her legs to keep her seat, and he panics at the pressure around his abdomen. He slams her right leg into the corral panel, but she can't worry about the pain. She is focused on not dying.

"Whoa!" she half shouts while searching for a safe way to dismount. Orion's hind legs come up high off the ground, throwing her forward with each motion.

He whips his body to the left while his rear legs pump to the sky again and Marni loses her grip on his mane. She's propelled over his head and lands on the ground only a few feet in front of him. Her mouth hangs open, but she can't inhale or exhale. All the air has been forced from her lungs.

The closeness of his hoofbeats on the dirt push urgency through her as she crawls to the panels. She shimmies under them and rolls to her back, watching Orion pant and snort. Carefully, noting what hurts on her body, she pulls herself up using the panels for support.

"Easy boy, you're okay." With one arm cradling her midsection, she opens the latch to re-enter the corral. Even though her hands shake and she just saw her world flash before her eyes, she has to get the halter and lead off of him. It's not safe to leave them on. A stabbing pain courses through her with each breath. She wheezes as she walks half bent over.

"Easy, Orion. We're okay. I told you it was a stupid idea." Marni tries to chuckle, but she winces. Surprisingly, Orion doesn't move as she gets closer to him. He lowers his nose. "I'm okay," she reassures him. After the halter is removed, she drops it to the dirt and stiffly walks to her apartment. She desperately needs ibuprofen and a hot shower.

Chapter Thirteen

Oil and grease stain Connor's clothes and the ATV engine lays in front of them in pieces. "Who knew something so small can cause so much fuss?" Jack pushes to his feet and holds the bad ignition spark in his hand.

"I'll get this put back together tomorrow. Mom will have dinner ready soon and she won't let either of us inside looking like this." Connor gestures between the two of them. Their hands are the same color as the dirty engine. Jack eyes Connor.

"You and Marni?"

Connor knew this was coming. "I don't know, Dad. We haven't exactly talked about it. I don't know what she plans to do about her job. Or her mom."

"Gwen is something else. I always told your ma she only needed a broom and a cauldron, then she would've put the Wicked Witch of the West to shame." Connor chuckles at his dad's disdain for Marni's mom.

"I'm not even sure Gerald likes her," Connor adds. Jack joins him in his laughter.

"Lord, forgive me for speaking ill of someone. I just hope Marni sticks to her guns this time. Gwen's been controlling that girl for too long." He clasps a hand on Connor's shoulder and gives him an encouraging squeeze.

"Come on, you're right about your mother. We have to get cleaned up if we want to eat."

Connor splits from his dad's company when he reaches his truck. He pauses and looks at the loft window. Catching a glimpse of himself in the side mirror of his truck, he pushes down his desire to go for round two.

Inside his cabin, he sees things from a different perspective. Marni could be here tonight with him. He just has to ask. Memories of her in his bed flood his mind, him between her legs, tasting her as she moaned under his tongue. He wants her now. Forget food. He smirks at his vivid imagination in the mirror and steps into the shower. He'd probably need a cold one before going to face Marni.

The water runs black down the drain and the heat of shower intensifies as it pelts the scars across his shoulder. He surprised himself when he told Marni the truth about them. That is a door he has kept shut for years. His parents and sister don't even know what all happened to him. He quickly finishes washing the grease from his body and puts on fresh jeans and a clean shirt. If he hurries, he might be able to steal her away before his mom rings the dinner bell.

His phone chimes and Hocks' name appears.

"Oh Connor, I want you so bad. Kiss me. Kiss me!" Connor squeezes his eyes shut as his best friend, and employee, makes lip-smacking sounds.

"Get it out of your system now. I'll deck ya next time."

"Easy, just joking. But seriously, when did that happen? You left the bar with Christy last night. Is ranch life so slow you can juggle two?"

"Speaking of last night, why the hell did you let me leave, anyway? I couldn't drive, which is how Christy ended up bringing me home."

"Hey man, I was just as hammered. Jasmine gave me a lashing from hell when she found me passed out in my truck, still in the parking lot. I tried to show her the bright side—at least I didn't drive."

"Well, you deserved it."

"Anyway, I called about tomorrow. What time are we starting and what's the plan?" Connor flipped through the mental index of everything that needed to be done around the ranch.

"We need to move the cattle to the east pasture. Think we can vaccinate and treat for pink eye, then move 'em in the same day?"

"Just us two? No. If you include those rodeo wanna-bes, maybe. It's about time they had some real farm work instead of Tonya's jobs."

"All right. I'll tell T tonight that *you* requested her hands tomorrow. She won't completely rip my head off if it comes from you." Maybe he'll ask Marni to tag along. She can out-rope any of them. The melody of Stacy's dinner bell echoing to his cabin interrupts his thoughts. So much for stealing Marni away before dinner.

He looks to the barn, hoping Marni just happens to cross his path. She must already be inside since she doesn't appear. He takes his hat off and hangs it on the hook. Tonya's in the kitchen telling her mom about her day with the wildies and that she found a few of the weanlings' homes.

Connor peeks his head in, searching for the infamous chocolate hair. Disappointment creeps up when she isn't there, either. He pours himself a glass of water, then sits at his usual spot while his family gets settled.

"Where's Marni?" Tonya asks and all eyes land on him.

"Why would I know?"

"Besides the fact that the entire ranch heard y'all this evening?" His cheeks turn beet red and he stares at his empty placemat.

"Tonya," his mom warns. "Have you heard from her, dear?" she asks, her tone softer now.

"Not since she got back from getting a new phone." Connor pushes himself up from the table. If this is his fault, he has to fix it. Maybe she regrets everything and now can't face him or his family. Maybe she is waiting to run back to the city again and leave him.

"I'll go check." He grabs his hat. The idea of her leaving causes an ache in his stomach so painful he doesn't think he'll be able to eat anything. The walk between the house and loft goes by too fast and he stares up the stairs. No matter what she says, he tells himself, he won't go find comfort in alcohol tonight. He'll need to feel this, to process it, and get over it—eventually.

The steps creak under the weight of his boots. He knocks but doesn't hear a response. The knob turns and clicks open.

"Marni?" He steps inside and scenes from earlier play through his mind. "Marni?" he says again, louder.

"In here." Her voice comes from the shower. If he had been paying attention, he would have noticed the water running when he was downstairs. He jiggles the knob, but it's locked. The shower knob squeaks as it's turned off. "Hold on." Her voice sounds off tight. Is she in pain?

The lock unlatches and Marni stands bent over with a towel wrapped around her. Her face contorts from the movement.

"What's wrong?" Connor looks at her clothes on the floor.

"I was stupid. I knew it was stupid. I'm not an eighteen-year-old girl anymore."

"Did I hurt you?" His voice is laced with worry and genuine concern. He's dead serious, and a giggle erupts from her.

"Ouch, can't laugh," she pants. "I can handle you just fine, cowboy. It was Orion. I may have been pro rodeo material, but it certainly wasn't for riding broncs." She sits on the bed and Connor watches her intently, trying to find the source of her pain.

"He bucked you off?"

"After my leg got slammed into the panels. My torso took the worst of it. It knocked the wind out of me, but I don't think anything is broken." He kneels down in front of her and gently places his hands on her thighs.

"Let me see." She hesitates but nods, and he slides the towel off her shoulders. Her knee is bruising already, but he doesn't see any signs of her ribs being hurt. He skims his fingertips below her breast and she sucks in a breath.

"Does that hurt?" His own voice comes out raspy.

"No," she whispers. He slides his hand across her abdomen and skims it around her ribs, gently applying pressure.

"How about that?"

"No." She bites on her bottom lip and captivates his gaze when his eyes land on hers. She closes the short distance between them; she tastes so sweet on his lips. He grips the comforter on either side of her hips to keep himself firmly planted. Even though her ribs are fine, she is still in pain and he can't do all the things he wants with her like this.

She pulls away, breathing heavily. The want for him and the pain mingle together.

"Stay with me tonight. Just so I know, you'll be okay." He pushes her hair behind her ear while he waits for an answer. She is one hundred percent fine with him taking care of her.

"Okay."

"Now for the lecture." He smiles and stands. "Why didn't you call one of us? How long have you been up here?"

"Not long. Can you bring my shirt?" She points at the wardrobe.

"Are you sure I don't need to take you to the hospital?" He helps her slide the shirt over her head, one arm at a time.

"Nope." She winces. "I just need a hot bath and wine. Kisses help too." She cocks her eyebrow up at him. Happy to oblige, he leans down and brushes his lips across hers.

"Better?"

"Much." She smiles. He slowly slides on her pants and helps her to her feet.

"You can't look at me like that in this condition. It's cruel." Connor pouts as Marni stares up at him with lust-filled eyes. She gently bites on her bottom lip. Connor lets out a huff and places his steely eyes straight ahead. "I will hurt you," he says to convince himself.

"You will have plenty of pent-up energy to take out on me later."

"How much later?" he pleads.

"Depends how much wine you have and how hot your tub gets." He doesn't have wine, but he knows his sister has a stash. He catches sight of the phone box and its contents scattered on the bed.

"I can handle that. Did you activate your phone?"

"Um yeah. I haven't listened to the thirty plus voice mails between Mom, Boston, and Parker, but it works. Why? Are you going to ask for my number?"

"Well, not now. You ruined it." A smile tugs at the corner of his lips.

"Give me your phone." He pulls his from his front pocket. Brimstone is his cover photo. She adds her number and sends herself a quick text so she will have his number, too.

"Seriously, if we don't get to the house, Mom is going to send a search party for you."

"Okay, okay, just one more." She pulls Connor down again and tastes him on her tongue. He growls and refrains from lifting her up and slamming her into the bed like he wants to. She breaks away and grabs his hand. "Okay, let's go."

***

"MRS. CURSTON, YOU DON'T have to do this," Marni fusses as Stacy fluffs more pillows than Marni knows what to do with. She places a dinner tray over her lap on the couch. Stacy insisted she couldn't sit on the hard kitchen chairs when she walked—more like hobbled—into the house. Her leg is really the main source of pain.

"I most certainly do. You're hurt. Why don't you stay here for the night? I hate the thought of you out there all alone and something happening in the middle of the night."

Marni glances toward the kitchen where Jack and Connor discuss cattle. Although everyone here is aware of her and Connor's recent attachments, she doesn't know if telling them she is planning to stay at his cabin is appropriate or not.

"That's really not necessary. I will be just fine."

"But I insist. It's the least I can do." Stacy plants her feet firmly, unwilling to take no for an answer. Marni takes a deep breath to tell her the truth when Tonya walks in, packing her plate of food, and sits on the couch next to Marni.

"What's up?" Tonya shifts her gaze between Marni and the stubborn look on her mom's face.

"Marni doesn't need to stay out there alone. I've offered to let her stay here."

"Well, I can stay out there with Marni. Then she won't be alone." Tonya forks a mouthful of potatoes in her mouth and Stacy's posture relaxes.

"Fair enough." Stacy walks back to the kitchen and Marni quickly tells Tonya the truth.

"I already know you're staying with Connor. I'll shack it up with Ginger tonight." Tonya smirks at Marni's confused expression. "Connor hasn't let you out of his sight since you've gotten back. You two have been attached at the hip. My brother may be slow in coming around to saying what he means, but when he does, he's in. One hundred percent."

Heat rushes to Marni's cheeks. Sure enough, when she glances in through the kitchen doorway, she catches Connor looking at her too.

"Now about Orion. He kicked your ass." Tonya pokes Marni with her fork and chuckles.

"I never could ride out a buck," Marni admits.

"How about we let the farmhands have a go? I know it's not the way you like to do things, but just let them ride out his buck and then you can take over." Marni will never tell her best friend she had the same thought sitting on the floor of the shower.

"Okay. But no spurs, no whips. Just let them ride out the way he moves and the moment he settles, they're done."

"They'll be super excited to show off for you." Tonya wiggles her eyebrows. "Also, I have to say this because he is my brother. If you leave again and break his heart, I will have to be mad at you. For a while. Third strike and you're out."

Marni looks at her, internally trying to math out how this would be the third time. The one instance is when she left for work, but what else is she referring to?

"I had to go back for work. Why does that count as two?"

"It doesn't. That was one."

"And the other time?"

"August 2012." Marni shuffles through her memories. That's the year she was supposed to go pro; instead, she went to college eight hours away and never came back.

"My mom. She forced me to leave. She wouldn't let me say my goodbyes."

"I'm not telling you to make you feel bad. You can't change the past. I'm just saying if you go down this road, please be very sure that this is what you want." Marni hasn't thought about anything long-term. Her life has been a whirlwind of changes. She's so caught up in chasing her desires that she hasn't pondered what she and Connor are.

"What does he want?"

"My brother's desires are not something I want to analyze. I have my thoughts, but you should talk to him. Before you two get in over your heads."

Too late, Marni thinks to herself. She wants to tell Tonya about how she has never felt this way about someone. The want and need to have him close. But by the way she just downed the desire conversation, a play-by-play is probably not something she wants to hear. Self-doubt creeps in now. What if this is just a fling for him and he grows bored with her?

"Okay, I'll talk to him."

Chapter Fourteen

CONNOR HELPS MARNI TO sit on the couch in his cabin. "I'll go run some hot water. Mom gave me a jar of white stuff she said to put in the water to help with the soreness." She snickers at his description of Epsom salt.

"I am capable of running my own bath."

He kisses her forehead. "I know, but I want to. Be right back." Connor disappears into the bathroom and Marni hears the squeak of the faucet turning. He comes back and scoops her up in his arms.

"Connor!" she squeals. "What are you doing?"

"Taking care of you." He smiles down at her as he cradles her against his chest. He puts her feet on the floor next to the tub. "I'm going to step out because if you undress, I don't know that I can keep myself from taking advantage of you." Heat rushes to her checks. "If you need me, just yell. I sat towels out for you and one of my shirts for when you're done."

"Thank you."

After slowly peeling her clothes off, Marni sinks down in the hot lavender-scented water and sighs as her muscles unwind. She flips through the numerous text messages and takes the time to listen to each voicemail. Parker's tell her she's made the worst mistake of her life and she'll regret this decision.

Boston's voicemails start out calm, offering to discuss this matter further with her, then leads into offering her better pay and substantial incentives. She has to listen to it a second time to confirm she heard correctly.

"Work remotely? Is he serious?" She assumes Jennifer, the owner, caught wind of her resignation and now it's Boston's ass on the line if he doesn't fix it.

Then Gwen's voicemails couldn't get an octave higher if she tried. Screaming at the disgrace her only daughter has become and how disappointed she is. She deletes them all except Boston's. She'd be stupid to not consider it. That was her career, her cushion to fall back on, and the reason she could buy this new phone out right without having to crunch any numbers.

The water cools and her toes and fingers look like shriveled raisins. Getting out of the deep tub proves harder than getting in. She tries to hoist herself up, but the strain on her side and putting weight on her knee takes her breath.

"This is embarrassing," she mutters. "Connor!" *I can't believe I'm stuck in his bathtub.* Footsteps rush through the cabin and he stops at the door, his face filled with worry.

"What's wrong? Are you okay?" He grabs a towel off the chair and comes over to the tub.

"I can't get out," Marni mumbles. He chuckles and bends over to help Marni from the tub. She secures her arms around his neck and his muscular arms wrap around her back. In one quick motion, she is out of the tub, pressed against Connor's clothed body.

He doesn't let go. She meets his gaze and there is hunger in his eyes. Hunger for her. Her stomach knots as his hand skims down her cheek and lands between her breasts.

"You're beautiful." He palms her left breast and chill bumps spread down her arms. She wants to kiss him, to have him do those fantastic things with his tongue.

Instead, he grabs the towel from the edge of the tub and wraps her body in it. "You hypnotize me." He smirks and gives Marni a quick peck before stepping back to give her space. She frowns at his retreat. "Don't look at me like that. You're hurt, and I could hurt you worse."

"Well, it would be worth it," she purrs. Connor shoves his hands in his pockets like it'll engage his turn-off button. By the bulge in his pants, Marni knows it's not working.

"Did you finally get your phone set up?" He nods toward her phone on the rug, clearly changing the subject.

"Yeah, I got through all the voicemails."

"Anything good?" Connor jokes.

"I'm the worst offspring in history, and Boston actually made me some pretty enticing offers."

Connor's stomach drops at the mention of Boston, but he ignores it. He can't control her and keep her here. She needs to make that decision for herself.

"Your mom is just pissed. She'll get over it."

"Probably not. You know how she is."

Oh, he does. He's witnessed the demeaning way she talked to Marni growing up. It was the textbook definition of verbal abuse.

Connor passes his t-shirt to Marni. Once she has it on, he leads her to the couch. He started a fire to knock the chill off the night while she was bathing.

"Well, screw her. She doesn't own you. She never has."

"Yeah."

"We are moving cattle tomorrow. Do you want me to take you to Mom and Dad's before we go?"

"Do you mind? I'll go stir-crazy here." He kisses her head, and she snuggles into the crook of his arm.

"I'd do anything for you." It's meant to be just a nicety comment, but there is a heavy weight of truth behind it. He really would do anything for her and she believes him.

"Connor..." She pauses. She needs to have this deep conversation with him and figure out what they mean to each other, but her throat tightens and cuts off her words.

"What is it?" He rubs his thumb up and down her arm while the fire crackles and dances.

"Thank you. For taking care of me." She blurts out instead. She can't do it tonight. Not when it could potentially ruin this secure feeling she has in his arms.

***

"CURSTON! THEY'RE SWINGING WIDE! Don't lose 'em!" Hocks shouts from the other side of the herd.

"Get up! Hey, hey!" Connor waves his arm and yells at the wandering cattle. Connor pushes Brimstone to cut them off and guides them back to the herd. They're riding over the last ridge now. They left immediately after breakfast this morning and now it's near dinner time. A few of the younger hands packed food. You'd think they would starve going a few hours without a meal.

Even though he rides daily, his ass is going numb and his knees are really acting up. The army did a number on his body, and on long days like this, he's reminded. His stomach growls and his canteen has been emptied for the last couple of hours. Brimstone is growing tired too. Luckily, once they get the cattle settled in the new pasture, it's only an hour ride back to the ranch.

"Long day, Boss." Hocks trots up alongside Connor.

"Either I'm getting older or this job is taking longer," he jokes.

"I think it's both." Hocks cracks a grin. The dirt of the day is caked to his skin.

"C'mon, let's get these poor kids home." The herd gets filtered through a fence gap and Hocks rides back to tell the other hands they're done for the day. They take off at a race back to the barn, and Hocks shakes his head.

"Remember those days?" Hocks asks.

"No, I didn't ride at their age. I was hauling thirty pounds of gear across a desert trying to determine if the kid approaching me wanted sweeties or to kill me."

Hocks winces at the nonchalant tone Connor uses to describe someone's worst nightmare.

"Sorry, I forget."

"Don't worry about it. You have to talk to someone. Keeping it bottled up and washing it down at night will catch up to you."

"It almost did." He remembers Marni catching him with Christy.

"Speaking of, how is Marni? I'm shocked she isn't here today."

"She and Orion had a misunderstanding."

"Oh, shit. Is she okay?"

"She's sore. She's been with Mom all day."

"What's going on between you two?" Hocks jokingly punches Connor in the shoulder.

"I don't know, man. She mentioned her boss gave her an enticing offer, so she might decide to leave again." They don't talk about their feelings much aside from ranching. Hocks doesn't miss the anguish in his tone.

"Have you asked her to stay? To really stay?" Connor remains looking forward as he responds.

"People have been telling her what to do her entire life. She submits to whatever others expect or want from her. I don't want to put her in a situation to do something just because I ask."

"But if you don't, how will she know how you feel?" Hocks uses a psychiatrist monotone and Connor cocks an eyebrow in his direction.

"I guess she'll have to ask." Connor picks up to a canter to put an end to this conversation. He pulls his phone from his pocket. No messages or calls appear on the screen. He hates the disappointment that hits him just because she hasn't reached out to him today. Could she be planning when to go back to the city in her idle time?

He can't contain the sigh of relief when he sees Marni's red Focus is still parked in the driveway. He hands Brimstone to Lucas, and Orion whinnies at their arrival.

"Marni hasn't been out to see him today. Is she okay?" Lucas asks.

"Why does everyone suddenly think I know all about her?" Connor snaps unintentionally, but his emotions about her are all across the board and the weight of Hocks' question has continued to weigh on him during the ride back.

"Sorry," Lucas mumbles and leads Brimstone to the crossties. Connor is starving and thirsty, but the layer of dirt caked to his skin takes priority. He checks the time; he has an hour before dinner will be ready. Plenty of time to freshen up.

He walks stiffly to his truck and, with a labored grunt, he climbs in. Part of him thinks food can wait and he can just pass out after his shower, but Marni will be at dinner. He wants to give her a reason to stay without asking.

His clothes drop in a cloud of dust on the bathroom floor. After washing away the day, he sits on the edge of the bed. It's really tempting to just lay back and sleep. The later it gets, the more his muscles and bones ache. He takes the bottle of pain pills from his top drawer the VA prescribed him as needed. He hates taking them, hates the way they make him feel, but on long days like today, he wouldn't be able to move without them.

Climbing the stairs to his parents' porch, he hears the women gossiping and giggling from the kitchen. Marni's laugh is distinguishable from his sister's dying-cat squawk. He pushes the door open and hangs his hat. Stacy fusses over some kind of casserole, she pulls out of the oven and Tonya sets the table. For a split second, he is confused when he doesn't see Marni.

"Long day?" He whips his head to the office desk in the bay window. Marni wears glasses framing her big brown eyes surrounded by papers that are covered in numbers that are more red than black.

Unexpected embarrassment overcomes him when he realizes she is looking at the ranch's financial records. He knows things aren't great right now. The price of beef is down, several years of drought in a row made them have to buy hay at ridiculous costs, and the price of feed and everything they need just seem to keep going up.

"Not really." He plops down at the table and Jack sits next to him. He stares at his plate, his eyes heavy, body sore, and now Marni knows the ranch isn't somewhere she would want to make her home.

"How'd it go?" Jack inquires.

"Hmm?" Connor is lost in his own thoughts and misses his dad's question.

"Moving the herd? Everything go smoothly?"

"Oh, yeah. All of them are accounted for."

"Good. A friend called today. They have some last-year roll bales they'll sell at a cheaper price. They need to make room for this year's crop. I told him I'd talk to you, then call them back tomorrow."

Connor crunches the numbers in his head. They didn't make what they expected from the sale, but he knows the prices will just get higher for hay the closer winter gets. This is the part of ranching he hates. The endless decisions he has to make to keep this afloat.

Connor glances at the array of papers Marni is shuffling through. "I'll look at the statements tonight before heading home and let you know." A headache is already forming. He anticipates he will be here all hours of the night, deciding what to slide where, so he can afford the hay.

"If I may, I have a proposition. I wanted to wait until I talked to my boss—well, ex-boss—but I've decided I want to do this regardless of what he tells me." Marni hobbles over to the dinner table. The soreness of yesterday's events have set it. From experience, she knows tomorrow will be the worst of it.

"What is it, sweetie?" Stacy's eyes sparkle with curiosity. All attention turns to Marni as she takes her seat. After looking over their finances, it's clear the horses will be too much for the ranch to support. She has to do something to save them and the ranch as a whole.

"Boston left me a voicemail trying to convince me to come back." She pauses and all of Connor's fears rise to the surface. He clenches his fist to keep from standing and leaving the kitchen. Stacy's face falls and so does Tonya's.

"Mar, you can't," Tonya speaks first.

"Let me finish." Marni raises her hand to stop Tonya. "He offered me a remote position where I can attend meetings via Zoom, and only in person if I choose." Marni's eyes meet each person at the table, but Connor is looking at his plate. "I would like to continue my work here with the wildies. Train them into cattle working horses and help bring in some income to pay for them. I plan on going back to the city—"

"No!" Tonya cuts her off. Marni shoots her a look.

"I'm going back to the city to discuss the terms of the remote job with Boston in person. I'll find a place in town and come work the horses when I'm not doing things for the firm. I also want to offer you this." Marni pulls a check from her back pocket. She wrote it this morning to help with expenses. It's the least she could do since they wouldn't let her pay to stay. With Connor in charge of the finances and having the final say, she slides the check across the table to him. "It's to help with the cost of the horses."

Connor eyes the check and shakes his head. "Absolutely not. This isn't your burden and your money is no good here." Marni's eyes harden.

"You can pay me back as we sell the horses if that helps your pride."

Stacy interjects when Connor's face flushes. "Marni, I think what Connor meant is we don't expect you to pay anything for staying here. And the horses aren't your responsibility."

"I know. I'm saying I want them to be." The corners of Tonya's mouth pick up. Stacy holds a hand to her chest and lets out a deep sigh.

"Really?!" Tonya squeals.

"If it is okay with *all* of you." She looks around the table once more. Connor's eyes are still glued to the check. The businessman in him says take the money and run—they really do need it. But all he can think about is what would happen if he and Marni don't work out.

"Well, of course it's okay! This is going to be awesome!" Tonya answers for everyone, but Stacy eyes her son. She can see the inner struggle he has with this decision. If he and Marni hadn't sparked, it would be a no-brainer. Now he is thinking with his heart and the what-ifs are taking over.

"Why don't we all eat and discuss this further later? Connor has had a long day and Marni has been reading numbers for hours now." Stacy tries to soothe over the chatter but Tonya shoots a glare at her brother.

"Are you seriously making this about the two of you?"

"I didn't say anything," Connor defends himself, but he looks at Marni instead. This is what she was worried about and the main reason she mentioned finding a place in town.

"It's fine, T. We can talk about it later." Marni rescues Connor from the speech Tonya was already working on. He doesn't touch the check, like it's laced with so many promises just waiting to be broken. Nobody speaks the rest of dinner, minus Stacy trying to ask questions to spark conversation.

Tonya and Stacy clean up while Jack retreats to the living room in his recliner. Marni struggles to stand from her seat.

Connor reaches for her plate. "Here, I'll get it." He takes her plate and hands it off to his mom. He pauses for a moment, watching her lean against the table as she walks, then stuffs down his worries about what his mom and sister will think. He wraps an arm around her waist so she can lean into him. She feels so fragile. No matter how exhausted he is, they have to talk about her offer and what it all means.

"Can we talk?" he whispers so his mom can't hear. Chills run down Marni's spine as she nods. Her mouth goes dry—is this the moment he admits he doesn't want a relationship? He sits beside her on the porch swing, careful not to jostle her too much.

"What happens if I accept your offer, then whatever going on here...stops?" Silence stretches between them.

"What *is* going on here?" Marni lifts her hand to his and intertwines their fingers. Connor leans his cheek onto her head. She feels like home; she belongs here, with him.

"I told myself I wouldn't say this. It's not fair to you." He lets out a long breath. Marni doesn't move, afraid she will break whatever courage he's worked up. "I want you to stay. I want you to come back to my cabin with me and wake up next to you every morning. I want to take care of you when you're injured and make love to you whenever we want. But how can I ask that of you when you are just starting to find yourself?"

His admission leaves her speechless. Having Tonya tell her how he feels is one thing, but hearing it from him has a fire burning in the pit of her stomach.

Connor has never felt so vulnerable. He just completely opened himself up to her and now all he can do is wait. She isn't used to guys not forcing or demanding her to do what they want. Or, like in Parker's case, manipulating her to think it was her choice all along.

"I don't know what to say. I know what you want me to say, but I can't make any promises right now. I do know I want to keep working with the horses and move here—to this town, not literally here. I want to give us a chance," she answers as honestly as she can. He grows tense at her long-winded answer. He hoped for a quick yes.

"Okay. I'll accept your check as an investment, and I will pay you back."

"If that's what it takes for you to accept it." The playful smile in her voice fizzles away as she lets out a ragged breath.

"You're in pain."

"A little," she lies. In truth, it's a hell of a lot of pain, but she loves being nestled into the crook of his arm and having his head lie atop of hers.

"Marni." He shuffles aside to give her more space. She sighs in relief as her ribs and lungs have more room to stretch. She lays her head down on his lap while he pets her hair. The sound of their heartbeats mix with the night owls hooting and the wind whistling through the trees. Marni revels in Connor's safe and warm touch, his arm protectively draped around her.

Chapter Fifteen

TONYA SNEAKS OUT THE back so she doesn't interrupt Marni spilling her guts to Connor or vice versa. As much as she loves her brother found someone she approves of and is no longer riding the blonde slut into oblivion, she still doesn't want to see him or her best friend getting all cozy under the stars. Her plan is working, though. Maybe not as smoothly as she had originally hoped, but she is giving her best friend something to fight for and find joy in.

The mustangs are saving her whether or not she sees it yet. She pops open a bottle of wine and drinks straight from it. Scrolling through her phone, she looks for potential booty calls to scratch her itch, but no matter how hard she tries, none of them seems interesting.

With a resolving sigh and two gulps of wine, she fills her claw-foot bathtub with hot steaming water and adds her relaxing bath salt concoction she bought from the local curiosities store. She's careful to keep all her purchases from there out of sight. Her mom—more closed-minded about witchcraft and all things taboo—wouldn't approve, even though it's just Epsom salt mixed with Himalayan salt, lava salt, some essential oils, dried lavender, and rose petals. She'd really lose her shit if she displayed all the pretty crystals and sage kits.

Her phone rings as she sinks down into the tub. Chester, a hope-filled high school fling, is attempting a video chat. Thanks to the red wine now coursing through her body, Tonya answers like it's a great idea.

"Holy shit! T! You're naked!" She angles the phone so only her collarbone and above are visible.

"I don't bathe in my clothes, Chester." She smirks and pulls her wine to her lips.

"Ah, you're drinking." He doesn't like that Tonya drinks nearly every night to combat her anxiety.

"Yeah, and?" she snaps.

"Nothing. I was just calling to see how you were doing."

"I'm fine, just like every other night you call." Tonya's tone bites at Chester's ears. He talks to someone away from the phone. "Where are you?"

"Ryan's. Do you want me to come out?" he asks. Tonya eyes her toes poking through the water. Her muscles finally relax and the combination of wine and salts has done their job.

"And leave my hot bath and wine? Definitely not." The video on the screen wobbles around the room. A door opens on his end, then the background noise quiets.

"Maybe I can take you out this weekend? Dinner?" She swirls the wine around in her mouth before swallowing. She doesn't have anything more than friend feelings for Chester, but he's made it clear he wants to be so much more than friends.

"Maybe. Have fun at Ryan's." Tonya ends the call and tosses her phone on the rug near her bed. It rings for the fourth time and she slides down into the water, drowning out the noise.

***

Stacy checks on Marni and Connor after giving them their space. Marni lays horizontal on the swing, her head nuzzled into Connor's lap, while his head is tilted back. Both of them are peacefully sleeping. She pulls a blanket from the linen closet and carefully drapes it across Marni. She unloaded a semi-truck on Connor at dinner and Stacy's sure they were up for hours discussing the terms and negotiating parameters.

Inside, Stacy finds Jack nodding off in his recliner with the news channel flickering.

"They fell asleep in the swing. She'll probably regret missing her pain meds and he'll wake up not able to move from his beaten body." Stacy lets out a huff in aggravation. The pain of a mother is watching your children endure so much and not being able to do a damn thing about it.

"Quit fussing. They're adults, not babies. They'll be just fine."

"Aren't we going to talk about her proposal?"

"They're getting hitched?!" Jack's sleepy eyes now widen. "What the hell did I miss?"

"No, you loon, the business proposal. About Marni and the horses."

"Oh, what's there to discuss?" Jack waves a dismissive hand.

"She wants to live in town. With the cutthroat gossip queens and hoity-toity, high-horse-riding, conniving witches that consider themselves the homeowners' association of the entire town." Stacy stomps through the hall to their bedroom. Jack follows, wearing a crooked grin at his wife's tantrum.

"Now dear, you're just angry that your jam didn't win the county fair last year."

"No, I'm angry that they failed to personally invite me to enter again this year, and I had to hear about it from Susan when Claudia and her cult followers handed out flyers in her shop." Her face turns red from not taking a breath while she yanks the decorative pillows from her bed and jerks the comforter back to the chest at the end.

"They just don't want your competition. We both know you have the best jam. It's all politics." Jack places a hand on her back and rubs softly.

"She's our daughter too, Jack. Regardless of what happens between her and our son. She can't live in town; she belongs here. She always has." Jack presses his lips together. His mind races, searching for a solution that will satisfy his wife and be the best for Marni.

"Come here." He pulls Stacy in and she rests her head against his chest. "We'll talk to Marni. She probably only mentioned town because she is worried about Connor." They stand there in silence while Stacy's heart rate simmers.

"You really think I have the best jam?" A chuckle comes from Jack's chest and it's music to her ears.

"Of course, dear. The others don't even compare."

***

Marni's eyes flutter open and confusion hits as she sees the sun coming up and feels a chill in her bones. A shiver follows, and she pulls the thin blanket around her chin. Connor is still sleeping, his face free of worry lines. He appears ten years younger.

She slides her hand from her head and rubs it across the zipper of his jeans. He stirs under her touch and a smile tugs at her lips at his response.

Why did I have to try and ride Orion? The two of them could be in her loft right now, and this way of waking him up could actually lead somewhere heavenly. Footsteps sound through the house and she pulls her hand back under her head. The screen door squeaks open, and Jack's eyes lock with Marni's.

Are you okay, he mouths to keep from waking Connor.

Marni gives him a smile, and he closes the door quietly behind him. Stacy will be up fixing breakfast soon, but she'll let Connor sleep as long as she can.

She replays last night. Her offer had even surprised herself. She hadn't planned to just spring it on all of them, but when Jack mentioned the hay and Connor's face was etched with stress, she couldn't wait. She'll need to ride into town the next couple of days and look for a place to rent. Susan at the coffee shop will probably be the best source to look.

Connor's morning wood pushes against her head since she got it all worked up. She enjoys the feeling, how he responds to her. This is something she had never experienced before. To actually have a guy want her to be a part of the sex and not just be used and tossed aside like her ex. She didn't know there was another way except what she read in romance novels and watched in movies. Vance was the only guy she had ever been with until Connor. The difference is day and night, and the orgasms...she thought she knew what those were, but she had been way wrong.

She is too shy to talk to Connor about this stuff. She certainly never discussed it in her previous relationship. Vance didn't like the idea of her having any kind of power and she'd pay the price. Marni hates herself for being the weakling she was during all of that. She always scoffed at movies when girls were the victims and didn't have the lady-balls to whack them in their sleep. Now she knows by the time they realize what is happening, the fear of retaliation is crippling and you can't see a way out.

"Good morning." Connor's husky voice startles Marni from her thoughts and she jumps, then is quickly reminded of her injuries.

"Shit," she chokes out as she lowers herself back down, catching her breath before she tries to move again.

"Sorry, I thought you were awake. Could've sworn I felt you rubbing...um, never mind."

"No—I was. I mean, yeah, I did—then your dad came out here. Sorry, I was stuck in my head." Her voice is tight, guarded. Connor angles her face.

"Hey, are you okay?" She wants to tell him. To unload all of this weight off her shoulders, the demons that constantly ride on her back.

"Yeah, just sore. You?" His eyes flick between hers. Clearly, he doesn't believe her, but he won't push her.

"Same. Can you sit up?" Marni clenches her teeth and contorts her face as Connor helps her up. He sucks in a quick breath of his own as he moves his legs and back.

"Are we old now? Like, is this it?" Marni scoffs, and Connor lets out a tight laugh.

"I hate to say it, but I don't think I could have had any pleasure with you this morning, even if you weren't hurt." Connor stands, his back and knees cracking in protest.

"I was thinking about the same thing this morning, she admits." His eyes are filled with want as he looks at her. Her hardened nipples tease him through her thin t-shirt and he has to adjust himself to another position in his pants.

Crunching gravel has both of their heads turning to the driveway.

Who would be here at this time of morning? It's barely six thirty.

Connor straightens his shoulders and pushes himself off the support beam. A red two-door BMW Coupe appears, clearly not the vehicle of someone snooping around.

"Impossible." Marni's hair stands on her arms and the blood drains from her face.

"Dad! Bring the gun!" His voice sounds like she is deep underwater and she is going to drown right there. In the back of her mind, she knows this is possible. There is really only one place she'd ever go if she left the city, and that is here.

Jack slams the screen door and hands the rifle to Connor. He tries to take Marni's arm and guide her inside, but she is frozen in place. Numb to the pain in her ribs, numb to Jack's touch and the cool air whipping her tangled hair across her face. Frozen and numb.

"Marni, go inside. I'll handle him." Connor's voice echoes around her.

It's not a him, it's her. She tries to speak but her vocal cords constrict and she reverts to the submissive girl she had worked so hard to put behind her. Connor wiggles himself free of Marni's grip and takes large strides down the stairs where the car stops. He cocks the rifle, and the sound sends a shudder through Marni. Jack stands next to her now, holding her steady. Without him, her legs would give out completely.

Tonya's truck slings gravel as she skids to a stop behind the car. A dust cloud follows close behind her and she carries a shotgun, her eyes out for blood. Stacy must have called her.

Do they really think coming out with guns blazing will do anything to deter the monster behind that black tint?

The door opens and Marni stares, watching the shit about to obliterate the fan all together. Connor stops short when red high heels and dress slacks step out of the car. Followed by long, straight brown hair and a blazer to match her pants.

"Feral as ever I see, Connor Curston. And Tonya, you look"—Gwen eyes her jeans and button-up shirt—"Well." Tonya's face scrunches with all the vile things she wants to spit at this bitch, but her mother raised her better so she almost bites her tongue in two instead.

Stacy rushes out of her kitchen to try and salvage the shit show she spied from the kitchen.

"Gwen! How lovely it is for you to pop by and visit! It's been so long." Stacy should definitely win an Oscar with her acting skills, Marni thinks. She is the only one even attempting to be nice at this point.

"Don't bother, Stacy. You've filled my daughter with lies and turned her against me. I've come to take her back to the city, to her career, before she ruins her entire life and ends up—" She pauses again. She used to do this when Marni was younger, as if daring her to insert what she thought her mother was going to say. "Well, ends up like Tonya."

Stacy's smile cracks slightly, but her voice is still sweet as honey.

"Now Gwen, Marni is welcome here as long as she likes. We wouldn't turn her away, you know that. Why don't you come inside and share a meal with us? Breakfast just got done and we can set an additional plate."

Gwen's eyes find Marni, who drops her head and wraps her arms around herself. Connor watches the exchange between them. What kind of mom makes their own daughter feel inadequate? How long does the verbal abuse take before one look can shut you down? His heart hurts for her. He wants to fight to protect her, but he can't actually use his fists against Gwen. He stands by helplessly.

"Marni, pack your things. We're leaving. Get in the car and your father can drive yours back for you." On cue, the passenger door opens and her dad steps out. His hair is more gray than brown now. Deep lines are etched into his features from years of unhappiness. Tonya steps toward Gwen, but a curt shake of Stacy's head has her closing her mouth and stopping her advance. "Marni, acknowledge that you heard me."

Marni looks at her bare feet. There is a rage building inside of her the others can't see. She's run this altercation through her mind over and over until she had it memorized. There are so many things she planned to say, but at this moment, words are pointless. Behind her mother's too-big sunglasses is a brown steely stare. Anything Marni says will be used against her and twisted to benefit Gwen. Her mom is a lawyer for a reason. An annoyingly good lawyer.

"No." Her voice comes out shaky. Not at all with the confidence she had hoped. Jack releases his hold on her, leaving her to stand on her own. She looks down at her mom from the porch.

"I said, *we're leaving.* Now." Gwen's tone is definitive, no room for refusal. Years of her mother using that exact tone flash through her mind. But one scene stands out above all the others. The day she ripped her from this place, her real family, the supporters of her dreams.

She isn't the reliant eighteen-year-old anymore. She has her own money, her own career, and now she has a business investment. She does not want or need her mother's approval.

"No, *you're* leaving." A hush falls over the ranch. Even the morning birds fall silent as Marni's words reach her mother. Marni fights back the tears. She will not give her crap excuse of a mom the satisfaction of seeing her cry.

"What did you say?" Gwen tilts her head like a predator.

"I'm staying here. I'm moving here. I hope one day you can accept that, maybe even support it. But don't worry, I won't be holding my breath or getting my hopes up." Her voice raises with vindication. Even though her breath is shallow and her flight instincts are screaming and ready to bolt, her voice is calm, strong, and the tears stay at bay.

Gwen's face falls and Connor, feeling the need to have Marni's back, crosses the war field that's been created between the porch and the red BMW. His boots crunch on the gravel and, just like with Parker, he moves to stand behind her. A lion to his lioness, protective and there if she needs him.

"So that's it. You throw it all away for some good dick?" Her words are a slap, but not more than the actual slap Stacy delivers across Gwen's cheek. She's had enough of Gwen talking to Marni like trash. Gwen's sunglasses fly off and one lens pops out when they hit the ground.

Tonya moves over to stand beside her mother now, daring Gwen to retaliate. Shock fills her eyes. She actually has the audacity to show a hint of sorrow when she looks back at Marni now.

Stacy straightens, shocked. Her hand tingles and stings from the contact, but she holds it still at her side.

"I think it's time you leave, Gwen," Tonya spits.

"Marni?" she whispers one last plea. It pulls at Marni's heart because at the end of the day, she is her mother. She birthed her, and is the reason she exists at all. Fed her, clothed her, paid for her education all without batting an eye. She raised her, but she also is the reason she sought love from a man who treated her just like her mom. That is what she thought she deserved. That is what she thought love was. Connor's hand clasps hers, not hard, softly, just enough to remind her she is not alone.

Gwen has a vulnerability in her eyes she's never witnessed before.

"Tonya's right, it's time for you to leave." Stacy is no longer playing the sweet hostess. Gwen straightens herself. With her shoulders back, her eyes lose all emotion.

"You're cut off. From any trust, any inheritance, any contact with me or your father. You are dead to us. You will not hear from either of us ever again. Don't come crawling to me when he breaks your heart and this fantasy in your head comes crumbling down." She turns on her heel and slams the door. The car spins in a half donut before lurching down the driveway. Hocks lies on the horn as she runs him off the driveway. The cherry on top of her exit.

Chapter Sixteen

Black spots plague Marni's vision. She can't breathe and her body shakes. Arms sweep her up and Connor lays her on the couch of the sitting room.

"Holy shit! Go, Mom! You bitch-slapped the fuck out of her!" Tonya shouts.

"Watch your mouth or I'll do the same to you," Stacy nags. Connor's blue eyes search Marni's.

Did I really just cut any ties I have with my parents? I should freak out. Maybe the fact I'm having a full-blown inner monologue with myself and not actually speaking shows just how badly I'm freaking out.

"My purse, my phone," Marni croaks. Someone, not Connor since he hasn't moved, obliges her request when her purse and phone come into view. With a shaky hand, she pulls up her online bank accounts. If her mom is in fact cutting her off, she is moving every bit of her funds from any account that has her mother's name tied to it.

For emergencies, in case something happens to you, dear. That is what she said when Marni opened her first and then second bank accounts. She pulls her check book out next and writes a new check with a significantly higher amount and hands it to Connor.

"Rip up the other one. Deposit this into the account the farm expenses come from. Don't argue." He rubs the back of his neck and gives her an uneasy look. She would be damned if her mom won this. Little do her parents know, she never touched the monthly amounts they deposited to her. Well, she is about to totally deplete the accounts all together now.

"Marni, this is a lot."

"I know, which is why I need you to go, like now, before my mom can call and screw it all up somehow." He kisses her forehead and grabs his jacket and hat. When she hears his truck roar to life, her chest feels lighter. An absurd number of giggles bubble deep inside of her and a hysterical fit racks through her. She wraps her arms tightly around herself to keep her sore abdomen together.

"Um, Mom?! I think Marni's lost it!" Tonya shouts for Stacy before coming to where Marni lays half sitting up on the couch. "Mar?"

Tears stream down her face from laughter.

She is free, actually free. Stacy's slap was the buttercream icing to the layered cake of her tormented life.

"I'm fine," she sputters between breaths. Her laughs sound more like a broken squeak toy with no sound. "Your mom—slapped—the shit out..." A new wave rolls through and this time Tonya's laughter is right with hers.

Stacy comes in with two glasses of water and eyes the two of them cautiously.

"I think you've both lost it." She rubs her still stinging hand on her apron and a laugh creeps up her throat as well. Jack stands in the doorway, watching the three of them cackle like wild hyenas, and he can't contain a smile. He never said much on the matter; he tried to talk to Gerald once about how Gwen treated him and Marni. The guy had the nerve to look him in the eyes and gave him a curt, "Mind your own," before leaving the workshop. He never came back.

Boots stomp up the porch steps and Hocks swings the screen door open, also carrying a gun in case he needs it. He stops once he spots Tonya, who is laying on the carpeted floor, holding her stomach and laughing with such force no sound escapes her mouth. Marni is in a similar fashion, and Stacy's slumped against the recliner, wiping tears from her eyes.

"Is it gas? Do you have a gas leak or something? Connor didn't even stop to say, hey? Is he chasing after the bastard in the red car? Does he need backup?" Jack slaps a hand on Hocks' shoulder and chuckles himself.

"Nah, son, we're celebrating liberation and emancipation." Hocks wears a smile, thinking they're all crazy, and leans his gun against the door frame before helping himself to the breakfast Stacy fixed.

***

"So WHERE ARE WE going today?" Marni can move more freely today, but she still isn't in any shape to ride Orion again. She hands Connor the hose to fill up the horses' water in the barn.

"You don't know what today is?" Marni checks her mental calendar and can't find anything important about today.

"It's the county rodeo. Tonight," He lifts several flakes of hay to put in the stall. "We're going to the fair to vote on Mom's jam, eat greasy food, and watch Lucas, Wes, and the others try to be cowboys."

"Really? You're into that kind of thing? I just thought with the crowds—" Marni lets her thought drop. She doesn't want to insult him, she just wants him to know she understands.

"It's a family event. And you're family." He winks from under his hat brim.

"I don't have anything to wear." Marni gestures at her worn blue jeans and discolored shirt.

"I think you look fantastic. What's the problem?"

"This will be the first time you and I...you know." Her cheeks heat.

"No, I don't know." He leans on the stall gate and crosses his arms.

"We're a couple, right?"

"Was I not clear when I fucked you—multiple times?" As if her cheeks could flush any hotter.

"Right. Anyway." She blows out a flustered breath. "This is the first time we will be out in public as a couple, and I want to make a good impression."

Connor stifles a laugh and places his hands on her hips to pull her close. "You are beautiful without trying to prove it to the town. But if you want to dress nicer, I'm sure Tonya has something you can borrow. Or you have time to run to town before we leave." Marni chews on her lip and lets Connor's Persian blue eyes land on her bottom lip, tucked between her teeth.

"If you keep doing that, you won't get out of this barn before I take you back upstairs." Connor nips Marni's exposed collarbone, and she leans into his touch.

"I wouldn't be mad about it."

"But then you won't have time to find an outfit." Marni rolls her eyes at his voice of reason.

"Fine. But tonight. When we get back..." She gives him a fleeting kiss on the lips before going to her car.

"She's something," Lucas whispers with his lips pursed into a silent whistle.

"Get out of here," Connor half scolds, half jokes and continues filling up the water buckets and feeding hay. He doesn't wait for Marni to come back. One thing he has learned from his sister, you can't rush a woman to get ready. He has a few hours to kill and decides to take Brimstone out for a leisure ride. He's halfway up the ridge when hoof beats catch up to him.

"Where are you going?" Hocks asks as he falls into step beside Connor.

"I thought Brimstone and I would have a relaxing ride. That's ruined." Connor smirks. Hocks places a hand over his chest.

"I'm wounded."

"Well, since you're here and I pay you, we might as well work. Let's ride to the back pasture and check the fences. There were some strong winds last night. It can't hurt."

Meanwhile, Marni huffs and shrugs out of yet another blouse that doesn't scream, *he's mine. Do not touch!* This is a small town, and without a doubt, Christy will be there somewhere. Even though Marni isn't particularly worried about her trying anything, she still wants to dress and look worthy of Connor.

"My brother does not care what you wear. He'd rather have you naked in bed." Tonya makes a gagging sound from the walk-in closet. "Nope. Still weird. Can't do it." Marni laughs at her best friend.

"It's not Connor. This is like my debut of being back. It's not often this town gets a new-comer, and even less often that one of their own moves back and snatches up the town's golden child."

"Ouch," Tonya scoffs.

"You know what I mean. He went to war. When we walk through town, everyone basically bows to their small-town hero."

"You get used to it. I don't even notice."

"Well, tonight, they're going to be noticing me and I don't want to look bad when they do." Marni slips on a white lacy blouse and a pair of dark wash jeans. The blouse is loose around the waist and tight around her breasts.

"What do you think about this one?" Marni asks. Tonya steps out of the closet and eyes her up and down.

"Turn," she orders and Marni obeys.

"I think you need different jeans. More of a faded look and flared. Definitely flared. Hold on." Tonya disappears into the sea of clothes now covering the floor of her bedroom and half her bathroom.

"Where did I—Oh! Here they are!"

Without warning, a pair of jeans hits Marni in the face and chest. She changes into them and hikes her leg to get a better view of her ass.

"These. Yes, these are the jeans." Marni praises Tonya's eye. "Now, what about you?"

"Already ahead of you." Tonya steps out in a sage green low-cut crop top and flared jeans of her own.

"Wow. You look amazing!"

"Let's hope my future husband thinks so, too." Marni's eyebrows shoot up.

"Who?"

"I don't know. I have to meet him first." Tonya fusses over Marni's make-up and hair. Marni tries to help where she can, but she is almost useless when it comes to cosmetics. A knock sounds at the door sometime later.

The women check the clock and they suck in a breath. Marni and Tonya finger comb their curly hair and snap necklaces and earrings into place. One last check of lips, and they open the door on Connor's third knock.

"Were you guys co—" His voice breaks off when he takes in the sight of Marni. She drops her gaze and fidgets with her fingers at the attention. Connor places his hand under her chin and lifts her head.

"Don't do that. Don't make yourself small. You deserve to be seen." Marni's caramel eyes pour over him. She rolls her shoulders back and stands straighter. Connor smiles and holds his hand out to her.

"Gag," Tonya jokes and walks between them to the truck. Since Connor drives a bench seat with jump seats in the back, Marni slides to the middle and Tonya sits on the passenger side.

"So little sister. Who are you trying to impress tonight?" Connor asks.

"I don't know yet. Why, anyone in mind?"

"I wouldn't wish your attitude on anyone."

Marni covers her laugh with a cough, but not before Tonya shoots her a glare.

"Anything I should know about the county fair?" Marni asks.

"Nothing's changed from when we competed. Even the announcer is the same, although he sounds like he smokes five packs a day now." While Tonya fills Marni in, Connor slides his hand across her thigh and gives her a gentle squeeze. His eyes fall to at the low cut of her blouse, and she takes the opportunity to turn more toward him. He grips her thigh harder and the tires of his old pickup flirt with the rumble strips on the edge of the highway.

"If you can't control yourself, I'm going to have to drive," Tonya muses. Marni sits back straight in her seat, sporting a victorious grin. Connor moves his hand to the steering wheel and props the other on the driver's door.

"It's crazy to me. Last time I was here, we were competing for our pro rodeo scholarships." Marni's smile fades at the memory of getting her acceptance letter and her mom refusing to let her go.

"We had our fastest time ever that night," Tonya added.

Connor stiffens. That was the night he knew. When he saw Marni swinging around with Dillon and the others in their grade as they threw their hats and celebrated, he felt it. He loved her then. He bought her the hat the following week.

"So, what should I expect? Last time, we had Kate and Presley to contend with."

Tonya laughs into her hand. "Oh, my gosh! I forgot about those two. Connor, do you remember when Presley cornered you in the trailer and took her shirt off?" Tonya's laugh turns hysterical.

"Did she now?" Marni raises her eyebrows in question toward Connor. He shifts uneasily in his seat and his cheeks turn red.

"Oh yes, she did! What was it you told her, Connor? *You're not my type*, which you can imagine a girl like Presley never heard a day in her life."

"And what is your type?" Marni's comment adds to his reddening cheeks.

"I'm about to make you both walk the rest of the way," he mutters and turns down a long gravel road toward the fair.

"Fine, but Marni could just call Dillon and get a ride."

Too far. Tonya took the joke too far with that. Connor's knuckles turn white on the wheel and Marni places a hand on his leg.

"No, I wouldn't," she reassures him. Tonya doesn't get the hint and snorts.

"Dressed like that, any man would be stupid to not pick you up." Tonya is looking out the windshield and doesn't see the uncertainty flash across Connor's face. His mind travels back all those years when Stacy came upstairs with the phone still in her hand. He had just wrapped the hat box and was checking how he looked in the mirror. Since Tonya had been accepted, he knew Marni would be, too.

He catches the look in Stacy's eye and turns to face her. "What is it?"

"You look very handsome," she purrs. Connor blushes but waves off his mom's words. The door slams open downstairs and something crashes to the floor. Stacy leaps to her feet. Tonya screams again, followed by another crash. The sound's coming from her room.

"Tonya!" Stacy runs now. Connor stops at her doorway as Tonya picks up another roping belt buckle and slams it onto the floor as hard as she can and screams like a banshee. Tears stream down her face and she falls into their mother, sobbing.

"She—ripped—"

"Ssshhh, honey. I can't understand you." Stacy tries to calm her. Connor bends down and picks up one of the discarded belt buckles she and Marni won together.

"Gwen—she ripped the letter. To-told Marni sh-she can't—go." Between her sobs, Connor realizes what has his sister so distraught. Marni's evil mother finally put an end to her rodeo career. She waited until it really mattered to Marni before doing it.

Connor sets the belt buckle on the shelf and walks back upstairs. One look at the hat box twists his gut, and he shoves it under his bed.

"Hey, where did you go?" Marni rests a hand on his forearm as they approach the fairgrounds.

"Nowhere," Connor assures her and lifts her hand to his lips.

Marni leans in closer to whisper, "She was just teasing. I wouldn't—"

Connor doesn't let her finish. "I know."

Chapter Seventeen

It's still early before the rodeo crowd rushes in, so it's easy to find Stacy and Jack at the vendor booths indoors. Stacy stages her jam with a bed of lavender sprigs and wildflowers they picked that morning.

"Oh, you made it! Tell me, what do you think?" Stacy studies the photogenic display.

"It's beautiful. Truly," Marni says.

"Looks great," Tonya adds.

"You really think so?" Stacy questions with her forefinger drumming against her lip. Jack wipes the sweat from his forehead and blows out a breath.

"Stacy, if ya keep changin' it, we'll be here all blasted day and night." Stacy swats at his arms and slightly angles a piece of the lavender a fraction, then sighs in acceptance.

"Okay. Who's hungry?" she asks the four of them.

"Starving." Connor flashes her a smile. It's been a while since she's seen her son this relaxed. By the way he always keeps one hand touching Marni on her hand, the small of her back, or her hip, Stacy knows she is the reason he is happy. She's practically bursting at the seams with the two of them.

"Staceeee," Jack whines and clasps her hand to drag her out of the stuffy vendor hall.

The smells of the county fair are just how Marni remembered. Sizzling steaks, beer, grilled onions and peppers mixed perfectly with the grease from the rides and arena dirt. Connor walks with their fingers intertwined and she can't help but notice the dumbfounded looks she receives from mostly women her age.

"Care to fill me in as to why I feel like the most interesting attraction at the zoo?" she whispers to Tonya.

"Because you're with Connor who is—well, was—the most interesting single attraction in this town." Connor grips Marni's hand tighter. He must notice the stares, too.

"Well, make them stop." Marni doesn't like having all the eyes on her. After years of hiding and having her mom be the center of attention, she likes the shadows.

"Can't. You have what they all want." Tonya flips her hair and stares down a couple who cower from her glare. Stacy and Jack stop at a vendor truck selling rib-eye sandwiches with all the fixings. Marni's mouth waters at the sight. The first bite sends juice rolling down her chin, and she chuckles from embarrassment before Connor wipes it with his napkin.

"Can't let it stain your top. Also, I'd be jealous if it got to rest between those breasts and not me. It would taunt me to lick it off, and I don't think that would go over so well." His voice is barely above a whisper, but Marni checks to see if anyone reacts to the personal things he just described.

"Who would complain? Your heart-eyed fans?" Marni teases. Before she can push him away, he slides his cowboy hat back just a hair and leans forward to plant a heat-exploding kiss on her exposed sternum. Her knees go weak and her sandwich no longer sounds appetizing.

"Let them," he coos before brushing his lips against hers. They follow his family as they walk around every artisan booth before making their way to the holding pens to look over the bucking broncs and bulls that will show their stuff later.

Someone grabs Marni around the waist and rips her from Connor's grip. Her scream sends Connor into a protective frenzy, and he reaches for the holstered pistol on his side. He whirls and sees Hocks lifting Marni off the ground. Her screams fade into laughter.

"Put me down!" She slaps at his hands and he gently places her down.

"Hocks, why do you have to be such a child?" Tonya snaps. Hocks only offers her a sideways grin that Tonya turns her back, hiding her face. Her stomach flips at the sight of him.

"Risky move on your part." Connor eyes him and Hocks lifts his arms, palms out.

"Just joking. Everyone knows you two are an unbreakable item. But if you get bored with him, there's a whole line of guys in this town just waitin'." He winks and falls in step with them. Stacy and Jack wander back to check on her jam, leaving the four of them.

"Including you?" Tonya snaps, still keeping her back to him.

"No. I have my eyes on someone else."

"What about Jasmine?" Connor chimes in.

"Eh. We had difference of opinions and she left."

"Sorry, man." Hocks shrugs and keeps walking. A somber air fills the silence until they reach the pens of livestock.

Lucas and the other farm-hands stand around on the panels, amping each other up for their events later. When the four friends arrive, the chatter dies down. Lucas is the first one to speak.

"It's good to see you, Marni. Sorry, Orion got the best of you. I'd love to help if I can."

"Thank you, Lucas. I'll probably take you up on that."

"How are you guys feeling?" Connor looks over the lot of broncs.

"I'm feeling great with my draw. Wes drew Dead Weight and I'm pretty sure he couldn't get any whiter." Wes rolls his shoulders and straightens his spine.

"Shut it!" he shouts at Lucas. He looks up at Connor. "I'm fine." Indeed, his face seems completely drained of color. Dead Weight must live up to its name.

"Well, it's one of the last events. Don't forget about your other two and practice with each other." Tonya gives the speech like she's done it a million times.

"We know," they say in unison.

"We'll be cheering for you." Connor tips his hat and they're on the move again. Marni's heart hammers in her chest at the feeling of being back here. Usually on the back of Brimstone, who was just as riled up as her.

"It's weird. I never really thought about what my mom took from me. But being here, feeling this place...she robbed me, didn't she?" Marni says it loud enough for Connor, Tonya, and Hocks to hear. They don't stop walking. Connor slides his hand to her hip and tugs her close.

"Your mom is a bitch," Tonya states matter-of-factly.

"Exactly." Hocks nods.

"You don't even know her?" Tonya argues.

"No, but if you say it, then it has to be true." He offers her another sideways grin, and he sees how she reacts this time.

Marni forces a smile on her face and shoves the memory of Mom down. They turn down the aisle, and Dillon stands there with a group of has-beens reliving the glory days.

Connor slows his steps but doesn't stop. Dillon glances at Marni and flashes a bright smile.

"Ladies." He tips his hat, cautiously watching Connor.

"Since when are you a gentleman?" Tonya snorts and playfully punches his arm, thankfully breaking the tension.

"You hurt me." Dillon laughs. Connor moves forward and the joking atmosphere deadens. Hocks steps up behind Marni and Dillon's friends mimic the motion. Connor acknowledges their movement and extends a hand out to Dillon. His eyes flick from Connor's outstretched hand to his eyes.

"We good?" It isn't an apology because, frankly, Connor will never apologize for punching him when he was forcefully kissing the woman he loves. He does, however, want no tension between the two of them, especially since they both are regulars at the same bar.

"Yeah, Curston. We're good." They clasp hands, and with one brisk shake, all the men's shoulders relax. Even Tonya, who Marni hadn't noticed, moved beside her unshielded best friend.

"Was that really necessary?" Marni whispers to Tonya.

"You don't know what he's capable of," she retorts and nods toward Dillon and his friends. "They do."

Marni stares, wide-eyed. She only knows the soft and gentle man who looks at her for confirmation at every turn. She never thought of the side that could take on all five guys by himself.

"He'd fight them?" she chokes out. Hocks hears the surprise in her voice and chuckles.

"Not just fight. He'd win. I'm just for show." Since Connor came back, Hocks was the only person brave enough to talk to the hardened trained killer Connor portrayed.

"I wasn't going to hit him," Connor argues.

Hocks just continues to smile. "You would have if he drew back."

Connor holds his hand back out to Marni, and she looks at the scars and callouses for a moment. She quickly takes his hand and smiles up at him with a new appreciation.

"What?" he asks, puzzled.

"Nothing." Her cheeks warm at the feelings stirring inside of her. She is safe. She will always be safe with Connor. Even from a drunk classmate. Hocks and Tonya joke in hushed tones behind them as they continue to walk around the fair.

"Do you want to ride anything?" Connor stops in the middle of the carnival rides.

She scoffs. "Those things are put together on hopes and dreams and held together by duct tape and super glue. Seriously?"

"You sound like Gwen," Tonya groans, coming up beside her.

"I do not."

"Do too."

Marni lets out a huff and steps into the closest line she sees.

"You don't have to. I was just asking." Connor shrugs while Tonya moves up behind her.

"Oh yes, I do. I am not my mother." Marni scowls at Tonya, who doesn't even look guilty of the accusation. The line moves forward and Marni finally registers which line she just happened to step into.

"Um, on second thought, maybe—" she stammers.

"Let's go, you big baby." Tonya urges her from behind, and in a blink, she is sitting in a swaying cart with Connor, Tonya and Hocks sitting on another. Marni's palms sweat on the metal bar across their laps.

"Are you okay?" Connor questions. He leans forward to see Marni's tightly shut eyes.

"Peachy." Her teeth clack together.

"You're not. I can tell him we want off. It's fine." He begins to move, but she places a hand on his thigh.

"No. I'm fine." She forces herself to sit back in her seat and takes a deep breath. Connor drapes an arm around her shoulders and shifts her closer to him.

"I could distract you." To prove his point, he brushes her hair across her shoulder and kisses her neck. Tonya gags from the car behind them, but Marni doesn't care. "If you want me to." He slides a hand on her thigh, skims his fingers under her top, across her abdomen. A shudder runs through her.

"Want me to stop?" She still hasn't been able to find her voice. The rise and fall of the ride's movements have her head spinning, but having Connor touch her, kiss her—she imagines herself anywhere but here.

"No," she whispers and opens her eyes to drown in the watery depths of his. Connor leans down and brushes a teasing kiss across her lips before gripping her inner thigh and sending pleasure up her spin.

Her world truly spun, but not from the Ferris wheel. The doors and windows Connor unlocked to her soul makes her feel lighter and happier. More than she has felt since the days she and Tonya competed, chasing after their dream.

She isn't here competing or chasing that high, but this. This high with Connor—it's worth chasing and never letting go.

She moves her lips to his chin, following his strong jawline to just below his ear. A growl rumbles from his throat and the corners of Marni's lips turn up at his response. She places a hand on his upper thigh, and the hard arousal she finds there makes her want more. Connor moves her hand back up to the railing.

"I can't exactly take you here, but you best believe me. I'll have you screaming later." The space between Marni's legs throbs at the husky, needing tone of his voice. He cups her cheek and places sweet, soft kisses below her ear, leading back to her lips, before he pulls back and studies her face. "That look in your eyes drives me wild."

"What look?"

"The one where your caramel eyes seem to melt and daze. You look so damn beautiful all the time, but that—that look takes all of my control." Marni blushes and pushes her lips to his again. She starts to tell him how she wants him, right then, but she's interrupted.

"Going again?" a deep male voice asks. Connor breaks the embrace, and Marni sees the carnival worker holding their gate open.

"No." Connor chuckles and steps out before helping Marni out. Her legs are jelly, and the burn in her abdomen and wetness between her thighs cry in desperation for him to calm the storm he fired up inside of her.

"Seriously, the entire ride?" Tonya fusses and Marni notices Hocks' reddened cheeks. She forgot they had a front-row show to whatever happened in their car.

"You didn't have to watch," Connor teases.

"Kinda hard not to," she retorts before storming off in the direction of the stands.

"I feel bad," Marni admits when she is out of earshot.

"Don't. She's just mad Hocks hasn't made a move yet."

"Really?"

"My little sister has been pining over that boy for about as long as I have you. Just never has worked out for them." Marni notices how Hocks and Tonya stride together as a couple. "Want to go and finish what you started?" Connor whispers into Marni's ear.

"I did not start anything," she defends.

"You were petrified. I had to do something."

"Heights. I don't like heights."

"I'm sorry. I didn't know."

"It's not your fault. I just couldn't handle Tonya calling me my mom. I'm not her. I will never be that monster." Connor stops her and stands to face her.

"She didn't mean it. You know Tonya."

"I know. She just never understood how I could let someone run my life like that. Looking back, I wonder the same." She intertwines her fingers through his and rests her head on his chest. When she opens her eyes, Christy is there, not even trying to hide her glare. She is sitting on some cowboy's knees next to a group of horse trailers and out-of-town competitors.

"Your fan club is here," Marni remarks. Connor groans and buries his head in Marni's neck.

"I'm sorry. Want me to go talk to her?"

"And say what? She'll just make a spectacle out of it. I have a better idea." Marni leans back, but leaves only inches between them. Connor stares down at her as she plucks his hat off his head, then places it on her own. A grin immediately forms, causing his dimple to show.

"Now kiss me."

Connor obliges her request and lifts her. Marni wraps her legs around his waist and she tips her head down to deepen their kiss.

"You're evil," Connor whispers against her lips.

"Just staking my claim." He lowers her back down and steals his hat back. There's something about cowboys and their hats. You simply don't touch them unless you are the girl their heart belongs to. The two of them don't glance back in Christy's direction before heading toward where Hocks and Tonya disappeared.

"There you two are!" Stacy flags Connor and Marni down before they make it to the stands. "Voting closes soon and I need you to get over there and vote for my jam! I already sent Tonya and Hocks. Now go!" Stacy shoos them off before searching the crowd for anyone else.

Connor keeps one arm across Marni's shoulders as they walk, occasionally kissing her temple and her hair. After all these years, she is back, and he has her to himself. He wants to pinch himself to ensure he isn't dreaming. They find Tonya and Hocks sampling jam. Connor doesn't even bother before grabbing a paper to vote.

"Aren't you going to taste them?" Tonya asks.

"Don't have to. I already know Mom's is the best." He and Marni place their cards in the box.

"You're right." Tonya makes a face at the last one she samples. "That one has enough sugar to kill a bee."

The announcer's voice comes through the broken speakers and fades. "We better go find seats. The events are about to start." Hocks motions for them to make their way back.

"You understood that?" Marni wrinkles her brow.

Connor laughs, but Tonya answers, "Nothing has changed but you around here." It's true. The town she left is just as it has always been, even the order of events at the rodeo. She was forced to leave and came back a shell of who she was. But never again, she vows to herself. She isn't letting go of anything she felt. No matter what.

Indeed, the rodeo is the same, but the competitors are obviously different. Most of the ones Marni had competed with are scattered through these bleachers.

Lucas and Wes enter the chutes for team roping. She and Tonya both scooted to the edge of their seats, hands folded over their mouths. Lucas and Wes nod and the steer shoots out. Both boys swing their lassos. Lucas is the header; his rope flies and lands its mark. A soft gasp escapes Marni. Wes releases his loop a fraction of a second later and it cinches up around both hind legs of the steer. In unison, Marni and Tonya leap to their feet and shout for the duo.

The boys pump their fists in the air and let out yells of their own. The two women exchange glances before leaping down the bleachers and over the fence to congratulate the two ranch hands. They reach the pair just as they slide off their horses and embrace them with hugs. The announcer comes over the speakers and dubs them the winners with the fastest time.

"You did it!" Tonya beams. Being down in the ring, looking at the crowd from here, Marni gets hit with the memories once more. Connor leans against the fence, just watching her, smiling. Ten years ago, he crossed that fence and came to congratulate her on her own win. She strides back over to Connor and he grabs her hands to pull her back up the concrete wall.

"You look sad," he whispers as he brushes hair behind her ear.

"I didn't realize how much I missed this. Missed being here. Everything I missed. I didn't realize the dream I gave up until now. I think part of me knew Mom would never let me go pro. Even with the acceptance, I never let myself hope or even dream about a future in rodeo. Not really." Tears spring to her eyes and Connor's mouth falls into a frown. He wants to take away the hurt and pain, but what can he do?

"I don't want to leave. Whatever happens with us. I don't want to leave this place, these people, this life. I want to stay for me." Connor kisses each of her salty cheeks and wraps his arms around her. He catches his sister's eyes from where she stands, still with Lucas and Wes, and she nods in understanding. She warned him today would be hard for her. All the memories from being here would resurface.

Chapter Eighteen

THE GROUP OF FOUR friends watch the remainder of the events. When it is time for bronc riding, Connor holds Marni's hand as they move down next to the fence.

"Just know you still have to work come Monday!" Connor shouts between cupped hands. Indeed, every farm hand has on their chest protectors and cowboy hats, intending on riding a bronc tonight. Marni's chest tightens at the sight of the wiry young men.

"Are they really going to ride those?" Marni's eyes wander to the snorting horses being shuffled into the holding pens.

"Well, they aren't going to pet them." Connor smirks.

"I know that. I just...I never knew anyone who did it and it's terrifying."

"I tried it. After you left for college. Made it five seconds and decided the army was less dangerous," he chuckles, but the laughter doesn't match the somber look on his face.

Marni watches the farm-hands through her fingers and doesn't take a full breath until the last one of them hits the dirt. A couple of them made it a full eight seconds. Dead Weight lived up to his name; Wes barely made it out of the gate before the horse kicked its rear legs to the heavens and twisted mid-air.

"You can relax now. That was the last one." Connor squeezes her knee and Marni lowers her shoulders away from her ears.

"Was it that stressful for our parents to watch when we competed?" Marni asks Tonya.

"Yes. It was." Stacy slides in next to Tonya with Jack close behind. She holds up a blue ribbon and gives us all a Cheshire cat smile.

"Did you really think you wouldn't win?" Tonya muses.

"That's what I tried to tell her." Jack gives her a lazy kiss on the cheek.

"I'll be back in a minute," Connor whispers into Marni's ear and stalks off toward the trailers.

"Mommy, Daddy! The fireworks are getting ready to start!" A child rushes in front of Marni to find their seat.

Marni turns halfway to search for Connor to see where he went, but she can't make him out of all the people walking to the bleachers.

Hocks leans in closer to her and whispers so no one else can hear. "It's the fireworks. They—the sound messes with his head."

Of course, Marni scolds herself. *Why didn't I think of that?* She takes a step after Connor.

"I wouldn't," Hocks warns, but she ignores him and jogs toward the trailers, looking for Connor. She pushes against the wave of people who are eager to see the show, bouncing off their shoulders like a bumper car.

Where the hell are you? She ducks under the trailer tongues, scanning to her left and right as she goes. She nearly gives up; maybe he went another way. Then, at the last trailer, he has his hands braced on the fender well.

"Connor." Marni exhales his name as she approaches. He whirls and she instinctively flinches, waiting for the slap for intruding. Connor holds a hand out.

"I'd never—what he did to you. I'd never do those things." Marni swallows the memory and takes his hand.

"I know. Just a reflex. I'm sorry." He pulls her into his chest and rests his cheek atop her head.

"Don't you ever apologize. You should go back. Enjoy the show. I just have some—I'll be up in a minute." Even as he speaks, he gets more tense as the minutes tick by.

"Hocks told me. I'm not leaving you out here alone."

"Marni, I'm not myself when they start. I don't want you to see me like that. Please go." He pushes her away to add distance between them.

"No. I'm staying." Connor drops his head and releases Marni to clench and unclench his fists. She steps forward and places her palms on each side of his face. "Look at me." He refuses, then caves when she doesn't release him.

There is so much pain in his blue eyes. A hell his mind is pulling him back into. "Kiss me," she purrs. He shakes his head, but she insists. "Connor, I want you to kiss me." He tangles his hand in her hair and pulls her closer to him. He ravages her mouth with urgency.

"Please, go," he pleads.

"No," she whispers and moves her mouth to his jawline, rekindling everything from the Ferris wheel earlier. Connor opens the trailer door and lifts her by the waist, shutting the door behind them.

Marni looks around the interior of the space. Before she can ask where they are, Connor pulls her against him and kisses her with hunger flashing in his eyes and claws at her shirt.

"If you rip it, I will have to go out of here shirtless." He slows and lets her lift the shirt over her head and slings it to the side. With one snap of his thumb and forefinger, he unhooks her bra, and it slips off her shoulders to the ground. His mouth sucks on her suddenly free breasts.

"Connor." Marni's head falls back, but he keeps her legs from giving out. The first boom startles Marni and she yelps. Connor's body shudders and he squeezes her tighter. She hooks her legs around his waist and tugs on the hem of his shirt, pulling it over his head.

Another boom, another shudder. Connor lays her down on the couch and hovers over her. His eyes are clenched shut as a round of consecutive explosions sound off.

Marni fumbles with his belt on his jeans and roars in triumph when she gets it and his pants' button undone. Connor is frozen, repeating something under his breath. Marni pushes her own jeans down her thighs.

"Connor. Connor, look at me." He raises his gaze, his eyes in a faraway place. "You're safe. It's just us." As if he just realizes they are both undressed, his eyes darken with desire.

"I don't want to hurt you." He rests his ear on her chest to listen to the drumming of her heart. The fireworks have paused for a moment, but the grand finale is still to come.

"You won't. I want this. I want you," Marni urges. Connor tucks a strand of hair behind Marni's ear and runs a hand down her bare collarbone to palm her breast. She arches her back for him. For more *of* him. His body responds to her silent request and with the next rumbling boom, he thrusts deep inside her.

His fingers dig into her hip bones. He pushes hard and fast, drowning himself in her. Letting her scent, the feel of her, her skin pull him from the depths of his hell. Even for this moment.

Marni clings to his shoulders, giving all of herself to him. Her name is like a prayer on his lips as he rides harder. He presses her down into the couch, not being careful with her in the slightest.

Repeated explosions mix with Marni's screams as Connor bites on her breasts, switching from side to side. He grips a handful of her hair and pulls her head back, nipping on her collarbone. He stands suddenly and pulls Marni to her feet.

"All you have to do is say no." Marni's breath is ragged, so she only nods. Connor turns her so her back is to him.

"Bend down, grab the back of the sofa."

She does as he says. A stinging sensation burns across her ass cheek as Connor slaps it. She yelps but doesn't move. It doesn't feel like Vance's slap. This feels like pleasure, not vengeance.

Connor presses his muscled chest against Marni's back to whisper in her ear. "I think you like that." Marni bites on her lip and giggles. Conner stands back and lands another slap. Shocks reverberate from her curled toes to her white-knuckled fingers gripping the back of the sofa.

Connor grabs her hips as her knees wobble. Another explosion, and Connor buries himself deep inside of her. Marni's never been taken this way, and she screams from delight and terror. Connor slows and wraps a hand around her long flowing hair before ramming himself into Marni, matching the rhythm of the explosions outside until they fade away and all he feels and sees is her.

Her flawless back arches for him. Her spine tingles with each reddening blemish on her cheeks. His teeth leave marks of his salvation. With each slap of him against her, Marni's own body shudders. For once, the explosions outside aren't those of grenades and tanks. They're the sound of everything he is. Every flaw, every scar, every nightmare, every hell he has endured—and now they're him and her. The two of them, hidden from the world, adding their own pleasures to the celebration outside.

Connor slides a hand around Marni's waist and circles her clit slowly until she rubs herself harder against him. Her moan is ecstasy to his ears. Her body writhes and spasms around him.

"Connor—I'm—" Her words cut off as she topples over the edge around Connor. The only thing holding up her limp body is his strength. The grand finale sounds around them, overlapping explosions and booms. Connor pumps harder and faster and slips out to spin Marni around and take her up against the wall. He pulls back out and comes up her abdomen, sweat glistening both of them, their breath ragged.

His blue eyes are clearer now. The etched lines around his mouth are softer. With the fireworks over, voices emerge around the trailers. Competitors coming back to load up and head to the next rodeo. Connor slides down to the sofa and cradles Marni to his chest. As her breathing slows, he revels in the moment just a little longer before facing reality.

He eyes the forming bruises on her skin. Trusting that if it was too much, she would have told him to stop. She gave him this. She gave him an escape. Something nobody else has ever been able to do for him. She dived into his hell and brought him back out again.

"We might not want to be found like this." He lazily traces a line up her arm.

"Probably not. Whose trailer is this, anyway?"

"I have no idea." Connor smirks. Marni pushes herself off of him, terror on her face.

"What do you mean? I'm naked!" She hurriedly throws her clothes on and slings Connor's at him. He chuckles and pulls his jeans on. Marni steps into the bathroom and cleans her stomach before pulling on her shirt and smoothing her hair.

"Would you hurry up?" she hisses. Connor stands in the middle of the room, not in a hurry in the least.

"Where did my hat go?"

"I don't know, but we have to get out of here!" Connor finds his hat next to the sofa and places it on his head. Marni opens the trailer door and peers outside. The coast seems clear as she steps out onto the grass. Connor jumps down behind her and catches her wrist.

"Come on, bef—"

Connor kisses her sweetly, gently this time.

"Thank you." He then presses his lips to her forehead. "I don't deserve this." His eyes fade back to that hell from earlier.

"No, I don't deserve this," Marni murmurs. She places his hand over her heart and cups his cheek.

"Hey guys." Tonya creeps up behind them and Marni's eyes go wide at the half-open trailer door.

"Hey! This—we—it's not—" Tonya raises her eyebrows and Hocks clears his throat.

"Are you driving the horses home or...?" he asks Connor as he points to the truck and trailer they had just snuck out of. Marni whirls between Connor and Hocks as they exchange glances.

"Your trailer?" She seethes through gritted teeth. Connor only shrugs.

Chapter Nineteen

Connor stands next to Brimstone, his mind reeling at the amount he deposited into the ranch account.

This can't be real. We went from sinking to swimming then—Hell, we're fucking floating without the need of a life raft.

Almost a week had passed since Marni gave him the check, and his mind feels empty from not balancing what he could afford to buy this week and what could wait.

"Earth to Curston." Hocks jostles him from behind.

"Hey. What?"

"Are you working today or admiring your horse's ass?" Connor shakes his head and swings his leg over. They ride past the house and the missing red Focus sends a quick flutter of worry through him before he remembers Marni did indeed go back to the city this weekend to discuss her employment with her boss and owner of the firm.

"Seriously, Connor, where's your head?"

"What are you talking about? I'm right here?"

"No, you're like a twitterpated, love-struck monkey." Connor punches his friend's shoulder playfully.

"Jealous?"

"Maybe a little." Connor gives him a deadly stare. "Not of Marni."

"Oh, sorry, man."

"Eh, I didn't really develop feelings for Jasmine, at least what she deserved. I see that in you, with Marni, what it means to truly care."

"It's fucking terrifying. I worry about her every second I can't place eyes on her. I'm sure the war makes that more intense. It's like I don't think she's real."

"I want that. I want to care about someone so much it hurts. That way I'll know it's real," Hocks says.

Tonya lopes up to meet them.

"Where the hell have you two been? Take the scenic route?"

"We were talking business. Why aren't you done yet?" Connor snaps.

"You try doing anything with these boys who can't rope!"

"Maybe you should teach them." Hocks gives her a daring smile.

"I'm not the header. You up for the challenge?" She smiles back. Hocks chuckles and tips his hat.

"I'll take that as a yes."

***

"Marni, lovely to see you. How is your mother?" Jennifer asks as Marni steps into her office.

"Well, honestly, we cut ties about a week ago and I'm dead to her...so there's that."

"Oh—uh, well." She stutters over her words.

"It's fine. Really. Long time coming." Jennifer nods and looks at her monitor. "Will Boston be joining us?" Marni didn't see him when she walked in, and everything in her office is still the same.

"No, it's just me. I wanted to discuss something with you before bringing him into the mix." That's cagey and weird for this office. The manager and owner are always in meetings together, or so she assumed. "Have a seat, please."

Marni sits in one of the office chairs and faces Jennifer, who's behind her desk. Her desk is immaculate even her stapler has its specific place. A manila folder sits alone in front of her.

"We're here to discuss your hasty resignation and your terms to come back." She says *hasty* with a hint of disapproval that, from a business standpoint, Marni knows she deserves. "Boston told me his side of what happened and I want to hear it from you."

"Yes ma'am. He called me into his office and told me to pack my bags and be at the airport for a weekend trip without asking me if I could or if I was even available. Then he told me if I refused, I would be fired. So I quit instead of him firing me." Her palms sweat. She managed to keep her tone even through her speech, but she feels like a snitch or something. What was his side of the story?

"I see." Jennifer taps her nails on the lacquer wood of her desk and opens the manila folder. "He told me he sent you some offers to entice you to stay, but you didn't reach back out to him about it."

"No, I didn't. I had planned on it, then I got injured by a horse and, well, you called before I called him back."

"Marni, you're a great asset to our firm. Don't think I haven't noticed how many times your name comes across my computer on the deals you make and investing you do. What will it take for you to stay?"

This is not the approach Marni expected from Jennifer. She thought she would have two options: to take or leave what was offered. She chooses to not hold back.

"I would like to work remotely and be made salary with an increase in my wages." Jennifer's features don't shift in the slightest. She pulls a paper from the folder and hands it to Marni. It is thick, embellished cardstock. It screams pricey and important. Her gaze falls to the page and the three-figure pay causes her voice to get stuck in her throat.

Are you freaking serious?! She struggles to keep from waving it around and shouting

"I can accommodate you to work remotely and mainly focus on the numbers and handling investments. I ask that you come in once a month for our monthly staff meeting. That'll keep your presence here so nobody will cause a stir in the order of things."

While Marni is getting the best news, she could have possibly expected. Her phone rings on her desk down the hall. Parker strides over and sees Connor's face flash across the screen.

"Hello, Marni's phone."

"Who is this?" Connor questions.

"You've reached Parker. Marni is...occupied at the moment and can't come to the phone. I'd be happy to tell her you called." A grin spreads on Parker's face as he paces around Marni's office, placing his hand on random objects.

"Where is she?" Connor seethes. He remembers the cockroach from when he visited the ranch.

"She's just in the other room—" He can't resist getting under the cocky cowboy's skin. "—about ready to scream my name." Parker hangs up and deletes the call record before blocking Connor's number entirely.

Connor shoves his phone in his pocket and his hands shake as he tightens his saddle around Brimstone. Rage fills every crevice of his body. It has to be a lie—Marni wouldn't do that to him. She wouldn't. As much as he tries to convince himself, doubt creeps in. What reason would Parker have her phone to begin with?

"You ready?" Hocks slides his rifle into the saddle sling and swings up on his mount. They drove to Callahan's farm after Connor got a call that a rogue mountain lion was picking off his calves and he needed help. It could just as easily have been Connor's herd, and neighbors help neighbors around their parts. They won't have service once they reach the mountains; he called Marni to warn her he wouldn't be reachable and to let her know what he was doing.

"Yeah, let's go." Connor and Hocks make up one of three hunting parties to find the feral animal and put it down before it can do more damage. Hocks notices his demeanor changed—whatever happened on the phone clearly has him on edge and lethal. Connor checks his phone one more time and tosses it onto his truck seat. No point in taking it with him. It would be only be a paperweight.

"What if Marni tries to call?"

"I'll call her when we get back. C'mon. We have a job to do." Connor's steely gaze even makes Hocks uneasy. He quickly grabs Connor's phone and shoves it into his saddlebag. He isn't sure what just happened, but he will not let Connor's stubbornness make it worse.

"We'll ride to the recent kill site and see if we can track the lion," Hocks says while leading at a canter. They have permission from the ranches that border the Callahans to hunt for the cougar. No rancher wants it wandering into their herds.

Connor's thoughts keep killing Parker in different forms and fashions. He feels sick to his stomach, imagining his hands on Marni. What if she is in danger and can't fight him off? She is supposed to be negotiating her job, but she is with Parker, who knows where, and he hasn't talked to her since she left yesterday.

"How many did Callahan say it killed so far?" Connor tries to distract himself and rides up next to Hocks.

"Five, in three weeks. That's unheard of. He thought it would get its fill and be on its way, but here we are." Connor scratches his beard. They pick up a gallop and ride over the ridge. The fields are flat, but on top of the ridge, they can see for miles. They slow to a halt and dismount when they get to the marker, showing the most recent kill site.

"Where did you say the other groups are going?" Connor leans over the blood and disturbed ground.

"You really are stuck on Marni today, aren't you?" Hocks repeats, "One group went to the mountain. Hopefully, they'll come across a den or even stumble upon it themselves. The rest are checking the other four kill sites. We're just assuming it's a lion. Nobody's actually seen it." Connor only huffs at his comment about Marni. He has half a mind to drive up there himself and confront her about the whole Parker thing, and possibly strangle the bastard.

He runs his hand over the set of tracks that head south, placing his fingers in each divot in the dirt. Standing, he walks a few paces with the tracks and sees the weight distributed evenly. Then drag marks offset the prints, with blood trailing behind.

"It's definitely a lion. Look here, it's dragging the calf with it."

"Do you think it has young? Could that be why it's on a spree?"

"Possibly. Young ones will do it too, when they get shoved out on their own. Basically, while learning how to survive, they think they have to kill every chance they get." Connor and Hocks get back on their horses and follow the blood trail.

"You know a lot about this stuff," Hocks observes.

"I had a lot of time to read while Tonya was dragging us to every rodeo across the state."

"You read about mountain lions?"

"No, I read about every predator in Wyoming and how they act." Their conversation dies as they pick back up to a canter. Connor gets lost in his head picturing Marni, her brown curls splayed across his pillow, her body rocking under his, her arms pinned over her head and ecstasy spreading across her face. Then Parker's voice rings in his head and he grips the reins tighter. He nearly runs into Hocks when he stops.

Hocks holds a finger to his lips and points ahead. They slide off and ground tie the horses. The two of them crouch behind a rock. Hocks signals to look at his ten o'clock through the scope. Connor lifts his rifle and scans the landscape. Roughly three hundred yards ahead, there is a pack of coyotes fighting over a carcass. Best guess, it's the calf carcass.

Connor nods to confirm they are going to shoot as many of the parasites as possible. They aren't as powerful as a lion, but they will kill a calf when they get the chance. The two men cock their rifles and set up their sights.

The sound of gunfire echoes throughout the valley. Connor grits his teeth and reminds himself he is safe. He's in Wyoming, not Afghanistan. He squeezes his eyes shut as Hocks takes a second shot. His hands shake, and his heart races in his chest.

You're home, you're home, you're home, he repeats in his head. He opens his eyes to see a coyote running away—it is pushing five hundred yards and will be out of range soon. He lets out a shaky breath and squeezes the trigger. The animal falls forward and remains still.

"Shoo, that felt good!" Hocks smiles as he stands. A cell phone rings and Connor looks back at the horses.

"Why do I hear my phone?"

Hocks meets his gaze. "I might have brought it to save you from making whatever is bothering you worse." Connor curses Hocks under his breath.

"Was that you guys? We heard shots," Paul, Callahan's son, speaks through the phone.

"Yeah, pack of coyotes. We haven't inspected the carcass yet, but I have a feeling it's the calf. The lion packed it in a good ways."

"Okay, Dad and Mitch are already in the mountains and are out of cell range. I'd say you guys are close to being out of range, too. We don't want anyone out overnight, so don't go too far before you turn back for the trucks."

"Ten-four."

He looks at his phone screen again. No messages or missed calls from Marni. He swallows his pride and tries again.

Chapter Twenty

Marni exits Jennifer's office, feeling empowered and like it's all a dream. She got the raise she wanted and the option to work remotely, which means bye-bye city life. She will keep her office for her once-a-month visit, too. She searches her purse for her phone. Odd, she thought, she had left it on the desk.

"Knock knock." A sing-song voice halts her search. Parker, who is no longer in a sling, leans in the doorway. His green eyes give her the once-over, as if looking for her weakness before he pounces.

"Parker." Her tone is dismissive.

"Are you looking for something?"

"Nothing that concerns you," she snaps. Parker's anger builds, but he keeps it pushed down. He needs to smooth things over with Marni, so he can have her again. Get things back on track before she returns to that rundown ranch.

"Maybe I can help. What are you looking for?" He steps into the office, keeping his voice soft, sweet, thick with innocence. Marni lets out a huff and gets down on her hands and knees, looking under her desk.

"It's my phone. I thought I left it on top here, but I can't find it anywhere."

"And you're positive you didn't take it with you?" The weight of Marni's phone pulls on his pocket as he walks over to her.

"Yes." Her eyes narrow at him.

"What about your car? Do you remember having it before you came in?" She tries to think back.

"Not specifically. I mean, I think I did, but I can't be sure." She pinches the bridge of her nose. All of this good news and she just wants to call Connor to let him know she is staying near the ranch.

"Let's trace back your steps. Did you use the bathroom before coming to your office?"

"Yeah..." She grabs her purse and the manila folder with her copies of the contracts and work agreements before heading to the bathroom.

"I'll find it. You can go back to work."

"You're saving me from paper pushing. I am quite content looking for your phone." He flashes her a smile. How can he be so nice like this but then so conniving at the same time? Marni doesn't let her guard down while he walks beside her. She heads into the bathroom and searches each stall.

Parker rushes back to her office while she is inside and places her phone between the chair cushions.

Marni sighs while looking in the mirror. Each stall has been checked and still no phone. Parker is still standing where she left him. Charming as the devil himself.

"Still nothing?"

"No. Seriously, you can go back to work. I'm just going to check my car. I can always buy another one." *Even though I've only had this one for three weeks*, she thinks to herself.

"Are you sure?"

"Yeah. Fingers crossed it's there." Parker gives Marni a smile and lets his hand slide down her arm before pocketing his hands and strolling back to his desk.

***

CONNOR AND HOCKS LOSE the lion's trail when they reach the rocks at the base of the mountain. A crevice breaks up the mountain and a small path, too small for the horses, winds its way deeper into the mountain.

"Let's scout that area. We'll tie the horses here." Connor pulls out his rifle.

"It'll be dark soon. We should probably set a marker and come back tomorrow." Hocks looks around warily. The sun is setting and shadows creep in all around them.

"We have a couple hours of daylight left. We can ride back in the dark," Connor insists as broken pieces of rock scrape against each other under his boots. He holds his gun at the ready, not wanting to give the big cat a chance to jump them. They speak with hand gestures, pointing at recently broken twigs and more tracks in the soft mud. Connor crouches and studies the new set of tracks they've come across. Still lion, but slightly smaller in size.

Hocks observes and furrows his brow. They are tracking a mom and her baby that looks close to weaning age by its paw size. She is probably teaching it how to hunt before he ventures out on its own.

Broken rock pieces slide down the side of the cliff and Connor's senses go on high alert as he jerks his rifle toward the movement. The hair stands up on the back of his neck; he can feel they're being watched. They've just become the hunted and in the cougar's territory.

The sun doesn't peek over this ravine and it's getting closer to nightfall with each minute that passes. More rocks clatter ahead, and the two men crouch down low and hold the stock on their rifles against their shoulders. Connor's breath is even hiding the uneasiness blanketing him. They can easily become cornered if a lion gets behind them. There is no way out on either side of the ravine. Connor follows the sound and a vicious hiss behind him makes him jump around.

A mature mountain lion eyes them and bares its incisors. The tip of its tail flicks back and forth. Connor readies his aim. A blood-curdling scream makes Hocks turn around once more, his back against Connor's. A juvenile male mountain lion is pacing in front of Hocks. It lets out a low growl and Hocks set his sights.

"What do we do?" he whispers to Connor. At the sound of his voice, both cats scream at the men.

"Don't miss," Connor states evenly. His finger hovers over the trigger as he tracks the cat with his barrel. A fraction of a second before he squeezes the trigger, a gunshot rings behind him. Connor squeezes his eyes shut as the smell of fired gunpowder takes him back to the war. His troop is storming into an abandoned building, but their intel was wrong. They're being ambushed.

"Connor!" Hocks' scream brings him back to the present. The enormous cat he'd been watching lunges at the two men now. Connor rolls, but its large fangs grab his calf and sink into the meat and muscle.

He tries to maneuver to get his aim, but it jerks his body around, keeping him face down in the rocks. Hocks swings his gun around and catches the cat in the head with the stock, stunning him, but the cat doesn't release its locked jaw.

"Shoot it!" Connor shouts as he fights to get free. Hocks aims and squeezes his trigger. Connor's body goes still. The jerking of his leg stops. Hocks drags the cat off of his body and rolls him to his back, checking for other injuries.

"Connor! Connor, look at me!"

An unknown explosion herds Connor's troops inside the abandoned building. Taliban soldiers storm every exit, boxing his men in. His ears rings from the repeated gunfire. Bodies drop left and right; blood slicks his boots and clothing. He can't hear the shouts of pain from his brothers, their dying breaths and screams, as the enemy wreaks havoc.

***

MARNI WALKS BACK INTO the office, once again tracing her steps. Phones don't just grow legs and disappear. Where did she put it? She scolds her crappy memory.

"I can recite account numbers and investments, but leave it to me to lose my lifeline," she mumbles. Parker meets her before she enters her office.

"Still no luck?" He leans against the door frame with his arms crossed.

"No, it's not in my car, it's not in the bathroom. I *know* I didn't have it inside with Jennifer. I'm going to search my office one more time and pray it just appears."

"I'll help. Four eyes are better than two."

What the hell? It can't hurt.

"Thanks." Once again, she scours her desk, under it and all around it. Parker is searching under the chairs she has sitting in front of her desk. She's about to say she knows it isn't there when he straightens his spine and swings her phone for her to see.

"Oh, thank God." Relief washes over her. When she opens it, she's surprised to see Connor hasn't checked in.

"Not God, just me," Parker smirks. Marni rolls her eyes at his joking tone.

"So I wanted to ask you," he starts, and Marni's defenses go up immediately. "I want to apologize for my behavior before and coming to the ranch. That was stupid." Marni doesn't see the point in holding a grudge. They are co-workers and civility will make things easier. "I've accepted you are with the cowboy and I miss working with you like before. Nothing more."

"I forgive you. Thank you for helping me find my phone." She lightly touches his arm before letting her hand fall away. She checks the time—she had every intention of driving home tonight, but at this hour, she wouldn't get there until early morning.

"Are you headed back tonight?"

"I was going to, but the meeting started late, ran long, and now after looking for my phone...I should probably just stay at my apartment." Parker's eyebrows shoot up at the mention of her apartment.

"You still have the apartment? I assumed you sold it."

"No, I still have it and plan on renting it out."

"You aren't going to be working here anymore?"

"I'm still working here. Just remotely and coming in once a month." That's good news, Parker thinks. At least she will be back once a month, so she isn't totally sold on uprooting her life and career entirely.

"Well, congratulations. I'm glad you're happy." She side-eyes his optimism.

"Er, thanks. Anyway, I'm going to grab something fattening and greasy, then head home for the evening. I'll see you later." She starts to leave. Parker notes how well she responded to the apology route he tried. Maybe he can build on that and convince her to let him take her out.

"Marni?" She pauses, and he catches up to her. "Can I take you out to eat? Not like romantically. More of an, I'm sorry I was an ass and congratulations on your new business venture? My treat." Marni debates it and checks her phone. Going out to eat with Parker was so normal. It used to be a regular thing.

"Let me make a call really quick."

Marni retreats to the bathroom and dials Connor. Regardless of his history, Parker and her work side by side on a lot of projects, and if he wants to apologize and put this all behind them, she is willing to. Out of respect for Connor, she wants to give him a heads-up.

The phone rings and the machine states that the caller she is trying to reach is unavailable. She sends Connor a quick text for him to call her and then lets Tonya know she is trying to reach Connor.

Outside the bathroom, Parker waits with his hands in his pockets.

"Okay, dinner." A smile that is a little too eager spreads across his face.

"You pick where we go." Parker holds the door for her as they leave the office.

***

"CONNOR!" HOCKS SHOUTS AGAIN, and Connor's eyes focus on him. His brows raise in confusion. Hocks takes his belt and makes a tourniquet just below his knee to help with the bleeding.

"What happened? Where did it go?" Connor looks around with wide eyes. He grabs his gun and twists around, looking for the cat.

"They're dead. We need to get you back. The muscle is shredded and you're losing a lot of blood." The long trek they made up the crevice is going to take twice as long, if not longer, back out. He has to get Connor on Brimstone and ride back to the trucks. Hopefully, he will get service sooner than that and can call for a medivac.

Hocks drapes one of Connor's arms around his neck. "One, two, three, lift." Hocks grunts under the weight, but he's able to get Connor to stand. The blood rushes to Connor's leg and soaks his pants, then trickles down in his boot. He breathes through the pain, flashes of him packing his troop members out of the rubble to safety after they killed the last of the ambushers. He looks over and sees Grisman, his leg blown off from the explosion.

"It's gone," Connor whispers.

"Your leg is still there. Stay with me, Connor." Hocks knows of his PTSD—he's watched Connor fight it before. Always triggered by gun fire or loud sounds. The mountain lion attack will probably take this to a whole new level for him. He slings Connor's gun over his shoulder for good measure, just in case he loses it.

"They're coming. It was a trap. They outsmarted us."

Hocks doesn't know what Connor is talking about.

"We got them, they're gone. We're going back to the horses and getting you to a hospital." Labored breaths come from both of them. Each step is painfully slow, with Hocks guiding Connor's one good leg for stable footing before moving his own.

"More. More are coming." Connor lays Grisman down behind the cover of a concrete wall. Bullets ricochet off the barrier, bits of concrete and dust filling the air around them. His eyes burn and blood mixes with the sweat running down his face. What remains of his troop looks at him, waiting for orders, waiting for him to make the life-or-death decision for all of them.

"I'll hold them off. You fall back. Get the wounded back to safety!" he shouts.

Baber crouches next to him and locks eyes with his.

"We come back together or not at all."

The others nod and grunt in agreement. Connor gives a resigned sigh and checks his clip before spinning and firing on the oncoming assault.

"So many more." His voice is gruff and his eyes are far away.

"Connor, listen to my voice. Focus on me. We are in Wyoming; we are walking back to the horses where we are going home. Hold it together. Think of Marni."

"Marni?" How could he think of her? The last thing he heard was Parker winning the war. She was with him, in the city, where she belongs, after all. "She's gone too."

A scream echoes throughout the ravine. The same kind of blood-curdling scream from the cat before.

"There is another one! We have to go faster!" Hocks half drags Connor along the rocky terrain. Stars scatter the cloudless sky, but the moon isn't high enough to shine over the cliffs.

"Baber!" Connor shouts, patting himself for a gun. "I'm out! Reload!" He swings his arms wildly. Hocks tries to bring him back to reality, grabbing at his arms to keep them down.

"Curston!" Connor's arms are being pinned, and his fight response kicks in. He shoves the captor back and falls forward when he tries to plant his weight on his mutilated leg. Connor looks down; Grisman's leg is blown off halfway up his thigh.

"It's gone! My leg!" Connor traces the lines of the missing leg.

Hocks can only watch as his best friend fights for his life, stuck inside his own mind. He crouches, a rustling sound surrounding them. Not another cat—they don't hunt in groups. A howl sends his hair on end and he shuffles closer to Connor.

"For the love of God, man, quiet." He begs his eyes to adjust to the night. Hocks pulls his rifle to the ready while Connor pushes himself to sit up against the rocks.

"What's going on?" Connor winces.

"It's wolves. I can't see them. Are you with me? Really with me?" He can't make out Connor's expression.

"Where the hell else would I be?"

"Afghanistan."

Connor sucks in a breath and grits his teeth. He hates his mind for betraying what is real from the fragments of his broken memories. "I'm here. Give me my gun." He grabs his rifle, takes stock of his shredded leg, and squints his eyes. It's time to buckle down and fight. His mind needs to get on the same page.

Wolves yip and chatter around them. A dried-up bush rustles next to them and Connor lifts his gun, ready for an attack. Teeth snap and a growl sounds close.

Hocks squeezes his trigger and Connor fires at movement to his left. Every gun safety course tells you to not fire until you can see what you're firing at, but this isn't a safety course—this is their life on the line.

"How many?" Hocks shouts as Connor pulls the trigger again.

"Don't know, reloading." He nimbly fills the rifle with bullets from his ammo vest; he kept it after retiring. They lose count of how many rounds they dispense. With each shift of movement, they fire. Connor keeps his head in the present. The very real pain of his leg makes it much easier. Finally, moments of silence fill the ravine after the last echo of gunshots dissipate. They both breathe heavily, waiting for another sign of a predator.

"I think they're gone." Hocks lowers his rifle. The moon crests over the peaks of the cliffs now, shining a light on the war zone the guys stand in.

Connor uses the stock of his rifle to push himself up. One lonely carcass lies on the ground, while barks and yips fade into the distance.

"We have to get back to the horses. Hurry." Hocks urges Connor up as they continue on. They stagger over the lifeless body.

Chapter Twenty-One

"ARE YOU ALL RIGHT?" Hocks asks. Connor knows the root of his question.

"I was back there. Taliban ambushed my troop. We lost twenty-two men that day. It was my call to stay and fight; we didn't stand a chance if we tried to run. Twenty-two men who took my order, followed my lead, dead."

Hocks stays silent.

"Grisman bled out—his leg had been blown off in the blast. Couple others got shot, nonfatal, but it was a massacre."

"You did the best you could. Nobody blames you and you can't keep blaming yourself."

Connor's foot slips on some rocks and Hocks tightens his grip around him. Sweat runs down Connor's back from the pain and the memories.

"Yeah," he responds somberly. They walk in darkness until the moon crests in the sky, then falls again over the cliffs. Connor's adrenaline fades and the gut-wrenching reality of their situation sets in. He can't feel his leg from the knee down and stumbles every other step.

"I have to sit down, just for a minute." Hocks lowers Connor and assesses his leg. The blood flow has stopped, but he knows it's the tourniquet keeping it that way. "How close are we?" Connor grits his teeth and forces a deep breath, trying to shove the pain to the back of his mind.

"Not much farther."

"You're a shit liar." Connor coughs.

The squeals of horses shoot through the night. Connor urgently pushes himself up. That isn't the normal chatter of neighing horses—those are cries for help, cries of pain. Hocks helps him half jog to where the ravine spills out back into the field. Minutes feel like hours. The horse's continual screams cut through the two men's chests. A howl joins the chorus and the hair on Connor's arm stands on end. His blood turns cold as the horses and wolves sing a ballad of death.

"No!" Connor screams. He tries to run to close the distance faster, but he falls forward and catches himself on the rocks. Hocks lifts him and they rush to the edge of the cliff. Wolves circle Ruger, who's striking and kicking at the canines that nip at his legs.

Hocks hands Connor his rifle. Gunfire sounds; the wolves flinch and turn their attention to the two men. Hocks drops one and the other wolves scurry around it. Connor squeezes the trigger, and another drops with a yelp. The remaining wolves retreat, Connor continuing to fire at them, hoping to kill more.

Ruger prances frantically and Hocks rushes to soothe him and check his injuries. Connor's eyes find Brimstone.

Shallow breaths expand her stomach as she lays covered in blood on the ground. Tears prick his eyes, and his vision blurs. He tries to blink them away as he pushes himself up and hobbles next to her head. Blood flows from the puncture wounds in her neck and her breath gurgles as blood aspirates her lungs.

Connor lifts her head into his lap and his tears splash on her cheek. He rubs a hand down her neck. "You're going to be okay. I'm going to make it better," He coos, but he knows, without a shadow of a doubt, her wounds are fatal. The whites of her eyes show just how much pain she is in. When Connor shifts his body, she lifts her head and tries to stand. He coaxes her head back down. "I'm going to take away the pain. You are such a good girl, Brim. You did a great job. You always did such a great job. I won't be able to find another as good as you in this lifetime."

His voice quivers, and he covers his mouth with the back of his hand as he sobs out. His heart is breaking in a way he never expected. To lose her is like losing part of himself. His teammate, his partner. He trusted her, and she trusted him. Now he has to do what needs to be done.

Hocks places a hand on Connor's shoulder and hands him the pistol from his holster. It feels so heavy and final in his hand. His palm wraps around the grip. Brimstone lets out a soft nicker, her breathing more labored now. Connor sets the barrel of the pistol against her temple. Tears flow freely down his cheeks and he wipes his face with his forearm.

"I'm sorry." He says it to her and Marni. Gunpowder ignites and the echo of that final shot seems to last for eternity. Connor rests his forehead on her shoulder, his tears mixing with her blood, and he cries out.

"When the memories were too much, we'd ride for hours until my head cleared. She knew all of my secrets. She took care of Marni years ago and—oh my god. Marni. This will kill her." Hocks crouches down next to him.

"We can't stay here. The wolves could come back." Hocks grips his friend's shoulder in solace.

"I'm not leaving her here for them to come back and finish what they started," Connor defends while stroking Brimstone's mane.

"Fine, I'll ride just far enough to call for help, then I'm coming right back. You better still be here and breathing. Clear?" Hocks' words come out harsher than intended, but fear tightens his chest. He doesn't want to leave Connor behind, but he knows he won't budge on this. He hands Connor his rifle and remaining ammo.

"If they come back, give 'em hell," he says through gritted teeth. He swings up on Ruger, the leather saddle squeaking under his weight. "I will be *right* back," he enforces before picking Ruger up into a gallop.

***

"THAT WAS NICE. SEE? We can be friends," Parker brags as he walks Marni to her apartment. She checks her phone again like she had throughout the night and sends another text to Connor. "Right?" Parker interrupts.

"I'm sorry. What were you saying?" Her far-off gaze lands on him and jealousy rises. It's clear she hasn't been listening or even thinking about him the whole night. They've nearly reached her door, and he is running out of time.

"Is something wrong?" Parker reaches a hand out and brushes it against Marni's forearm down to her hand. Her brows furrow and she looks down at her phone, helplessly.

"I think I've messed up. I'm sorry. I have to go." At that moment, she turns away from her apartment towards her car—to the ranch, to home. To Connor.

In a move so swift, Parker grips her hand and pulls her back in. He cups the back of her neck and presses his lips to hers. Not gently, not a question of if it's okay. He is taking what he wants, and it enrages Marni.

She shoves him back with both hands before raising her hand. Unlike Stacy's, Marni's is a fist, and she swings up, catching Parker square in the nose. Blood pours almost immediately from the impact. He grabs his nose to stop it from throbbing in pain. Marni doesn't wait around for him to recover. She slips out of her heels and races down the hallway, passing the elevators to the stairwell.

A stabbing pain grows through her hand and she cradles it to her chest. Once she reaches her car, she locks the door and sits inside. She calls Connor again, pleading that this time he will answer. Fear sinks its talons in her and she shakes with it when, once again, she is met with the same message. Until now, she didn't want to seem like the needy girlfriend who calls her boyfriend's sister, but she can't wait any longer.

"T?" she chokes through a sob.

"Marni, it's okay. They'll find him." Her head spins.

"W-what?"

"They are out riding right now looking for him and Hocks. I'm sure he is okay. With no cell service out there, they probably just decided to camp for the night." Marni wipes snot and tears from her face. She starts her car and pulls out of the garage.

"I don't know what you're talking about."

"Wait, why are you crying then? What happened?" Marni signals her blinker and turns on to the main road before answering.

"Parker kissed me. I punched him, but I'm pretty sure my hand is broken."

"How the hell did that happen? Where are you? Why were you with him?!" Marni squeezes her eyes shut and resists the urge to scream out at her own stupidity. She had once again let him manipulate her into getting what he wanted.

"He took me out for dinner to apologize. Then he kissed me, forcefully. I left Connor a message to let him know and now he won't talk to me. I screwed up, T." Tonya lets out a deep sigh through the phone.

"Connor and Hocks left this afternoon to help hunt a rogue mountain lion at Callahan's ranch. They were supposed to meet back up at dusk, but they haven't come back. Cell service sucks out there and we can't get a hold of them. But like I said, I'm sure they're fine. They're both resourceful and they have their guns and horses. The other two hunting parties are still out looking for them. Mom and Pops refuse to let me help in the search."

Marni's head spins. She didn't even know where Connor was. That's why his phone wasn't working.

"Okay, I'm headed back now."

"Are you sure you're okay to drive all night? You won't get here until the morning."

"I can't stay here. I certainly won't be able to sleep with Connor missing. If I get tired, I'll pull over. I promise."

"All right. So, how did the meeting go?"

Marni tells Tonya about the meeting, her raise, and the fact she is moving for sure.

"That's great!" Tonya celebrates. "I'm pretty sure Ginger is starting to like me. She let me pet her a couple of times." Marni didn't want to haul her back to the city for the overnight trip and Tonya offered to watch her.

Tonya doesn't hear Marni's response when she pulls the phone from her ear.

"Marni, hold on for a second. I have another call. It might be the guys." She clicks over before Marni can say anything.

"Hello?" Tonya answers.

"T, it's Hocks. I've already called 911, but I need you to get to Callahan's place. A lion attacked Connor and they're going to fly him to the hospital, but Brimstone..." His voice breaks and he clears his throat. "Wolves got her, and he refuses to leave her side. He wants to bring her home and bury her on the ranch. Can you drive the rollback out here? I'm leaving a marker for you." Hocks' words sound so far away. Tonya isn't one to let her emotions take over, but her stomach twists and her lip begins to quiver.

"How bad?" Tears prick at her eyes.

"I'm not sure. It got his left leg and wolves have been attacking and retreating since. The EMTs are tracking my phone, so I need to ride back so the helicopter can find us. Have Paul show you where the most recent kill site is, then drive south toward the mountains. There will be a split between the cliffs; that's where you'll find me. I'll see you soon." He disconnects the call. Before she can ground herself, the line flips back to Marni, who is singing along to the radio.

"Hey, you're back." Tonya forces a smile and stuffs down her fear as she grabs her keys and slides her boots on.

"Um, yeah, some guy trying to sell me car insurance." Marni is already distraught about Parker. She doesn't want to add Connor to the list. Especially not when she has six hours ahead of her.

"At midnight? Those telemarketers have no class," she jokes and Tonya chokes on a chuckle.

"Yeah. Hey, I'm going to get some sleep. If you get tired, call me. Don't push yourself too hard and wreck."

"Oh, okay. I'll see you soon."

Tonya fires up the rollback and races down the driveway, passing her parent's house. Her dad staggers down the steps with his jacket half off, hopping in one boot. He holds a hand out to flag Tonya to a stop.

He slides into the passenger seat and doesn't say anything as the old truck roars in protest at Tonya's quick acceleration.

***

THE HELICOPTER BLADES WHIRL overhead and Connor leans over Brimstone to shield his eyes from the dust. Hocks gestures for the EMTs to follow him. They lay Connor on a stretcher and place straps across his body.

"What about Brimstone?" Connor shouts to Hocks over the roaring blades.

"Tonya's bringing the rollback and we're taking her home. She's on her way now."

"Marni?" Hocks had tried to call her from Connor's phone, but it went straight to voicemail. He shakes his head and Connor's face falls. He'd be sure to ask Tonya about that when she got here.

Ruger stands next to Hocks as he settles beside Brimstone. He slides her bridle off and unbuckles her saddle. He holds both rifles close, peering into the darkness, not risking the wolves getting to him if they come back. The agonizing pain he saw etched on Connor's face will haunt him for months to come. The way his face contorted from the flashbacks of Afghanistan...he'd never seen his best friend in such a raw state.

***

TONYA REACHES THE KILL site and turns the wheel so she is heading south toward the mountains. The helicopter flew overhead while they were on the highway and she knew it was Connor. Paul didn't say much when she picked him up, and her dad still hasn't said a word. Eerie silence fills the cab, and she feels like she is suffocating on the what-ifs and unknowns.

They bump over the rocky terrain, the roughness of it forcing her to go much slower than she wants to. If she can just read Hocks' face, get a feel for how bad Connor really is, then maybe she will be able to breathe again.

Jack places a hand on Tonya's free arm. A twinge of selfishness hits her. She is worried about her brother, while her parents are worried about their only son. She offers her dad a comforting smile and looks back as her headlights shine across two horses. One standing, fully tacked, the other lying on the ground. Hocks pushes himself up from the dirt, raising one arm to shield his eyes from the headlights.

"Dear God," Jack murmurs.

Tonya throws the truck in park and leaps to the ground. She doesn't stop running until she can make out the shadows on Hocks' face. Exhaustion makes his eyes heavy, but she doesn't see any grievance underneath. Connor will be okay. She wraps her arms around her brother's lifelong best friend. He folds into her, letting her be his strength for a time.

"You're...okay?" she asks into his chest. He swallows the lump in his throat and eases back as Jack approaches.

"I'm okay. Here." He hands over a bridle. Realization dons on her and she places her hand over her mouth. Her heart slams into her chest at the sight of Brimstone, bloodied and lifeless. Her hands shake and tears roll down her cheeks.

"Wh—what did this?" Jack stammers. Tonya crouches next to her and rubs her hand down Brimstone's cold neck.

"Wolves. We followed the lion tracks through there," Hocks gestures toward the path. "And then we were jumped by a pack. They must have found them tied. We left them vulnerable...We hadn't seen any signs of wolves. I'm so sorry." He kneels next to Tonya and Jack clasps a hand on his shoulder.

Tonya's red eyes break his heart as they look up at him. "Ruger? Is he okay?" She stands and walks over to Hocks' gelding. She rubs down his neck and body. There's blood on his front right leg.

"It's not deep. He fought them off well. Landed some solid blows." Tonya eyes the two dead wolves laying in the shadows. Hocks had moved them before they arrived, hoping to ease the unsettled feeling gnawing at him.

Paul pulls the winch from the rollback and stands respectfully until Jack gives him the go-ahead. The winch whines as it drags Brimstone's body across the ground and up the metal bed. A trail of smeared blood is all that is left on the rocky ground.

Tonya has flashes of her chasing after Marni on Brimstone during their roping days. Her chest tightens, and she chokes out a sob. Marni was the only one who could control her outburst at the gate until Connor came back from the war. It was like she chose him as her person. Nobody, not even her, could make sense of it.

She turns and squeezes her eyes shut. She will not break down, not yet. Not in front of her dad and Hocks. A hand rubs her back, and she jerks to see Hocks' deep green eyes settling on hers.

"He's going to be okay," Tonya states, not questioning it. She can see it in Hocks' face.

"He's going to be okay," he confirms. Her stiff shoulders slump forward and her knees wobble. "Not here," Hocks murmurs as he steadies her against his body.

The whining of the winch stops and the bed lowers back down. The finality of metal slamming into metal echoes around them. Tonya disassociates from her emotions and lifts her brother's saddle from the ground, and sets it on the bed of the truck.

She grabs Ruger's reins and hoists herself onto the bed. Hocks follows her.

"I'll drive," Paul offers. Jack slides back into the passenger seat.

"Go slow for Ruger!" Tonya shouts as he fires up the engine. She clucks once at Ruger, and he picks up a walk, occasionally switching to a trot to match the speed of the truck. The ride is rough and Paul bumps over a rock that slides her sideways. Hocks wraps a hand around Tonya's waist and pulls her closer to him than he meant to.

"Sorry," he mumbles. Tonya shrugs it off. She doesn't put any space between them and he doesn't shrink back. It's then she sees the blood soaked into his shirt and pants.

"Is that...?" She points at the stains.

"Yeah, I had to basically drag him back."

"I know about the episodes. How bad did it get?"

Hocks sighs and rubs his other hand on his pant leg. "He got lost pretty bad. He told me about his troop being blown up and he was yelling, like he was back there. It was terrifying to watch. I couldn't bring him back." His fingers absentmindedly rub her hip as he tells her all of this. "Tonya, where is Marni? Connor kept calling and nothing. I even tried before I called you and it went straight to voicemail. She hasn't even texted him today. He's torn up over it, but you know him. Bottles everything up until he explodes."

"What do you mean? I was talking to her when you called and she said she couldn't get a hold of him. She called crying because..." Her voice trails off and deep in her gut, she knows Parker has something to do with this. Some way, somehow, that slippery serpent is behind it.

"Crying?"

"Her douche-bag co-worker kissed her, and she punched him. She was crying because she's worried she screwed up whatever is between her and Connor. It's all very confusing." Hocks recalls Connor complaining about a guy that came to the farm that works with her.

"Did you tell her anything?"

"No, she's driving. I don't want her to wreck trying to get here faster. She can hate me for it, but she'll forgive me once she sees he'll be fine." Tonya lays her head on Hocks' shoulder. He stiffens but decides to roll with it. He rests his head atop hers. The bumpy terrain keeps him from nodding off like his body wishes he would.

Chapter Twenty-Two

PAUL PULLS THE ROLLBACK up to Callahan's barn. Mitch and his other farm hands stand by anxiously.

"Jack, I am so sorry. If I'd known—" Mitch starts, but Jack holds up his hand.

"There is no blame expect the predators of the west. Would you mind stabling Ruger here tonight? I need to get Stacy and Tonya to the hospital."

"Of course. I'll have Paul and Luke take Brimstone over along with the backhoe and dig her a final resting place. If you and Stacy need anything, don't hesitate to call."

Hocks unhooks his trailer and the three of them get into his truck. He steals glances at Tonya through the rearview mirror and quickly looks away when she catches him.

She doesn't ignore the heat that rushes over her from his attention. He is extremely attractive, and she has always had a crush on him since they were young, but she was Connor's *little sister* and could never get a second glance from him.

Stacy is waiting on the porch with her purse as they pull up. She appears to have aged ten years since breakfast.

"He's okay, just banged up. Hocks saved his life." Tonya strokes her hair while they hug.

"Thank you, Hocks. Thank you." Stacy's vision blurs with tears. She slides up next to Tonya in the back seat and Hocks turns back down the driveway.

"He's okay, Stace. Our boy is okay," Jack reassures her with a smile. Tonya's phone rings and Marni's name appears on the screen.

"Everyone, quiet." She hits accept once all is silent. "Hello?"

"Hey, I hope I didn't wake you. I was getting sleepy."

"No, you didn't. How close are you?" Tonya looks at the clock on the front of the truck. It is getting close to six, and the sun will be up soon.

"I'm roughly an hour and a half away. I might have to go to the ER after I get there. I can't close my hand anymore. I swear, if I'm permanently crippled from Parker's bloodied nose, I'll be pissed."

"You broke his nose?" Tonya laughs.

"I'm not sure if it was broken, but blood started gushing out of it instantly. I slipped out of my heels and ran."

Tonya looks at her mom, who is watching her curiously. Right, she has to tell Marni about Connor.

"Mar, I need to tell you something and I need you to promise not to freak out and wreck or anything."

"What happened to him?" Marni's gut instincts tell her it's about Connor.

"He is fine. He was air-lifted to the hospital. He and Hocks found the lion, and it attacked Connor before they shot it. It's just his leg. We are on our way now. Can you meet us there?" There is silence from Marni's end. Tonya pulls her phone from her ear to make sure it's still connected.

"T, you swear he's fine?"

"Hocks assured me his life isn't in danger. I don't have much more information, but you can get your hand looked at, too."

"I'll be there in thirty minutes." She disconnects before Tonya can remind her she promised not to freak out.

"You didn't tell her about Brimstone," Stacy whispers.

"I don't know how," Tonya admits.

***

MARNI STOMPS THE GAS pedal to the floorboard and her tiny economy car revs like a leaf blower.

"I'm so stupid! I was having dinner with Parker! He was lost in the mountains and getting eaten by lions!" Tears stream down her face. She doesn't fight them. She blinks them free so she can focus on the next car to swerve around.

Anger swells inside of her. She targets it all at Parker, but in reality, she is angry at herself. She let Parker walk all over her again. She put herself in that position so he could make another move, and now her hand hurts so damn much she can't grip the steering wheel. Vivid images of Connor lying cold, bleeding out, haunt her vision. Her chest tightens, and she prays to God that he is okay.

Honks drone like it's her battle cry as she narrowly fits through two trucks, barely escaping a collision. Her heart drums at the close proximity and she forces her hand on the wheel to stop trembling and eases off the gas just a tad. She checks her phone for the fifth time since she hung up with Tonya. Waiting for some kind of update. In a ditch effort, she tries calling Connor's phone again. Nothing.

"I'm so sorry!" she sobs out to the crowded highway. "Please, please be okay. Please." Images of what could be between them crawl into her mind. Riding side by side through the pastures, her on the back of Brimstone riding down the aisle and Jack giving her away on his own mount. Getting tangled under the sheets of their king-size bed in his cabin, the smell of cedar and gun oil clinging to her for eternity.

She clings to the happy maybes as she takes the exit off the interstate to the hospital where her future either ends or begins. Tonya said he was fine, but she could've just said that, so she'd drive smarter. She buckles down her emotions and prepares for the worst. By the time she reaches the hospital entrance, she only then realizes she is still barefoot.

"Shit," she mutters, but she isn't turning back now to go buy a pair of shoes. She gets wild looks, with her mascara smeared across her checks, her eyes puffy and red, and her bare feet shuffling along the cold tiled floor. The lady at the desk wears a bored expression and lazily lifts her eyes to give Marni a once-over.

"Name and emergency?" she asks in a monotone voice.

"His name is Connor Curston. He was bitten by a lion. I'm family," she adds hastily as the woman opens her mouth. She clicks something on her computer then pushes a buzzer, opening the wide double doors. The smell of disinfectants and death flow out.

"Room six," she mumbles, barely catching Marni before she rushes through the doors. She darts her head left and right, checking each room just in case the lady at the desk had it wrong. The door to room six is cracked, and it's dark inside. Rhythmic beeping sounds from the room.

She pulls in as deep of a breath as she can muster and tries to smear away the ruined makeup. Taming the stray hair from her face, she peeks inside and sees Connor asleep. His left leg is bandaged from his knee to his foot. An IV is hooked to his left arm, and he wears a hospital gown that catches him mid-thigh. His hair has the impression of his missing cowboy hat, and small cuts and bruises litter his arms.

Marni claims the empty chair next to him and hugs his hat to her chest. Nothing beeps frantically on the monitors, so that has to be a good sign. She watches the rise and fall of his chest.

He's alive. He is alive; she repeats in her head.

Her phone chimes with a text from Tonya.

We went for a coffee run and breakfast. Text when you're close and we will meet you.

I'm here. He's sleeping right now. I'll just wait until he wakes up, Marni responds.

If you want me to bring you something, let me know.

Marni tucks her phone back in her pocket and a new wave of relieved tears stream down her face. *He's going to be okay.* Will he still want her after what she did? She can't resist the urge to reach up and brush his cheek with the back of her palm.

He stirs from her touch and shoots up from the bed, whipping his head around wildly. The whites of his eyes grow until they land on Marni. Realization hits and he shifts his gaze to his bandaged leg and the IV in his arm. He relaxes back to the bed and sucks in deep breaths.

"S-sorry," Marni stutters quietly.

"No, you're fine. I just forgot where I was. What are you doing here?" He eyes her holding his hat like her life depends on it. Parker's voice comes back to him. "*Why* are you here?"

Her mouth opens, then shuts at his tone. He doesn't want her here. That much is clear from his voice. "I'm sorry, I'll go." Tears well up in her eyes and the sight hurts Connor more than his leg ever could. She places his hat back on the seat and stands.

"No, wait." He lets out a huff. Marni stops and turns to look at him. She cradles her bruised and swollen hand. Connor sees it for the first time. He shoots back up in the bed and props himself on one hand. "What happened?" His eyes fill with worry. He looks her over for other injuries but doesn't see any. Had Parker done the same thing to her as her ex?

"It's nothing. You are in way worse shape. Are you okay?"

"I'm fine. Now tell me what happened," he repeats with more vindication. When she doesn't answer, he pushes again. "Was it Parker?" His name raises bile in the back of his throat.

"Why would you think that? I mean, I punched him, but why would you jump to that conclusion?"

"You punched him and broke your hand?" Connor repeats, making sure he doesn't have some kind of brain damage and he heard her wrong.

"He kissed me. I think I broke his nose." She looks down at the floor like she is waiting to be scolded.

"He answered your phone. I called to let you know what I was doing. He said..." Connor pinches his nose between his eyes. "He said you were at his place, doing...you know." Marni's face contorts from white and meek to red and full of rage.

"That bastard! He stole my phone the whole fucking time!" She throws her purse to the floor and paces like she really wishes Parker's face would appear so she could punch it again.

"What are you talking about? Stop pacing, you're making me dizzy." Connor tries to sit up, but the bandages prevent him from moving.

"I thought I lost my phone and after looking for over an hour, he magically found it where I know I didn't leave it. I left it in my office during my meeting. He must have gone in there and took it. And I went and ate with the fucking asshole!" A nurse rushes in to see Marni flailing her arms around.

"Um, miss, are you all right?"

"Fucking fantastic!" Marni shouts through gritted teeth.

"She's fine. Sorry, we'll keep it down." Connor encourages the nurse to leave. She finally takes the hint and actually closes the door this time.

"I'm so sorry, Connor. I didn't know. If I had, I certainly wouldn't have gone to eat with him." Her head falls into her hands and then she winces as the pain shoots through her mangled one.

"Come here." He gestures her over. She slides up next to him and lays her head on his chest. He brushes her bare arm and kisses her forehead.

"I was so scared," she whispers and warm tears wet his chest.

"I'm okay. Just a scratch." She nuzzles closer to him and he notices her bare feet on the bed. "What happened to your shoes?" She chokes out a laugh.

"When I saw blood pouring from his nose, I couldn't exactly run in heels, so I left them."

A chuckle rumbles inside his chest and he kisses her again. He inspects her hand and pushes the nurse call button.

"Are you in pain?" Marni leans up.

"No, but you are getting that hand looked at." Marni sits up and shimmies her skirt back down her legs.

"Connor, what happened out there?"

"War can screw you up more mentally than physically. I was back in Afghanistan. I froze, and it cost me. Then, when we were coming back to the horses, wolves flanked us. We scared them off, but they found the horses." His throat tightens and his words lodge in his throat. Marni's brown eyes widen as she makes assumptions.

"Ruger got free; he fought them off until we got there." Connor sniffs as tears run down his cheeks. "Brimstone—she—by the time we got there, she was in bad shape. There was so much blood." He chokes on a sob and bites his bottom lip, trying to keep his composure. More tears fill Marni's eyes—the horse she trained and competed with, that got her pro qualified, that had listened to every sob story over a guy and ran away with Marni's worries across the ranch. "I'm so sorry, Marni. I couldn't save her."

Marni wraps her arms around him and leans into his chest. Their world falls apart together, both grieving for the love of a horse that saved them from themselves.

"It's not your fault." Marni is surprised her voice comes out steady. "None of it is your fault." The door cracks open and the nurse pokes her head in. Connor doesn't hear it and Marni holds up a finger to ask for another moment. He leans back, his Persian blue eyes that she loves to drown in, holding her gaze.

"I love you," Connor whispers. She's not even sure she heard him. She shifts her gaze between his eyes.

"You do?" she whispers back. His eyebrows shoot up, astounded.

"Of course I do. This isn't just me testing the waters. I've known for a long time." Marni's muscles melt into him.

"I love you." She brushes her lips against his. He tightens his hold around her waist. Happiness courses through him when she speaks those words.

"You are coming to stay with me as soon as we break out of this place, got it?" His demanding voice tickles Marni into a giggling fit.

"Whatever you say."

The nurse pokes her head in again and Connor spots her.

"She needs her hand looked at. She punched an asshole and broke his nose." A wide grin spreads on Connor's face, one full of pride. The nurse hesitates for a beat, then approaches Marni and asks to look at her hand.

***

CONNOR LIMPS TOWARD THE freshly covered grave under the pine tree at the back of the ranch. He let himself break on Marni before. Today, he looks down somberly and places a handful of yellow and purple wildflowers and his cowboy hat on Brimstone's grave.

"You were one of the good ones. Run free now." He sniffs back the tears that burn his eyes and backs away so Marni can take her moment to pay her respects. She holds a belt buckle in her hands as she walks forward. Tears flow freely down her face. She drops to her knees in the fresh dirt.

"I never got to take a ride on you since I came back." Her throat tightens, and she tries to swallow the lump that forms. "You really were the best horse a girl could ever ask for." She places the belt buckle on top of the wild flowers and rests her hand there. "I'll take care of him now. Thank you for everything you've done over the years. You won't be forgotten. Run wide open until we meet again."

She pushes herself up and backs into Connor's chest. His arms harness her and he kisses the top of her head. The river babbles nearby and birds sing a somber melody. They walk back over to Turbo and Clover, a dun mare who has more whoa than go. They swing their legs over and ride side by side at a walk back to the ranch.

Tonya spots the two of them from the front of the barn and leans into Hocks. She bounces with excitement on the balls of her feet.

"If you don't stop, you're going to give it away." Hocks nuzzles her ear and takes her hand to try and still her.

"I can't help it. I've been dying to show them both!" He gives her a quick kiss on the cheek and smiles down at her. "What was that for?" They were both still new to this whole thing. Hocks and Tonya grew up together just as much as him and Connor. The timing was just never right, until now.

"Because you're adorable, bouncing around all giddy." He kisses her again.

"I am not adorable. That will *never* suffice. That is an insult to women everywhere." She scoffs and folds her arms.

"You're sexy as hell when you pout. Is that better?" He tickles her ribcage and she giggles. Marni exits the barn when Lucas takes Clover and gawks at the sight of Tonya and Hocks on the porch.

"Connor?" Marni nods toward the pair of them. "When did that happen?"

"I didn't know it did, but I'm not mad about it. It took them longer than us and that's saying something." He beams at Marni and steals a deep kiss that pulls Marni to her tiptoes.

"Hey!" They pull apart and turn to look at Tonya running to them. She hugs her brother first, then squeezes Marni tightly to her before pulling back to look at her braced hand.

"Sorry, I forgot. How does it feel?"

"Not bad. I must have strong bones since it's not broken." She chuckles. A pretty bad sprain, but that was all.

"Okay, well, we have something we want to show you!" She grabs Marni's good hand and pulls her toward the barn. The men fall behind Tonya's brisk walk.

"When did that 'we' thing happen?" Marni raises her eyebrows.

"I guess the night Connor got hurt." She tries to recover when Marni makes a face. "Not like that! When we left the hospital, he brought us home and Mom offered to let him stay in the guest room. He had been awake for like forty-eight hours. He texted me the next night, asked if I could talk. He couldn't sleep, kept having nightmares of the shit him and Connor went through. We both needed to feel something besides the stress of it all, so we...you know. Fucked."

Marni's eyebrows shoot up and she lets out a slow whistle. "And?"

"And it was amazing. Like romance novel amazing. We haven't really labeled anything or even talked about what it all means. We are just in a fog of bliss, I guess. I really like him." Her cheeks blush and Marni knows this is the real deal. Nobody gets under Tonya's skin, ever.

"Where are you taking me?" Marni asks when Tonya stops at the tack room and pulls out a blindfold to tie around Marni's eyes.

"It's a surprise," she says. Connor laughs behind her.

"Why isn't he blindfolded?"

"Because it's not my surprise."

Connor's lips suddenly brush hers, and her skin tingles as he moves his lips to her ear.

"This might just have to come back to our bed with us." The space between her thighs throbs at his husky voice. Tonya grabs her hand and drags her forward, away from Connor's sexy talk.

"Not in front of me." Tonya feigns a gagging sound.

"T, slow down! I'm going to fall!"

Orion whinnies close by and Tonya pulls Marni to a stop.

"Well, I'll be damned." Connor gasps next to Marni.

"What? What is it?!" Tonya tugs Marni's blindfold free and she blinks, adjusting her eyes to the bright sun.

"I—wh—how?" Marni can't believe her eyes. Lucas is sitting in a saddle. On Orion's back. His head is lowered in a relaxed stance.

"You did all the hard work. He did go through four ranch hands before he quit bucking." Lucas swings down and leads Orion to the gate of the corral. He hands the reins over to Marni.

"You got it in ya?" Connor slides his hands in his pockets and nods toward the pastures. Marni places her palm on Orion's blaze. He licks his lips and pushes into her.

"Hey, pretty boy, what do you say? Wanna run?" Horse hooves clop and she turns to see three other horses tacked. Hocks, Tonya, and Connor all mount up and look to Marni expectantly. Her saddle squeaks as she swings her leg over. Orion's power thrums beneath her.

"Think you guys can keep up?" She can't contain the giddy, light-as-air

through her.

"Let's make it a bet. You win, you move in with me. I win, you move in with me." Connor winks from the back of his chestnut mare. Marni's heart flutters and her cheeks warm.

"I like those odds."

The four of them line up and Lucas stands with the blindfold Marni was just wearing, waving it in the air. Orion pulls on the bit—he's ready to fly.

"On your mark..." They all gather their reins. "Get set..." Marni squeezes her legs against the saddle. "Race!" Orion launches off from his hind-quarters, and thundering hooves stampede across the grassy field.

Connor is on Marni's left, Tonya and Hocks on her right. Orion pulls on the reins to go faster, his wild heart wanting to truly run. In that moment, all she can hear is the four-beat drum of his hooves. She drapes the reins across his neck and he stretches it out, reaching farther.

Marni opens her arms wide and in ecstasy as she and Orion take the lead. Her fully trusting him, and he fully trusting her.

Bonus Chapter - Tattered Heartstrings

TONYA NEARLY COLLAPSES AS she falls to her bed. Tears leak from the corners of her eyes.

He's safe. He's alive. He's okay.

It's been two days since the accident, but her body is still coiled up for a fight. Connor is stable in the hospital. Marni is with him. Thank God her hand isn't broken, or she'd be driving to hunt down that sick psychotic Parker tonight instead of trying to breathe. Her phone lights up and Chester's name dances across the screen. She knows if she doesn't answer, he'll just keep calling or worse—show up.

"What?" she snaps.

"I just heard. Are you okay?"

"Shouldn't you be asking if Connor is okay? He's the one who was attacked. Not me." Tonya pries her boots off with her toes and they fall to the floor with a thud.

Chester sighs on the other end. Tonya checks the time. *Why does he always call so damn late? Better yet, why do I always answer?*

"Is he okay?" Chester finally asks. Tonya's mind reels back to the site of Brimstone and Hocks standing there like he'd seen a ghost. He held her the whole ride back to Callahan's ranch. His deep green eyes, so full of concern, an emotion she hadn't seen him hold before. Fear? He'd dropped her and her parents off a couple of hours ago. Part of her wished he'd asked to stay, but that's how it's always been with her and Hocks. The moment she shows interest or returns his coveted flirting, he runs away.

"Tonya?" Chester questions and she blinks away the memory.

"He's going to be fine. Cougar nearly took off his leg."

"I heard his horse didn't make it. I'm sorry." Tonya huffs and sits up. That horse was more to him than people will ever realize. Tonya saw it when he came home. She saw the ghosts in his eyes, heard his screams at the images in his head. The first time she found him reenacting what could only have been a horrible experience, he was hiding behind his porch railing, clutching an empty pistol, claiming *they* were coming for him.

She sat there all night until the sun came up and Connor woke. He made her swear she wouldn't tell her parents, and she didn't. Tonya shouldered his burden and eventually convinced him to ride with her and she watched the way Brimstone seemed to chase the monsters away for him. Eventually, when things got bad, he'd saddle up and be gone for hours, but she never had to worry because Brimstone had him.

"Clearly you're not okay. I'm coming over." Chester interrupts her thoughts again.

"Look I'm fine. Just tired. It's been a long night."

"It's been almost five years," Chester's voice gets thick with emotion.

"Yeah, I know." Tonya's throat tightens, and she shakes away the unwarranted push of pain. She can't take on more, not tonight. "Goodnight, Chester." She hangs up before he can protest and peels out of her clothes. Her skin feels too tight around her body, her chest feels too heavy.

"No, please, not tonight." Tonya rushes to the fridge and bypasses the wine and lonely beer. She grabs a fifth of bourbon and pops the lid off and chugs several gulps. The burn lightens the weight in her chest and her limbs warm as the liquid spreads. Her ring tone cuts through the silence and she glances at it curiously. She designates everyone close to her a specific song to know if she should answer, mainly to know when it's Chester and she can ignore it.

She picks up her phone and Hocks' name appears on the screen.

"Hello?" she whispers.

Silence.

"Hocks? Are you okay?" Tonya sets on the edge of her bed and cradles the bourbon between her thighs. Hocks' heavy breathing comes from the other end. Could the hospital had called him first, did something happen? "Is it Connor, is he—"

"He's fine. I'm sorry—I—I shouldn't have called. I just..."

Tonya holds tightly to the phone. *Just come back,* she silently pleas. She could use the distraction and has been fantasizing about having Hocks in her bed for years.

"Do you want to talk?" she asks.

"I don't know. I went home, but everything hit me and I can't—I don't want to drink alone. I usually drink with Connor, but ya know."

What demons is he running from?

"You can come here," Tonya offers and holds her breath for his answer.

"Your parents—"

"Turn your headlights off. They'll never know. Connor does it all the time." Only a partial lie, yes Connor does it all the time, but Stacy always knows.

"Okay, I'm not far. I'll be there soon."

"I should probably get dressed. I was fixing to take a shower with my good friend Jim Beam."

Hocks grips the steering wheel and drops the phone to his lap. He's watched Tonya grow up as his best friend's little sister, but damn, he's also noticed how she *grew* up. She's not a little kid, and he's damn near tired of running from how he feels about her. He takes a deep breath of courage and lays it all out there.

"I'm better company than Jim Beam, or maybe you like to have two men take care of you?" He internally rolls his eyes at the sound of that line. The longer he waits for a response, he wonders if he read the night at the fair all wrong. Like always, he flirted with her and got close, but normally when he left, he'd feel guilty for looking at Little T that way. Maybe it's because Connor has Marni now and he didn't let the fact that she is his little sister's best friend.

"Hurry up, stud," Tonya whispers and Hocks presses the gas pedal harder.

Tonya shoves her clothes and random items in the cabin under her bed, in her closet, in the storage under the stairs. What remains is a slightly looking together cabin. She had stripped off her bra and panties at one point, but her nerves got the best of her and she slipped into an over-sized T-shirt that landed right below her ass cheeks.

The sound of tires on gravel crunches outside and Tonya's breath hitches at a truck door closing. Her hand hovers over the doorknob and she waits for the knock.

Hocks stares at the porch steps. Once he crosses this line, there is no going back. He isn't dumb enough to not know what is going to happen tonight. He places his palms onto the hood of his truck and leans into them.

Fuck, why is this so hard? He knows what *he* wants. But if any of this goes south, things will be awkward as hell. But Connor took the chance. Can't he do the same? Isn't T worth the chance? Of course she is.

He places one foot on the step, then the next.

Tonya has one palm flat against the door. Her chest heaves from anticipation. *Come on,* she begs. She will not open that door until he knocks. He's here, this is his move.

Hocks presses one palm to the door and leans his forehead on the wood grain.

"T?" he says into the night.

"Hocks?"

A smile forms on Hocks' lips and he wants with every fiber in him to rush through that door and wrap her in his arms.

"Are you sure?" He doesn't have to explain what he is asking.

"Yes," Tonya says without hesitation. The door knob turns and she pulls the door open. Hocks stand with his hands braced on either side of the door frame. His dark brown cowboy hat causes his vibrant green eyes to pop into the shadows. Sandy brown scruff lines his jaws and Tonya wants to run her fingers over it.

Hocks hardens at the see-through white T-shirt barely covering her. Her nipples pebble through the material and he grips the door frame harder to keep from tackling her. Neither of them move for a few moments. They study one another with new eyes filled with intent.

Tonya takes a step back and Hocks comes in. The air around them grows thick with desire and want. Each of their bodies yanking on each other.

Tonya picks up her bourbon off the table and throws it back, then offers it to Hocks. "Liquid courage?"

"I don't need that to tell me this is the right choice," Hocks says, and he slips out of his jacket and boots. Tonya had lit her oil lamps displayed throughout the cabin, shadows caused by the flickering flame dance across their features.

Tonya moves toward him and brings the bottle to her lips again, swallows, then sets it down. "Me either. It just makes everything better."

"If you need that to make sex worthwhile, you haven't been with the right man," Hocks informs her. He lifts his hand and brushes his thumb down her cheek and across her plump bottom lip. One look into her eyes and he sees the flame the bourbon kindled into a wildfire. She leans into his touch and Hocks snakes an arm around her waist. Her eyes flutter and he closes the distance between their lips. On the surface she tastes of the bourbon, but there's a honey sweet flavor underneath and he sucks on her lip, bringing it to the surface.

Tonya pushes to her toes, and he tightens his grip around her. His tongue dances with hers and she can only imagine of his skill working over her clit. Hocks raises the hem of the T-shirt and cups her ass. Desire pools between her thighs and it takes everything in her to not hike her leg around his hip and beg for more.

"I need you to know this isn't a spur-of-the-moment thing," Hocks rasps out between kisses. He moves down her neck and brings a hand up to move the shirt off her collarbone so he can nip at the tender skin. "I've wanted you for a long time."

Tonya's eyes roll back in her head with every touch from him. "Then take me," she pants and moans when he places another bite on top of her shoulder. Hocks repositions his hands under her ass and lifts her to his waist. Tonya yelps in surprise and wraps her arms around his neck. Her bare pussy rubbing against his shirt covered abdomen.

"Bed or shower?" Hocks asks when he enters her bedroom.

"Both," Tonya says with confidence and Hocks tosses her onto the bed. Her shirt rises to show she is commando, and he growls his appreciation. "Like what you see, Stud?" Tonya muses and dips a finger down her center and rubs it around her clit.

Hocks rips his shirt off and quickly works on his buckle and pants. "Hell yeah, I do."

Tonya sucks in a surprised gasp when his cock springs free. "I didn't know you were packing," she mulls and licks her lips. She rolls to all fours and crawls to where he stands at the base of the bed.

Before Hocks can finish taking his pants off his ankles, Tonya wraps her mouth around the tip and her hand around the base of this cock. He fists his hands into her hair to keep his balance and revels in the feel of her working his dick from base to tip. Her T-shirt falls up her back revealing her bare ass and Hocks can't wait to take a bite. Tonya flattens her tongue and licks from base to tip and pops her lips. She looks up at Hocks through her eyelashes and he steps out of his discarded pants.

He places a finger under her chin and pulls her up on her knees. Gripping her waist, he lays her back on the bed. It takes so much energy to go slow with her and not just blow his shot in minutes. Which is what would happen if he let himself fuck her now. He crawls up between Tonya's thighs and he already knows she is dripping wet for him. He doesn't hold back when he finds her clit and gets the taste of her on his tongue. He goes to work hard and fast; he wants to her to come now, so quick that she'll see stars.

He bites down on the sensitive bundle of nerves and Tonya's back arches; she fists the sheets in her hands. Hocks puts three fingers inside of her and she moans out as he stretches her with slow circles. His tongue never stops, her legs tremble and he knows he has her. He thrusts his fingers in and out quickly, then bites down on her clit as her orgasm explodes from her body and she tightens around him.

"So fucking good," Hocks purrs and kisses the inside of her thigh before pulling his fingers out. He moves to suck her juices off himself, but Tonya grabs his hand and brings it to her lips. She takes one finger tentatively and the black iris' in Hock's eyes expand like a predator. His cock stiffens to the point of pain and she slowly sucks on each of his three fingers. She drops back to the bed and reaches between her legs and squeezes his dick.

"Your turn," she encourages and Hocks covers her mouth with his. Their tastes and smells intertwine in this space. Hocks thrusts inside of her and she stretches around his thickness, a breathless gasp escapes her at his size. She claws at his back to go deeper, harder. She wants to get lost and forget about everything else but this moment.

Tonya reaches between them and circles her clit, and the orgasm builds immediately. Hocks' corded muscles flex with each thrust and Tonya bites down on the top of his shoulder. He pushes himself back and gives her a lupine grin. He dips his head and sucks a nipple into his mouth and bites down. Pain mixed with ecstasy pushes Tonya over her second orgasm and she pinches her clit with the sensation.

She clenches around Hocks' cock and he thrusts deep inside of her and circles his hips. He pulls out and groans as he comes up her abdomen and between her breasts. He holds himself up, suspended over her, waiting to see regret or disappointment flash across her features. He never felt good enough for T and that's another thing that always held him back.

Tonya pushes himself up to his elbows and presses her lips to his. "You promised me the shower?" She points and Hocks chuckles.

"Anything for you, Darlin'," Hocks states. Tonya gives him a soft smile of approval. Maybe something wonderful came from this horrible circumstance. Maybe it is their chance for their happy ending.

About the Author

Lacy Chantell is a new upcoming author. She resides in Kentucky and owns a small business. She is a mom of two toddlers and lives on the family farm with her husband. She loves to read all genres, ride her horses, hiking, pretty much anything outdoors. Inspiration hits her everywhere she goes for new book ideas and she is excited to keep telling stories for others to enjoy. Romance and Fantasy are her favorite genres to write, and she loves to put her characters through hell for them to get their happy ending in the end.

Follow her on her social media accounts or join her newsletter to keep up with releases and her future works.

www.lacychantellpublishing.com

Additional Works

Cowboy Romance

Curston Ranch Series

Wild Heart – Book One

Tattered Heartstrings – Book Two

Wildflowers & Wild Horses – Prelude/Book Three

Langley Ranch Series

The Reason Why – Book One

Printed in the USA
CPSIA information can be obtained
at www.ICGtesting.com
LVHW091916140824
787872LV00015B/118/J